"I don't think any man in his right mind would want to escape marriage to you."

"Says a man who doesn't know me." Grace rolled her eyes at Zeke.

"I know enough, Gracie. I know enough," he said softly.

Grace blinked and stared at him. "You actually sound like you mean it."

His dimples flashed. "I do."

Grace sighed a happy sort of sigh that left a smile on her face. "I could kiss you for that."

His blue eyes collided with hers. Held.

Grace was afraid to breathe. Afraid to move.

His gaze lowered.

Her lips tingled in response.

Another long, breathless moment.

Then he looked away.

The
AMISH
WEDDING
PROMISE

A Hidden Springs Novel

Laura V. Hilton

FOREVER

NEW YORK   BOSTON

Copyright © 2019 by Laura V. Hilton
Excerpt from *The Amish Secret Wish* copyright ©2019 by Laura V. Hilton

Cover design and illustration by Elizabeth Turner Stokes
Cover copyright © 2019 by Hachette Book Group, Inc.

Forever
Hachette Book Group
1290 Avenue of the Americas, New York, NY 10104
read-forever.com
twitter.com/readforeverpub

First Edition: December 2019

Forever is an imprint of Grand Central Publishing. The Forever name and logo are trademarks of Hachette Book Group, Inc.

The publisher is not responsible for websites (or their content) that are not owned by the publisher.

All Scripture quotations are taken from the King James Version of the Holy Bible.

ISBN: 978-1-5387-0064-8 (mass market), 978-1-5387-0062-4 (ebook)

Printed in the United States of America

OPM

10 9 8 7 6 5 4 3 2 1

To Loundy: my favorite song.
To Michael: my adventurous one.
To Kristin: my darling daughter.
To Jenna: my sunshine.
To Kaeli: my shower of blessing.
In memory of the real Duudi Cliff: Cliff
Hall. May you rest in peace. Thanks
for being like a grandfather to my
children.
And in memory of my parents, Allan
and Janice, and my uncle Loundy and
my grandmother Mertie, who talked
about their Pennsylvania Amish
heritage.
To God be the glory.

CHAPTER 1

"Get to the shelter! A tornado is heading this way!"

The male voice, accompanied by the incessant blaring of a vehicle horn, didn't wake Grace Lantz. She was already awake, her arm wrapped around her sister's shoulders, both of them kneeling beside their shared bed.

"Dear Jesus, please calm storm like in story we read in Bible class," Patience said as she leaned into Grace, shivering.

Too bad real life wasn't quite so cut-and-dried. Grace hadn't been able to sleep due to troubling thoughts about her imminent marriage, and she was already praying, *Is this it, Lord? Did you want me to come to a complete and total end of myself? Well, I have. Now what?* So when Patience awoke due to the storm, it'd been a simple matter to slide to their knees.

The horn blared again, followed by a pinging that sounded like hail hitting the window glass.

The bedroom door slammed against the wall as their older brother Jon barged into the room. "Come on. Hurry now."

"I finish prayer," Patience whimpered and stayed by the bed.

Jon huffed and looked at Grace. "The storm's pretty bad."

"Amen." Grace finished the prayer for her sister, snagged her hand, and pulled her to her feet.

Jon led the way with the dim, flickering beam from his flashlight's dying batteries as they rushed downstairs to the small basement. They all bypassed the big monstrosity of a wood-burning furnace with vents leading up through the *haus*. *Mamm* had already laid out sleeping pallets on the side of the basement that didn't leak. *Daed* and Jon never seemed to find the time to apply sealant to the one wall.

"Please, Jesus. Save us from the storm." Patience sank to her knees and prayed out loud.

"Amen." *Daed* sat beside her and patted her arm. "We should all pray for safety."

"And try to get some sleep," *Mamm* added, looking pointedly at Grace. "Tomorrow's a big day."

And with that, Grace's thoughts swirled back to the wedding, to the backless benches sitting in neat rows in the barn. The wagon waiting—the one that carried the benches from *haus* to *haus* each church Sunday, wedding, or funeral. Her stomach clenched, roiled. She sank into the softness of the quilt pallets *Mamm* had prepared. It was her last *nacht* as an unmarried girl. She was supposed to be excited, thinking about tomorrow *nacht* alone with Timothy, but were these prewedding jitters normal? The doubts? The fears? Her married friends never mentioned them. The—

An angry roar, like a train rushing past, filled the air. But this train was filled with scary thumps, bumps, and a sucking sound that seemed to squeal and scream.

Patience prayed the same words louder, probably so *Gott* could hear her over the strong winds. "Save us from the storm, Jesus."

How could Grace comfort her younger sister when she was filled with fear, too? Not because of the storm. Illinois tornadoes always seemed to miss them. How many nights had she spent in this basement due to false alarms? She wouldn't have even bothered to go downstairs if it weren't for Jon coming to get them.

Instead, the wedding demanded Grace's attention. Maybe she should pray, but how could she when her thoughts spun as fast as the wind outside?

An eerie silence filled the air. Grace raised her head. *Daed* met her gaze. "Try to get your sleep, Gracie. It's your wedding day tomorrow."

Jah. It was. And she wanted to crawl over and curl up in *Daed*'s arms and ask him all the questions that still whirled in her mind. But she was a grown woman plus, she needed to take care of Patience.

Grace pulled her sister into her arms, lay next to her on the pallet of quilts, and held her close until her breathing evened.

Ich liebe dich, Timothy. Really. That was her last thought before her eyelids closed.

She woke to *Daed* shaking her shoulder and holding a lantern. She rubbed her eyes and stared up into his grim face. "*Daed?*"

"You need to come upstairs." His mouth worked as if he wanted to say more, but nothing emerged.

"Is Timothy here?"

Daed gulped and shook his head.

Her breath lodged in her throat. "You're scaring me." The words were whispered so she wouldn't wake her sister and *Mamm*.

"Just come."

Grace pushed to her feet and followed *Daed* from the cellar.

He stopped and pulled open the backdoor. The sun wasn't even up yet. The sky was just barely lightening.

She sucked in a breath.

The barn was gone.

The backless benches were gone.

The buggies and wagons were gone.

And the big tree with the swing hanging on it lay uprooted across the driveway, the open family buggy perched neatly on top.

* * *

Zeke Bontrager pulled his best friend's transistor radio closer and adjusted the volume.

The other two men in the loft with him fell silent. They'd spent the night there just in case the mare needed help delivering her new foal. She hadn't. The foal had been safely born a half an hour ago and was nursing when the men left the stall to try to catch a few hours of sleep in the loft, if they could, with the violent thunderstorm raging outside.

"A line of severe thunderstorms moved through the

region during the overnight and early morning hours. Eleven tornadoes have been confirmed, with widespread straight-line wind damage resulting across much of Illinois and eastward before the storms weakened over northwest Ohio," the broadcaster's static-filled voice said.

"*Jah*, I heard that Hidden Springs, located near Arthur, Illinois, was really hit hard last night." His brother Eli picked up his hat from the loft floor and twirled it on his finger. Such a show-off.

"I wonder if they need help. If they do, maybe we could volunteer," Zeke said. Perhaps this would be an opportunity to show *Daed* that he was a hero and not just a goof-off, as *Daed* was so fond of calling Zeke. He glanced down to the dark barn floor below. How long before people would be up and he could find out about arrangements?

"I think we should go." His friend, Hezekiah Esh— better known as Kiah—turned the radio off as it started blaring music with a strong bass beat. "I don't want my *daed* to find out about the radio. He'll take it away and lecture me about how a preacher's son needs to set a good example, even if he's on his *rumspringa*."

"*Jah*, and how will you explain knowing about the tornado?" Eli scoffed.

Kiah frowned. "Since it just happened…maybe he won't ask. Chances are he'll have heard anyway. Just not from a radio." He shoved the forbidden device farther away and covered it with some loose hay.

"I agree. We definitely should go." Zeke stood and brushed the straw off his pants. "I'm sure the Mennonites are already on it. Maybe they'd let us join in."

"You'd get to go anyway since you worked search and rescue before." Eli frowned. "Me, I'd have to ride in on your shirttails if I'm allowed to go at all. My boss threatened my job if I take any more unnecessary time off. And since I have no search-and-rescue experience, he'll see it as unnecessary."

"Your own fault. You're the one who decided that float trip was more important than work." Zeke frowned. Eli needed to grow up. Maybe if Zeke was gone for a while, his brother would learn to stand on his own.

"Hey, it was a once-in-a-lifetime experience. And *you* went, too." Eli swatted him with his hat.

"As a guide." Zeke swatted him back. Why did he always resort to such childish behavior around Eli?

"Boys." Kiah's *daed* stood at the foot of the ladder. "We need to talk."

Kiah peered down. "The horse is fine, *Daed*. We were with her up until a little bit ago. Did something go wrong?"

"I just peeked in. You did a fine job. It's not about the mare."

Kiah grimaced and kicked more straw at the radio.

Zeke raised his eyebrows.

Eli scampered down the ladder first, no doubt because, as he often told Zeke, he was only guilty by association and, therefore, not guilty at all. "Whatever it is, I didn't do it," he said when he reached Preacher Thomas.

"*Nein*, and you won't. Go on, now. And put your hat on straight." The preacher waved him off.

Eli straightened his hat and trotted out the barn doors. "See you at home, brother. When you get released from your punishment."

"Grow up." Zeke followed Kiah down and then stood silently beside his best friend, his gaze fixed on the ground. There wasn't any point in confessing to the radio sin until they knew what the preacher wanted. But he couldn't think what else he might have done.

"Our brothers in Hidden Springs need us. A couple of vans are leaving in less than an hour. And since you both want to go, you will. But I expect to hear you made a positive difference there and didn't get into trouble. I also expect you to act like mature young men."

Zeke caught his breath. Kiah's *daed* had heard their conversation? And he implied he thought they were immature? Okay, maybe they were, but they'd been alone. No girls to impress. No one around to judge. Or so he'd thought.

"You'll be assigned to one of three jobs: search and rescue, cleanup, or reconstruction. Possibly all three, depending on the need."

Zeke raised his gaze enough to peek at Kiah.

Kiah's Adam's apple jumped. "We'll be as good as gold, *Daed*."

"And don't think I don't know about the radio."

* * *

Grace didn't know where to start. She mindlessly helped *Mamm* with breakfast and cleanup, then slipped into her tennis shoes and ran out to find *Daed* and Jon. It was surprising Timothy hadn't shown up to check on her and her family yet—or for the wedding, which was supposed to be at eight thirty that morning. Nobody had, for that matter. But maybe word had already gone out that the wedding would be postponed until the next available Thursday, since their barn was gone.

And maybe Timothy's family had suffered even greater losses. Should she go check on them? Probably. But she'd have to walk five miles...unless *Daed* and Jon could lift the buggy off the tree. She'd wait until after lunch. That would give Timothy time to do the protective future-husband thing and check on her first.

Jon and *Daed* tossed the remaining rubble off to the side of the place where their barn once stood. There was a mess, but considering everything lost, not that much remained. A shingle or two, broken pieces of boards. A broken hammer—the iron part was there; the wooden handle was missing. The chickens were gone. The hog had been killed. The cows were missing with no word on their fate. And one horse—out of three—wandered around the pasture, none the worse for wear.

"Can I help?" Grace skidded to a stop beside *Daed* as he crouched down to gather a handful of nails.

Daed sighed and pointed toward the *haus*. "We have some broken windows. Sweep up the glass, and Jon and I will work on getting the glass replaced or the windows boarded up next. Then help your *mamm* with Patience. She doesn't handle change well."

The understatement of the year. But Grace wanted to be useful. Not just sweeping up glass. Or doing laundry, because if the glass shattered, some might have sprinkled over the bedding.

Cleanup chores the morning after a tornado was not how she imagined her wedding day. She'd imagined Timothy gazing lovingly into her eyes, touching her hand gently, and whispering sweet nothings. Something that made her feel loved and cherished, even if he'd never treated her that way in…well, ever. He'd been more pragmatic. *We're a good match.* And they were. But…was it wrong to want sparks? To want to be with him? To dream of their wedding with longing instead of dread?

Maybe something would change when they saw each other after this terrible disaster. He'd be more demonstrative. She'd be more receptive.

She could hope.

"I thought I'd run over and check on Timothy's family after lunch, if it's okay." Grace glanced at *Daed*, then toward the end of the driveway.

"I'm surprised he hasn't come by yet." *Daed* glanced toward the road, too.

Jon chuckled. "He probably thought to make his escape while the going's good. At this rate, little sister, I might be married before you."

Considering his wedding would be in two weeks, it was probably true. Weddings were held only on Thursday mornings during the fall or in the early spring. She and Timothy might have to wait until next year. But maybe her unrealistic expectations for flutters and sparks would fade by then.

She glanced toward the road again, as if Timothy would come around the corner. Too much to hope for, probably. Though Jon had already gone to check on Aubrey's family. She glanced at her brother. "Aubrey—"

"Aubrey and her family are fine; *danki* for asking. No damages." Jon smirked.

Daed frowned. "Be nice, Jonathon."

"Sorry, *Daed*. Sorry, Gracie."

Grace sighed. "I'm glad they had no damages." She caught her breath. Maybe Timothy's family had more damages than hers. "You passed by Timothy's place on the way there, though. Are they...?"

"I didn't see any damage at their property," Jon said. "But the road was a mess getting there, and I had to be careful of downed power lines. I ended up cutting through the woods, pastures, and fields, and I didn't really look too closely at their place."

Maybe Timothy hadn't wanted to make the effort that Jon had to. Timothy did like to take the easy way, and cutting through pastures wouldn't be as simple as the road. However, if he suffered from prewedding jitters as badly as she, maybe he *had* made his escape. She might be suffering from doubts and insecurities, but being jilted wasn't an option. She'd be talked about and teased for days. Weeks. Months. Who knew?

"Gracie? Gracie, where are you?" Patience called from somewhere inside.

Grace headed toward the *haus*.

Bride Jilted during Tornado.

Or: *Groom Rides Tornado to Freedom.*

Perhaps she spent too much time peeking in *The Budget* for news.

But if he had left, she'd what? She had no idea.

After courting three years, there was no turning back. Period.

CHAPTER 2

Zeke climbed out of the van and stretched. It was only about a four-hour drive from Shipshewana, Indiana, to Hidden Springs on the outskirts of Arthur, Illinois, but being cramped into the back seat of an overfull vehicle had taken its toll. At least he'd had plenty of time to pray that he'd somehow be a hero in his *daed*'s eyes. And they weren't even there yet. Instead, they were taking a bathroom and refreshment break at a fast-food restaurant.

After he'd ordered a hot mocha, they got back into the van.

Zeke reclaimed his window seat and looked at the scenery. Now that they were closer to Hidden Springs, signs of damage were everywhere. A church was gone, but the sign remained. The words read HE CAN CALM THE STORM. Zeke snorted. *Jah*, He could, but apparently He didn't want to.

Trees were down all over the place, shoved partially

off the road, and men in orange vests and hard hats worked around downed power lines. Zeke supposed they'd turned off the electricity so they could move the lines from the road and work on them, but he didn't know for sure. Electricity was foreign to him.

The driver pulled into a large parking lot at a school. A few cars, pickups, and vans were already parked there, and someone carried a box filled with towering stacks of paper cups inside. Someone followed with a large yellow picnic jug.

Zeke forced his cramped legs into movement and climbed out of the van. Hopefully, his duties wouldn't require him to climb into the back seat of another *Englisch* van. He'd prefer a horse and buggy. Or to travel by shank's pony, though someone in the van had mentioned the Amish and Mennonite host families might provide transportation.

Kiah jumped out of the van and moved to stand beside Zeke. The Red Cross hadn't arrived yet, but considering this was a disaster, they no doubt would arrive in a few days. Until then, the Mennonite missionaries they'd ridden with were in charge of giving directions. Or rather, whomever they reported to here in Hidden Springs.

Today, the sun was shining, and other than the stray shingles, siding, and chunks of insulation lying in the parking lot, Zeke didn't see any damage at the school.

"Leave your bags in the vehicle until you meet up with your host family." The Mennonite driver paused in front of them. "Go on inside, report, and get your assignments."

Zeke nodded and followed the others in his group who'd already headed in that direction, Kiah by his side.

As they neared the building, a large, white Siberian husky mix with dirty, matted fur approached. He looked well-fed but was minus a collar. Most of his group ignored the dog, but Zeke crouched down, hand extended.

An older Amish man came around the corner.

An injured *Englisch* man wearing ratty jeans and a green T-shirt and smoking a cigarette kicked at the animal. The dog cowered. "Stupid stray."

"You shouldn't be cruel to him," Zeke said, peering up. "You're displaced, too. In fact, we all are for now."

The man grunted, crushed out his cigarette, and went inside. The Amish man smiled and said something under his breath that Zeke didn't catch.

The dog sniffed his fingers, wagged his tail, and licked Zeke's hand, then sat in front of him, staring up at him with one pale-blue eye, one brown.

Zeke stood. "You can be my dog while I'm here. I'll find you a good home. I think I'll call you Shadow."

Kiah had gone into the building without Zeke, so he turned and followed his friend. The dog stayed on his heels until he reached the door; then he stopped and sat.

"You're well trained, aren't you, boy?" Zeke patted the dog's head. "Stay." He went inside, followed by the Amish man.

A square folding table stood just inside the door. A piece of paper taped to the front read, SIGN IN HERE. Someone's smartphone lay abandoned on the table, along with a pen, a stack of index cards, and a half-empty paper cup of black coffee. An unoccupied gray folding chair stood behind that, and about half of his group loitered there, staring at the abandoned paper. Zeke joined them. No one seemed to know exactly what to do.

The Amish man walked past and disappeared through another doorway. Since Zeke didn't know him, he probably was a local.

"The driver went to find someone in charge," Kiah said. "I hope they put us together."

"Me, too." Zeke would much rather be with his friend than with his distant cousin Vernon, who was also on this trip. He and Vernon barely tolerated each other.

Zeke glanced around the gymnasium. Pullout bleachers and basketball hoops were on the perimeter of the room, while colorful tape circles, lines, and half circles marked the open area. Over by the far wall, someone had set up a few cots, along with a long table and more gray folding chairs. A few *Englischer*s sat there, holding phones or computer tablets. The driver stood beside the table, talking to a lady in blue jeans and a gray T-shirt. Aside from the colorful tape on the floor, the whole windowless room appeared bland. The woman gestured to a door at the side of the room, and the driver went in that direction, disappearing from sight.

A few minutes later, the same older Amish man from outside reappeared. He was small, slight of build, wiry, and had a bustle in his step. He hurried up to their group, the driver behind him.

"Welcome! We're so glad you're here to help us." Despite the lack of size, his voice boomed. "Follow me, please, and we'll let you know where you're going and what you'll be doing. This way." He turned on his heels and hurried back the way he came from.

Zeke glanced at Kiah, and they followed.

"This way," the man said at the doorway, and he took off at a fast trot down a long hallway with lockers—also gray—lining the beige walls.

"Apparently color interferes with higher education," Kiah said.

Zeke laughed, earning a glance from a brown-haired young *Englisch* man about their age, wielding a wide broom. He wore ragged jeans with holes in both knees and a bright-green T-shirt with a name of a soft drink printed on it—the same man who had kicked the dog. His hair was longer than most *Englischer*s', with unruly curls throughout. A large white bandage was wrapped around the top of his head and a red gash marred one cheek. His eye was swollen shut. Maybe he was the janitor?

The Amish man led the way into what must be a classroom, though it was unlike any Amish classroom Zeke had ever seen. Tables instead of desks. A computer at the teacher's desk. A screen instead of a chalkboard.

A skeleton, taller than the man who took them there, stood guard beside the desk. Next to the bony hand, another half-full cup of black coffee waited.

Zeke stumbled to a stop and scratched his neck, staring at the staging of the bony hand and the coffee. This was getting weirder and weirder.

"The school is being used as a meeting place for the volunteers and a temporary lodging for the families who'd lost their homes," the Amish man explained as he approached the desk and sorted through a mess of papers. "Ah, here we are." He started calling out names and handing an index card to the person who answered.

"Ezekiel Bontrager."

"Um." Zeke cleared his throat and forced his attention away from the bony hand. "Here?"

"Don't be afraid, son. If you know the answer, just

shout it out." The man chuckled. With a tilted head, he surveyed Zeke for a long, silent moment as if gauging his worth. "Ezekiel Bontrager," the man said again with a look that made Zeke want to be a better man. "You'll do."

What? Zeke frowned. Had his reputation followed him here from Shipshewana?

The Amish man shuffled through the cards, pulled out another one, and handed it to Zeke. It had the name Seth Lantz written on it along with an address. "Roads are bad out that way. Lots of damage. You'll likely end up walking partway. Be sure to avoid downed power lines. Seth knows you're coming, and he'll give you and your buddy a place to stay and your assignments."

His buddy? Zeke edged closer to Kiah and glanced at his card.

His best friend's card had a different name.

Could they trade with someone so they had the same destination?

"Don't ask to trade." The slight, wiry man shook his head. "I was told to keep you boys separated."

Well, that was unfortunate. But it probably was wise if the organizers wanted them to interact with the community instead of each other.

Zeke would make the best of it. "The place I'm staying... Any unmarried daughters?"

The thin, wiry man smirked. "Twelve sons. Ain't it a wonder?" He laughed as if he'd made a joke. But his eyes held a measure of something. Mischief, maybe.

Zeke didn't get it. But apparently a pretty girl to spend his downtime with wasn't in the forecast, either.

The Mennonite missionary who was also in the room eyed Zeke sternly. "There'll be no dating on this trip.

Period. You are here for assistance only. That no-dating line is drawn in quicksand. Not mere sand. That means it won't be overlooked. Immediate punishment."

* * *

Grace cleaned the entire upstairs, sweeping and scrubbing the floors. She made the beds with fresh sheets, including the ones in the spare rooms. They might be asked to house an Amish family whose home became uninhabitable due to storm damage. *Mamm* took the sheets to wash and hang outside.

After finishing upstairs, Grace packed the sandwiches and cookies, prepared in advance for the evening singing after the wedding-that-wasn't-happening, into a picnic basket. She tried not to think about how, in other circumstances, she and Timothy would likely have been kneeling in front of the preachers at this time. She glanced at the wall clock. It was eight thirty. It didn't matter. Timothy wasn't here, the guests weren't here, and the barn was gone. Disasters trumped weddings.

With a sigh, she loaded the basket into the back of the buggy that had been rescued from the tree. A couple of Grace's married brothers fired up chain saws to turn the downed tree into firewood.

"Where are you going?" *Daed* looked away from the branches he trimmed off with loppers. He lifted his eyebrows.

"To take sandwiches and cookies to, uh…" She frowned.

"Rescue workers. Of course. Good idea."

Her oldest brother, Reuben, who had a daughter almost her age, nodded. "I'm sure they'll appreciate it."

Well, actually, she'd thought to visit Timothy's family, but rescue workers would be better. It would just serve as a bitter reminder that the wedding would need to be rescheduled if she gave the sandwiches to Timothy's family.

Daed sighed. "Does your mother know you're getting rid of the sandwiches and cookies? We might be taking in a couple workers. I told the bishop we would if needed. Plus, we'll need to have a barn raising."

"She knows. She told me to get rid of some of the sandwiches and cookies and told me to take Patience with me to distract her. She hasn't stopped crying over the barn and the missing animals." In fact, they hadn't seen a single one of their cats or their dog since the tornado. Maybe it'd calm her down if she called for the cats or dog while on the road. At least it'd make her feel helpful.

"You might need this." Reuben put a chain saw next to the basket in the buggy. "It's fueled up. Lots of trees down, but don't get near any downed power lines. I heard they can kill up to twenty-five feet away if they are activated. Or was it thirty-five feet?" He glanced at their brothers.

They shrugged.

"Whatever. Just stay away. We don't want anything to happen to you." Reuben turned his attention back to the tree.

"Are you going to check on Timothy?" another brother, Joseph, asked.

That was the plan, but she hesitated to admit it. Timothy should've checked on her. Especially by now.

The brothers all sighed, probably reading the answer

in her eyes. They always said they knew exactly what she was thinking.

"Don't judge him too harshly. Maybe he just couldn't get away. Or maybe they had more damage than I saw. I wasn't looking too closely," Jon reminded her. "Be careful with the chain saw."

She nodded and went to the house to get her sister. Hopefully this would work to calm her down because Patience was trying her patience.

The roads were worse than Grace imagined. Jon hadn't been kidding. Trees were down everywhere. Most of them she could simply drive around, but some blocked the whole road and she had to stop and clear a partial path. But taking Patience through the pastures—where they might face an angry bull or an overprotective cow—wasn't an option.

As they reached the road going toward town, an electric company truck was parked on the edge of the ditch, along with a big truck with a basket on an extended arm rising up into the sky.

Patience stopped crying long enough to stare at it.

Grace wanted to gawk, too. She was tired, hot, and sweaty and hoped this meant the rest of the way to Timothy's house was already cleared. She parked the buggy and climbed out. "Stay here, Patience. I'll be right back." She grabbed a few plastic bags full of sandwiches and cookies and approached the workers. "Do you want a snack?"

"Thank you, miss." One man took a couple. His coworkers gathered around.

After Grace passed out the sandwiches and cookies to the workers, including a couple for the man in the cherry picker, she turned to the first man. "Can I get through hcrc, or are the lines, um, still dangerous?"

"They're deactivated, miss. You can get through."

"Thank you. Oh, you haven't seen any loose cows or horses, have you?"

He shook his head.

Should she ask about dogs or cats? But considering how many people let their pets run wild, that would be a waste of time. "Thanks again." She waved and got back into the buggy.

Patience was still quiet but sniffling. "I saw a dog."

"Ours?" Grace glanced at her sister.

She shook her head. "Swartzes', I think."

They owned a couple of beagles.

Grace expelled a breath, clicked at the horse, and drove on. She turned at the corner, away from town, and at the next road turned again.

And stopped. Another huge tree blocked the road.

Patience started crying again.

Grace slumped, staring at the tree and fighting the urge to hold her sister and cry with her.

Or maybe turn around and go back home.

This might be why Timothy hadn't checked on her.

But not checking on her because of a downed tree made Grace feel like she wasn't worth the effort. And that wasn't a message she wanted to convey. Or receive, for that matter.

Too bad it was received. Loud and clear.

Unless he had another, better reason.

And with that hope, Grace firmed her shoulders, climbed out of the buggy, and grabbed the chain saw. Again.

She turned to Patience as she passed the front seat. "Call for the dog and cats while you wait. I'll hurry."

Patience whimpered, said a half-hearted "Here, kitty, kitty," then resumed crying.

At least she tried.

"I want to go home!" Patience howled.

The chain saw roared to life, drowning out her sister. Sort of. Because the words still echoed.

Grace probably should've left her sister at home. But *Mamm* had asked her to take her along.

This was not easier on Patience or on Grace. At least at home Patience would've had some semblance of normality, even if the barn was missing. And the animals gone.

Grace batted her *kapp* strings behind her shoulders, tried to ignore her quivering muscles and the blisters already forming on her hands, and went to work. Best cure for depression—work. At least that's what her *grossdaadi* always said.

A vehicle stopped beside the buggy and honked. She glared over her shoulders, but then turned to face the van. The chain saw still rumbled. Maybe they'd get the message that she was working as fast as she could. All things considered. If they wanted to get through faster, they could get out and help.

An Amish man climbed out of the back seat. "I'm looking for Seth Lantz's house," he shouted. His straw hat shadowed his face.

Grace yelled back, "You passed it. Turn left at the corner. Go down the road about three miles, turn right, and it's the second mailbox on the left."

"Back that way?" He pointed.

"*Jah*. He's my *daed*."

The man glanced from her to Patience, then to the still-roaring chain saw. "How about I get out here and help? Looks like you need it."

"I've got it under control." She stiffened. But oh, *jah*, she needed help. Badly.

The man ignored her. Or maybe he received her unspoken message. He trotted back to the van and retrieved a duffel bag and a dog that looked familiar...

A dog that barked and jumped up in the buggy beside Patience and snuggled against her. Grace blinked. Their dog.

Patience threw her arms around his neck and cried into his fur.

Grace wanted to do the same. But maybe she could have a well-deserved, but private, meltdown later.

The man said something to the driver. The driver backed up, somehow avoiding the drainage ditches on either side of the road, and turned around, leaving the man there.

"He's going to take the man I've been partnered with to your *haus*, so we'll be reported in, and let them know I'm helping you." The man tossed his bag into the back of the buggy and approached. "Looks like your, ah, friend knows Shadow."

"She's my sister, Patience. And his name isn't Shadow. He's our dog. Where'd you find him?"

"At the school. What is his name?"

"Slush."

He grinned. "Like melted snow?" He held out his hand. "I'm Zeke. Well, Ezekiel, but my friends call me Zeke."

She lowered the chain saw to her side, letting it die. "Grace Lantz. Almost everyone calls me Gracie." She slipped her hand into his.

Sparks rocketed through her.

Her gaze shot to his.

His eyes were blue. Vivid blue.

And they widened as he stared at her.

Her face heated as she jerked her hand free.

* * *

Wow. And *wow*. Zeke had never had *that* reaction to a pretty woman before. And she *was* pretty. Light-brown hair that was messy and escaping the confines of her *kapp*, hazel eyes, full lips, pink cheeks, and…He let his eyes drop. Tree bark and sawdust clung enticingly to her curves.

She'd probably be embarrassed to realize she looked so disheveled.

He reached for the chain saw, but she shied away. "Let me help," he said. "Can you comfort her?"

Her eyes slid toward her sister. He followed her gaze. What was her name again? Patience? From the brief glance he took, she had special needs. Her arms were still around the dog's neck, and it seemed as if Slush grinned at him.

He couldn't help but grin back, happy the dog was back with his people.

"I'm not sure if anyone can help at this point, if Slush isn't helping, but I'll try." Gracie relinquished the chain saw. "*Danki*."

"So twelve brothers, huh?" he asked as she started to walk away.

She stumbled to a stop, turned, and frowned at him. "How do you know?"

His face heated. "I might have asked if Seth Lantz had any unmarried daughters."

Her eyes narrowed and a shadow filled them. "And...?"

And he suddenly wanted to find out the reason for the shadow so he could make it go away. "The man I asked said, 'Twelve sons. Ain't it a wonder?' He didn't mention you. Or Patience." He gestured toward the buggy.

Gracie frowned. Sighed. "Patience is special. She'll never marry. And today's my wedding day."

The words fell like a boulder, knocking the breath out of him.

She turned and trod away, leaving him staring after her. Speechless.

Questions formed. Died.

The one girl who had ever caught his attention this way and she was married?

Wait. No. Something didn't fit.

He yanked the cord and the chain saw rumbled to life.

Some problems were easier to take care of than others. And right now a downed full-grown tree was a smaller problem than figuring out why Gracie's comments didn't fit.

Except, she didn't say she was married. She introduced herself as Lantz. She said it was her wedding day, yet she wasn't at the wedding.

The tornado cancelled the festivities.

Her groom wasn't there. Here. With her.

Zeke turned his head enough to watch Gracie climb into the buggy next to the still-smiling dog and Patience.

Her groom wasn't there, but Zeke was.

It might've been his imagination, but it seemed Slush's grin widened and the dog winked.

Zeke winked back.

CHAPTER 3

Grace cuddled next to Slush's side and stretched her arm across the seat to touch Patience's shoulder. She gently rubbed it while trying to think of comforting things to say that might encourage her sister to stop crying. At least the wails had died down to sniffles. Probably a headache and stuffy nose, too, if Patience was anything like Grace.

Their rescuer was helpful. And pleasant to look at. A firm jaw, well-shaped lips, vivid blue eyes that made her heart pound into overdrive, and wide shoulders that appeared strong enough to bear her burdens. And the way his muscles flexed, stretching the pale-blue fabric of his shirt taut— *Oh my.*

She probably shouldn't gawk at the view, but wow. *Gott* sure did nice work when He created him. Even his name, Zeke, seemed exciting.

Not that it mattered. She wasn't available—unless

Timothy had bolted, and she refused to believe that was true. But maybe she could fix Zeke up with one of her friends while he was here.

On the other hand, a man like that probably had a serious girlfriend back wherever he came from. And he wouldn't have time to date here, even if he was available. He was here for relief work. To help *Daed* and the community clean up and rebuild. To clear the roads and...and to find missing people.

She gulped. She shouldn't ogle the man. Even if he was super nice looking.

He turned off the chain saw and faced her. "I forgot to ask: Do you want the logs saved for firewood? I could bring your wagon back to collect it."

That'd be lovely. Except, they didn't have a wagon anymore.

Something about her expression must've cued him. He frowned. "How substantial is your loss?"

She couldn't begin to guess. And she didn't want to tick them off when Patience was listening. Especially since she'd finally begun to calm. Grace glanced pointedly at her sister, then shrugged.

Zeke's gaze slid from her to Patience and back. He nodded and yanked the chain again, returning his attention to the tree while Grace's attention remained fixed on him.

"Slush needs bath," Patience whispered.

Grace nodded. "We'll give him one when we get home." Or at least Patience could. *Mamm* would probably need Grace's help with supper preparations if this man was staying with them.

"He handsome. What his name?" Patience shifted to look at Grace over Slush's head.

"Zeke." His name came out on a breathy sigh. Grace's face heated. But Patience didn't seem to notice.

Zeke hefted a log and tossed it into the woods. About fifteen minutes later, the road was cleared enough for her to go around the fallen tree. He turned off the saw and loaded it into the back of the buggy.

Grace twisted. "Do you want a sandwich?"

"Sounds good." He opened the picnic basket. "Wow, there's a lot in here."

"They wedding sandwiches and cookies," Patience volunteered.

Zeke nodded, but his gaze shifted to Grace.

Something she couldn't identify flashed in his eyes. Her breath caught, and for a moment the world disappeared. Then his lips flexed and his gaze filled with something...pity? Or was it compassion?

He lifted the straw hat off his head, revealing dark-brown—or maybe even black—hair. It was short, as if he'd recently had a haircut.

And that settled it. The man was more than handsome. He was gorgeous. Swoonworthy, her *Englisch* friends would say. Or maybe they'd call him eye candy.

Grace was inclined to agree.

He swiped at sweat beading on his forehead, then replaced his hat before climbing into the back seat of the buggy. He leaned forward. "Where to next?"

Grace gulped. "To check on my groom." The words were raw, ripping open wounds that hurt.

Zeke leaned back. "Why isn't he checking on you, Gracie Lantz?"

Because she wasn't worth the effort.

She tried to swallow the stubborn lump in her throat as she picked up the reins.

And even though it hurt, it seemed that was the hard, brutal truth.

* * *

Zeke wished he could see Gracie's expression. Judging by the way her back stiffened and her chin rose a couple of notches, he'd hit a nerve. Not intended. But if the groom wasn't checking on his bride the day after a bad tornado—not to mention their wedding day— something was very, very wrong. If the groom was alive, he should've been fording rivers and climbing mountains—not that either was necessary in the well-bridged plains of Illinois—at the very least, chainsawing his way down the road to make sure the lovely Gracie Lantz was okay. To offer comfort if needed. And to provide additional help for the family.

And since the groom hadn't come, then . . . well.

Zeke sighed. Worst-case scenario, the groom was no more.

In which case, maybe it'd be best if Gracie didn't continue her mission to check on him.

On the other hand, the worst-case scenario had better be the case, because there was no wrath greater than a scorned woman's. Maybe that wasn't exactly how the saying went, but it was close enough.

At least Zeke was there to offer comfort, assistance, friendship, a shoulder to cry on, or whatever else was needed.

The "Twelve sons. Ain't it a wonder?" comment suddenly made sense.

If he—or anyone—hurt Gracie intentionally, he'd be staring at not one, but twelve business ends of pitchforks.

Best keep their relationship, such as it was, to assistance only.

Zeke shook his head and turned his attention to Patience, who still snuggled Slush. "Is Slush your dog?"

The girl's almond-shaped eyes turned to him. "She family's. We've cats, too." Her words were thick, slurred. Definitely a special child. Tween. Maybe early teens.

Gracie guided the horse and buggy around the tree. The road seemed mostly clear ahead. Except for a tree half across the road from the other direction. And a pile of some sort of rubble.

"Cats. How many?" He could go with that. He looked back at Patience.

A branch from a low-hanging tree brushed its leafiness against his head, dislodging his hat. He grabbed for it. Too bad he hadn't thought to look up for hidden dangers.

"You cute." Patience giggled. "You think, Gracie?"

Gracie turned her head and glanced at her sister. "The heart is what matters, Patience. You know that."

Jah, true, but he would've liked to know what she thought.

Not that it mattered.

Patience turned to look at him. "The heart is deceitful above all things, and desperately wicked: Who can know it?"

Zeke was impressed. His special cousin could spout off Bible verses like that, too.

He forced a grin. Why couldn't she recall a more pleasant verse? Maybe one about how *Gott* looks at the heart and not the outward appearance?

But then, he'd fall short there, too, because *Gott* would know why Zeke had to prove himself in so many different ways. And he'd be judged.

And fail.

Because...

Zeke shook his head as he pushed the thought away. He forced his attention back to Patience. "My family has three cats. They live in the barn. Mice catchers. We have a dog, too. He's a mixed breed. Someone dumped him and we took him in."

Patience twisted in the seat and beamed at him as if he were some sort of hero. "You good man."

At least that's what he heard. Her voice was thick from crying and hard to understand.

He'd go with it. "*Danki*."

"I'm not sure how many cats we had," Gracie said. "They adopted us. Most were wild and wouldn't let us near. But there were two that allowed us to hold them."

Had. Were. Past tense. Zeke's brow furrowed. "How much damage did you have?" he asked again.

Gracie glanced at Patience and shook her head.

"Our barn gone. And all the church benches." Patience beamed at him as if it were a good thing.

Okay...

Zeke studied the firm set of Gracie's shoulders. Her family had so much damage and she was out delivering sandwiches and cookies and checking on her groom? A man who should've been checking on her?

Respect flowed through him.

*   *   *

Finally, Grace angled the buggy into Timothy's drive-way. She stared around at the seemingly untouched barn and house, the buggies parked outside the barn, the horses in the pasture.

Jon was right.

It both comforted her and horrified her at the same time.

He was safe. His family and home were fine.

And no one cared enough for her to check on her family.

Or to show up for the wedding-that-didn't-happen.

But in their defense, maybe they heard that her family's barn had been lost and didn't want to embarrass *Daed* by making him explain that under the circumstances, the wedding would be postponed.

The Amish were sensible, forthright, and obvious. No point in pretending something that wasn't. Well, at least in some cases. In others, they were master pretenders.

She straightened her back and parked.

She'd pretend that being ignored or forgotten didn't hurt.

Something brushed her shoulder, and she turned in time to see Zeke pulling his hand away. Had he intended to touch her in comfort but changed his mind? It would be improper for him to touch her. Physical displays were discouraged. Among anyone.

And yet, deep in her heart, she wished for a bit of physical comfort like she'd offered Patience earlier. Just the idea that he'd thought to offer comfort soothed her and helped her move out of the buggy.

The door to the house opened as Grace climbed out.

Timothy's *mamm* rushed toward her, arms out-stretched. "You came! Isn't it horrible?"

CHAPTER 4

Zeke shifted on the uncomfortable seat as the heavyset woman dressed in black engulfed Gracie into a smothering hug. It appeared as if Gracie's nose was buried in the woman's neck as she moaned, "Horrible, horrible, horrible," over and over.

Worse, Patience began to cry again—howl, really—when she stared at the woman suffocating Gracie.

Slush's grin faded, and he gave Zeke a canineworthy glare, which communicated, "Fix this!"

Uh, sure. But how? And what happened that was so horrible?

He reached forward and awkwardly patted Patience's shoulder. "There, there."

It worked about as well as he expected—not at all.

Slush gave him a disgusted look, nosed his hand away, and burrowed against Patience's side.

Not that it worked any better. Except Patience hugged Slush again.

Zeke glanced around at the long rectangular chicken *haus*, wrinkled his nose at the stench, and then turned his attention to the two women beside the buggy.

Gracie pushed away. "What exactly happened, Lavina?"

"Timothy and two of his buddies went out buggy racing last *nacht*. Last hurrah before he had to settle down, you know."

Zeke winced. *Ouch*. But then he, Eli, and Kiah might've done the same.

"None of them came home. I guess they got caught in the tornado. His buggy was found in the middle of the bishop's living room, but there was no sign of Timmy."

How on earth? Zeke's mouth dropped open.

"Except his pants. No suspenders, no shirt, just his pants. I had them marked with a *T*, you know."

Gracie's face flared red, but she shook her head. "I didn't know."

Lavina ignored her. "The bishop lost his roof, the horse made her way home, and we found her in front of the barn this morning, but there's no sign of Timmy. Or his friends."

Gracie paled, but other than pulling Lavina into her arms again, she didn't make a sound. At least none that Zeke heard over Patience's wailing.

But this "mission" had turned from assist to search and rescue, to probably recovery.

Somehow Zeke would need to get word to someone in charge so the other members of his group knew.

Maybe the Amish guy at the school . . .

But he could hardly call the school and ask for a man that way. Too bad he hadn't paid close enough attention to catch his name.

Probably Zeke's new roommate had. Vernon Graber played by the rules, got straight As when they were in school, and even now had the respect of all the church leaders in Shipshewana. And he and Zeke barely tolerated each other. They probably placed him with Zeke to make sure Zeke stayed on the straight and narrow.

Something that wouldn't happen if he were rooming with Kiah. They'd be too busy having fun, goofing off, and maybe racing a few buggies of their own.

Because all work and no play made Vernon a dull boy. Dull man. Whatever. One who was to be married in three weeks, which was more than Zeke could say for himself. Unfortunately, he was to marry a woman Zeke used to court before Vernon swept in.

But then again, he hadn't yet met the woman who made him want to give up his sometimes immature ways and start acting his age.

His gaze landed on Gracie. Lingered.

Even if she were no longer taken, a long-distance relationship would be tough. Of course, the usual confines of the courtship ritual were frustrating, too. But for a woman like Gracie, he'd consider taking his chances with long-distance dating. Maybe he'd even uproot himself and move nearer.

The thought surprised him. Even more surprisingly, it felt right. But then he shook his head to clear his thoughts. She'd just received horrible news about her groom.

No point wasting his time thinking this way.

He pulled out his cell phone and uploaded his list of contacts. Did he have any of the Mennonite missionaries listed from previous trips? If he did, he'd let them know about the change of status.

Of course, he couldn't find a single one of them listed. He'd have to get their numbers from Vernon. *If* he carried a cell phone. And that was a big if. They were allowed, but not all Amish carried them.

How many times had *Daed* misquoted the verse in 1 Corinthians and told Zeke to put away childish things and become a man? And keeping contact information current would be an adult thing. Letting things slide would definitely not be.

Zeke blew out a puff of air. Slush turned to look at him, his head tilted as if in question. It was time to be the man. He needed to be the hero here and help Gracie find out what happened to her groom. To reunite the young lovers. Then turn and walk away.

The thought hurt.

But it was the right thing to do.

* * *

The good news was that Grace hadn't been jilted on her wedding day. The bad news was she might not have a groom. It was an out-and-out miracle the horse survived being picked up by a tornado. She wouldn't expect two miracles from the same twister. Besides, how on earth would a force of nature remove a man's pants?

Her face heated again. The very thought of it.

And for that matter, what had possessed Timothy to go buggy racing on the eve of his wedding?

Grace's chest hurt. Her eyes stung. And she didn't know what to say to Lavina. How did one find words of comfort for this? The only suitable refrain was the one Lavina had returned to uttering, over and over and over. "Horrible, horrible, horrible."

Should she offer to sit with the family and do basic household chores, or should she take her sister and Zeke and go home?

Since Patience had resumed her wailing, maybe going home would be the best thing. Timothy and his family had never had much patience with Patience.

Grace's throat hurt from unshed tears, but she gave Lavina another hug. "Let me know if you get any news. Perhaps he and his friends took cover in a storm shelter. Or maybe he's at one of his friends' houses even as we speak."

Lavina stopped chanting "horrible" and peered at her, hope erasing the bleakness in her eyes. "Do you really think so? You're a regular angel of mercy, Gracie."

Nein, she didn't think so. She managed a smile, one that probably looked as sick as she felt, and turned away. "I'll keep looking. Do you want some sandwiches and cookies? To help feed your guests?" Timothy had mentioned out-of-state family coming in for the wedding.

"That'd be appreciated, Gracie Lou."

Her middle name wasn't Lou, but she didn't correct Lavina as she reached into the picnic basket and handed several large resealable storage bags to her would-be mother-in-law. Then she climbed into the buggy.

"Thank you," Lavina gushed.

Grace nodded. "You're welcome."

"I'll help her find Timothy," Zeke offered.

Grace turned away and patted Patience's shoulder. "It'll be okay."

The words were more for Grace, but it worked to reduce Patience's wails to gasps and sniffles.

Slush licked Grace's cheek.

Warm breath tickled Grace's other ear.

"Do you really think so, Gracie?" Zeke mimicked Lavina's words in a whisper, his voice heavily underscored with skepticism.

Was giving false hope to Lavina a lie?

Grace shrugged, her shoulder bumping against Zeke's chin as he moved away. Sparks shot through her.

More important, was it a sin to be physically attracted to another man on her wedding day? Especially right after learning her groom might be dead...and in clear sight of her would-be groom's mother?

* * *

As Gracie drove home, Zeke scrolled through his contacts on his phone again, just in case he'd overlooked something in all the previous drama.

He hadn't.

Rule number one in search and rescue: Keep your team close at all times.

Okay, maybe it wasn't rule number one, but it was definitely somewhere in the top ten. And due to his own failure, he didn't have a way to get in contact with any of them, except Kiah and Vernon—and the latter only because they were partners on this trip.

Zeke sighed. It wouldn't do any good to call or text Kiah, because he'd be unlikely to have the information, either.

On the other hand, whoever Kiah was partnered with *might* have the information.

Zeke thumbed a quick message: I need the phone number for the Mennonite in charge.

A minute later, the phone chirped with a message. Why? You bailing on me? The number followed. Along with a name: Daniel Zook.

Ha. No. I'll tell you later. Thanks.

And then the dilemma—call Daniel Zook and risk Gracie and Patience overhearing or...

The buggy lurched over something big, and Zeke's cell phone fell, skittering across the floor. He dived from his seat, hitting his knees on the lower surface and wedging his shoulders between the front and back seats. He carefully reached over the chain saw and grabbed his phone as the wheels bumped over something else. It seriously needed new shocks. He clutched his phone and somehow managed to shove the device into his pocket. He'd call later.

He glanced up and met the brown-and-blue gaze of Slush. The dog's mouth was parted in a wide grin as if he were laughing.

Zeke would laugh at himself, too. He got off the floor, sat, and reached forward to rub his hand over Slush's dirty, matted fur. The dog seriously did need a bath. If they didn't have anything else for him to do this evening, he'd give him a bath himself. After experiencing who knew what horrors, the dog deserved attention.

Gracie took a corner too fast and he slid on the seat. She drove like he did back home when he was in a rush. Were her emotions driving her to distraction and she just wanted to get home before falling apart in front of her sister? Probably.

His hand shifted from the dog's back to the seat behind Gracie. The back of his fingers brushed against her shoulder. Tingles worked up his arm.

He pulled away and directed his attention toward the devastation lining the road. Siding. Shingles. Insulation. Sheets of mangled metal. Houses reduced to nothing but rubble. Maybe the buggy shocks weren't a problem after all. The road was in bad shape.

A group of electric workers waved as they passed. "Thanks for the sandwiches and cookies."

Gracie waved back.

Then they passed a very beat-up mailbox that dangled precariously from its post. She turned in on the dirt drive. There was a smallish, two-story farmhouse, considering there were twelve sons, and no barn. No shed. No animals, except the horse pulling the buggy Gracie drove, and the dog.

A fallen tree being sawed into pieces littered the driveway. And about a dozen men, most of them bearded, looked up as Gracie pulled the reins. "Halt."

Slush stood, his tail wagging but low and slow as if he was confused or unsure about something. The destruction? Possibly.

One of the Amish men, this one beardless, approached the buggy. "You found the dog. And your groom."

Gracie made some sort of noise.

Zeke's heart rate surged into a gallop.

Patience grinned. "Her *new* groom."

CHAPTER 5

Grace struggled for a breath as Jon's gaze shifted from her to Patience, then to Zeke.

"Who are you?" Jon's brow furrowed as he put down the chain saw and approached the buggy. "You aren't who I expected. Where is Timothy?" His gaze returned to Grace.

She would be surprised if Jon really had expected her to bring Timothy back. She opened her mouth to try to find an explanation, but sudden, unexpected emotion clogged her throat.

Behind her, Zeke cleared his throat. "I'm Zeke Bontrager from Shipshewana. I was told to report to Seth Lantz. I'm part of the crew that came with the Mennonite missionaries, and I'm not anybody's groom." He angled a glance at Patience.

"I'm Gracie's brother Jon."

Slush climbed over Grace's lap, his toenails digging

into her legs through the fabric of her dress, and he jumped out of the buggy.

Jon put his hand on Slush's head as *Daed* came over, crouched down, and petted the dog. "Welcome home, boy."

Patience turned to stare at Zeke. "You Gracie's groom," she insisted.

Grace's face burned. She forced herself to focus on her brothers and *Daed*. "I don't know where Timothy is. His buggy is in the bishop's living room, but he's gone."

Daed frowned.

"Timothy's *mamm* said he was racing buggies with his friends," Grace whispered.

Daed's eyes widened. He turned his attention to Jon. "Let this be a lesson to you, son. Don't go racing the *nacht* before you marry Aubrey."

Jon nodded. "That would be a given."

Zeke climbed out of the buggy. "Did my cous—eh, partner arrive? Vernon Graber?"

"*Jah*. He's . . ." *Daed* waved his hand toward the house and shrugged. "Guess he figured we had the tree under control."

Zeke nodded. "If you tell me what you need, I'll get to work. There are the trees we cut to get the buggy through, if I could borrow your wagon . . ." He glanced around. Grace followed his gaze. No wagons. Her brothers had come on bicycles and scooters.

It would seem obvious for him to help with the current tree, but fourteen men working on one tree was a bit of overkill.

"I could go out looking for Timothy . . ." Not that he'd know where to look.

"I hear they are organizing a search. They'll update us if we're needed. *Englischer*s are heading it up." *Daed* glanced toward the road. "They have special people—I believe they said National Guard. From past experience, we're in their way."

"I'll carry your bag in and help *Mamm*." Grace held her hand toward Patience to assist her out of the buggy.

Patience grasped her hand and clambered out. "I give Slush bath."

Slush tucked his tail and howled. A long, mournful sound.

Daed turned to Zeke. "Instead of worrying about the wood, fill the bucket with water, find the dog shampoo, and help Patience with Slush."

He nodded. "*Jah*, sir." He glanced at Patience.

"Keep in mind you'll be wetter than the dog," *Daed* warned.

Slush made a series of short, sharp barks, looking at *Daed*.

Grace stifled a giggle. The dog was the only one who could get away with back talk. She turned her back to the men, grabbed the picnic basket and Zeke's bag from the back—one of her brothers had already snagged the chain saw—and turned toward the house.

Mamm had coffee percolating in the kitchen, but she wasn't in the room. A male voice came from upstairs. Probably the Vernon that Zeke had mentioned.

Grace put the leftover sandwiches and cookies on the table, left Zeke's travel bag on a chair, and carried the picnic basket to the basement. She slid it onto the shelf where it belonged and turned to go upstairs as Patience and Zeke came down.

Holding hands.

Well, more accurately, Patience tugged Zeke's hand. "This way."

Zeke flashed Grace an easygoing grin full of mischief. It was enough to make her wish she were giving Slush a bath. He and Patience were going to have fun. Slush, not so much.

At least not until the end when he retaliated by shaking all the water off his fur and drenching anyone nearby. Then he'd go lie down in the sun with a big grin.

Grace decided to stay in the basement to chaperone. Zeke seemed like a very nice man, but *Patience* was holding his hand. Grace would have to warn her—again—against touching a man. It was frowned upon, even by courting couples, though some did touch, hug, or kiss when the chaperones turned their backs.

Grace could count the number of times on both hands that Timothy had touched her in the three years he'd courted her.

Kissed would be half that.

Despite herself, her gaze went to Zeke as he let go of Patience's hand and lifted the metal tub down from the nail on the wall. His muscles pulled the back of his shirt tight. He'd touched her twice in comfort or accidentally since she met him. She'd felt more sparks in those accidental touches from Zeke than in all of Timothy's intentional ones. What would it be like to be kissed by him?

Ach, her shameful thoughts. Grace fanned her face with her hand, then went to get the dog shampoo and handed it to Patience. But despite her internal scolding, her gaze shot right back to Zeke.

He turned, catching Grace staring at him.

"Sure you don't want to help, Gracie?"

She wanted to, *jah*, but there was probably something sinful about having fun with another man on your wedding day, even though her groom had disappeared.

One of the preachers would be able to point to chapter and verse—or find something in the *Ordnung*—to fit the situation, but Gracie's brains had packed a suitcase and headed south at some point.

She managed a mute head shake.

"It be fun, Gracie," Patience said.

It would be. But…"*Mamm* needs me. *Danki* anyway."

"Too bad, Gracie. You need to know Zeke if you marry him."

Zeke's face turned a fascinating shade of red that Grace was sure she rivaled, but he chuckled.

"*Jah*. What she said."

* * *

Zeke could almost imagine *Daed* shaking his head in dismay at Zeke's rather flippant agreement, but he wasn't sure how exactly to handle Patience. Sure, he had a special cousin, but Jonah was male and didn't make comments about Zeke marrying some girl he'd just met. He also didn't cry so easily. And in light of Patience's overabundance of tears, it seemed wiser to agree now and try to explain the situation later. If and when he found the words.

Better yet, maybe Gracie would explain.

He followed Patience and Gracie upstairs, trying not

to notice the sway of Gracie's serviceable maroon dress. She turned to go into the kitchen where a woman he assumed was her *mamm* now puttered, pouring Vernon a cup of coffee. A plate of sandwiches and cookies sat in front of him. Snacking instead of working.

Giving the dog a bath wasn't much better, but that was what he was told. At least he was working.

He shouldn't judge. Vernon hadn't bought anything to eat or drink at the fast-food restaurant, so he probably was hungry. And Zeke had eaten a couple of sandwiches in the buggy on the way here.

Zeke turned and followed Patience outside.

Slush lay sprawled on the grass, an almost stubborn expression on his face. He opened his mouth and eerie howls filled the air.

"Up. Now," Patience demanded, finger pointing to the dog.

The dog made a series of short barks, somehow doing it without getting up. He finished it up with another howl.

Zeke stared, fascinated. Who knew a dog could have a temper tantrum?

"Slush," Patience said firmly. "Up. Bath."

The dog commented back with more short, sharp barks and another howl. He didn't move.

"Let's go." Patience stomped her foot.

Slush glared but got to his feet with a huff.

Zeke followed them to the corner of the house where a water spigot was located.

"Hose in barn," Patience directed.

"Sure." Zeke nodded. But since the barn was gone, the hose likely was too. He hesitated to say so, though, in case it restarted her tears.

One of the men, probably one of her brothers, approached. "The hose is in the pile of junk over yonder. Not going to guarantee its condition, though, since it had a nail driven straight through it." He kept his voice low, probably so Patience wouldn't hear and get upset.

"*Danki*." Zeke headed that way. He found the hose, uncoiled it, but the man was right. It was in terrible condition. Good thing it was warm, with temperatures supposed to be in the mid to upper sixties, according to the weather report he'd heard in the van earlier.

He carried the hose over to the spigot and attached it as Patience set the tub where she wanted it and ordered Slush in.

Not that Slush went willingly. He voiced his opinion before obeying and after he got in. Just like Zeke and Eli. They tended to protest when asked to do something they didn't want to do, too.

Zeke turned the water on, and Patience squealed as water shot from everywhere, as if it were a sprinkler hose.

The backdoor to the house opened and Vernon and Gracie stepped out. Vernon glanced at Zeke, his expression heavily lined with judgment, as if Zeke's job was women's work—and it was—and that were all Zeke was good for, which it wasn't. Zeke resisted the strong temptation to turn the hose in that direction just to see Vernon dance, but it wouldn't win Zeke any friends. It'd probably earn him a well-deserved lecture and maybe an early trip home.

He needed to go home a hero, so perhaps—

No matter. He'd be unlikely to be recognized as anything more than a screwup even if he saved the whole world from certain disaster like some comic book super-hero. Which he wasn't.

Gracie said something quietly to Vernon, who bestowed a charming smile on her, and he went to join her brothers and *daed*. And Vernon would probably know all their names before he did a lick of work.

Zeke figured he'd get to know them in time. Standing there while twelve people tossed names at him at once would only serve to confuse him.

"Pay attention." Patience jerked the hose from his hand.

Right. Zeke turned, just as the dog's grin faded and he let loose another long, pitiful howl.

"You soap. He not hold still," Patience said. She aimed the hose toward the washtub and Slush's feet.

Slush moaned, long and loud enough that any neighbors nearby would think the animal was in agony. Shoot, Zeke was right there and he almost believed Slush was dying or something.

"He hate baths." Patience glanced at Zeke.

That would be a given. But Zeke nodded. He dared to venture close enough to pat the dog's head. The look he got in return could only be called pitiful. And miserable. Definitely miserable.

"You poor thing," he crooned. "You'll feel so much better once you're clean. And the sooner we get started, the sooner we'll be finished." He reached for the dog shampoo and soaped the dog up. "Do you have a wire brush for him?"

"That Gracie's job." Patience started rinsing the dog off.

"I won't mind if he does it." Gracie's voice startled Zeke. He hadn't known she was still near.

"Maybe you'll sit with me while I brush." The words

came out without conscious thought. He liked the idea, though, but it would be a very courtship-type thing to do, and they weren't courting. "Slush, that is. Not you." His tongue tripped over itself in his hurry to retract. Not that it worked. He cringed. He sounded like an idiot, because if he was brushing Slush, then of course Slush would be sitting with him. He clamped his mouth shut before he added something even more stupid. Like maybe suggesting a walk later.

Patience giggled. "He not mean Slush."

Gracie blushed. "Maybe I will."

Really? His heart pounded.

"And we'll outline a game plan to find Timothy."

Right. The missing groom.

And with that Zeke was slammed right back into his place.

* * *

Grace went to fetch the dog brush from the basement shelf, then returned to the back porch as Slush violently shook, sending water flying in every direction.

Patience squealed.

Zeke made a grunting sound.

Grace tried not to giggle, but it escaped anyway, as Slush grinned happily and strutted off, tail held high.

Zeke spun to face her, as if something in her giggle had lit a spark of... well, something. His eyes filled with humor and maybe a challenge.

She shivered and backed away.

He took a step toward her, then stopped, the light dying in his gaze.

Disappointment stabbed her.

What would it be like to be courted by this man?

Shame flooded over her like the waters of the local creeks during the spring rains. She shouldn't think that way when she was engaged, promised, almost married...

Ach. Acute pain butchered what was left of her emotions. Tears stung. A lump clogged her throat. She dropped the brush on the porch floor and blindly fled toward the backdoor, stumbling over her feet and uneven boards, and *oof.* An unseen step flung her forward.

She threw her arms out to catch herself, but the next second strong hands closed around her waist, hauling her up and back.

She came to rest against a firm but wet chest. Male hands stayed loosely clasped, but the tingling warmth of them filled her along with a very pleasant male scent of pine and fresh air.

A breath tickled her ear. "Don't worry, Gracie. We'll find him."

Was it wrong that she didn't want to? Well, she did, but...

"You'll be married in no time." His voice dipped, probably in an effort to be comforting.

Instead it was... sexy.

She shivered and stepped out of his grasp.

Jah, Timothy would be found. They would be married.

And she'd forever wonder what might've been.

CHAPTER 6

Zeke detached the hose, coiled it up, and returned it to the trash pile. Most of the water had come out of the sides instead of the end anyhow. He was almost as wet as the dog. He tried not to think of the look on Gracie's face before she started to run off and especially not how it felt to hold her soft, warm body against his chest when he caught her.

How would they go about finding her missing groom—the fool who was racing buggies the night before his wedding?

Zeke emptied the metal tub and set it upside down on the porch, then picked up the abandoned brush Gracie had dropped. He glanced at Slush, now lying on his side in the sun. Zeke would love to lie in the sun and dry off, too. Maybe even take a nap, since he hadn't gotten any sleep in over twenty-four hours. That wasn't an option.

He clicked his tongue. "Slush, come. Come on, boy."

The dog raised his head with a huff and glared at him.

"Okay, buddy. You win. For now." It'd be better to brush the dog's fur when it was dry anyway.

Gracie had fled, probably to regain her composure before they made the game plan to find Timothy. He shouldn't have teased her. Or flirted. She was promised to another man. Even if that gave him a strange feeling inside. Even though he wished he'd met her first.

Patience went inside to change her wet dress—or so he assumed, since she didn't say. Should he change? He grimaced. No. He'd only brought along one change of clothes. Best let them dry naturally.

Maybe Daniel Zook knew about the missing men and would already have an update Zeke could give Gracie. He wandered around to the side of the house to make the call. It went to voicemail.

"Daniel, this is Zeke Bontrager, one of the Amish men with you on the trip. I just discovered that three young men were racing buggies when the tornado hit, and they are all missing. One buggy was found. Call me."

He disconnected and went to join the men gathered around the tree. Vernon wasn't among them. He glanced around but didn't see him.

Seth Lantz must've noticed, because he cleared his throat. Zeke turned to find all thirteen men staring at him. Twelve of them with beards. It was rather disconcerting to be the recipient of so many stares. He forced a smile. "Sorry. I was, um, wondering where Vernon was."

"We sent your friend to see if he could find any of our cows or horses."

They weren't friends, but okay. Zeke nodded. "How do you want me to help?"

"You can fix the mailbox, if you'd like, then since you volunteered, you can comb Slush. We're almost finished with the tree; then we'll have dinner. Oh, and there's a hammer in the small tool kit in the kitchen."

Zeke nodded. The mailbox might require more than a hammer. That aside, was he given wimpy jobs because he somehow needed to prove his worth? He tugged at the cold, soaked material clinging to his chest.

"After dinner, you can help Gracie. She might want to visit her friends to find out if they'd seen Timothy. Or to find out how they fared." Seth's mouth set in a firm line, and he narrowed his eyes in warning, a mirror image of most of the looks *Daed* had given Zeke over the years.

He straightened, tempted to make some flippant response or ask them point-blank if they thought he was worthless, but he bit the words back. For some reason, he wanted to earn this man's respect. Just like he wanted to win *Daed*'s respect. And *Gott*'s.

"Don't hurt her. She's strong, but she's in a very fragile state right now. Do you understand?" Seth warned.

"*Jah.* I understand. I'll do my best to find her groom." Even though he didn't want to.

Gracie's *daed* nodded, but a strange light filled his eyes. "You also seem to relate well with Patience. Her world is in turmoil right now, so be gentle. It'll help the rest of us to know she's happy."

Zeke could see why. Her tears were messy, loud, and hard to handle. He adjusted his hat and tried not to shiver as a gust of cool air hit his drenched clothes. He also tried to school his expression. How could he return home a hero if he wasn't able to do anything heroic? "I have a special-needs cousin, and I've worked with many special-needs children at a camp, so that's why I sort of understand Patience. I worked with the boys, though." And they didn't cry so easily.

Seth nodded. "We appreciate that."

Vernon would get a bigger hero's welcome if he located the family's missing livestock. All Zeke had done was find the muddy dog.

He shouldn't compare himself to others. He could almost hear his preacher *grossdaadi* quoting Bible verses about that. Several of them. Unfortunately, none of them came to mind, and he didn't want to stew over them while thirteen Amish men armed with chain saws, clippers, and handsaws stared at him.

They were a peaceful, nonviolent people, sure, but accidents happened. Sometimes accidentally on purpose.

He took a deep breath. The quicker he got the mailbox fixed, the quicker he'd be out of accident range and the sooner he could get on to a real job. "Where in the kitchen would I find the hammer?"

Seth smiled. "It's under the sink in a small toolbox. Belonged to my wife before we married."

A couple of the men chuckled and elbowed each other.

Strange. Were they baby toys or something?

He wasn't sure how to react. Probably the best way would be to go along with it. And laugh with them if the joke was on him in some way.

Zeke eyed the men; then, with a nod at Seth, he turned and went inside the house. The kitchen was void of life, so he opened the under-the-sink cabinet and found not one but two toolboxes. Both were small, and the light-blue one was stacked on top of a light-pink one.

He lifted the blue one out and set it on the counter. Since it was on top, it'd make sense that it was most often used. He opened it. And stared. It *was* full of baby toys and rattles. He picked up a yellow-and-red hammer and shook it. It made noise.

Zeke chuckled. Patience was too old for these, so some of the twelve brothers must have children.

He returned the hammer, closed the toolbox, and picked up the pink one. He set it on the counter next to the blue one and opened it.

His chuckle turned into a cough. Seriously? Every single thing in the toolbox was *pink*. Pink! No wonder Seth had stressed that it belonged to his wife, and the men had grinned and elbowed each other.

The joke was on him.

But he was man enough to handle it.

Maybe.

Not if Vernon saw him wielding a pink hammer. Zeke would be the laughing stock of Shipshewana for months.

Of course, the manly tools probably had been kept in the barn and were literally gone with the wind.

He stared at the two boxes. Then, with a sigh, he firmed his shoulders, picked up the pink box, and walked out of the house.

The twelve Lantz brothers chuckled. Their father just smiled.

Zeke nodded, accepted a small handful of nails from Seth, and marched out to the mailbox.

He had the post pounded back into the ground and most of the dents knocked out of the mailbox when Patience came out. Her dress was dry. She carried a small brown bag in her hand.

"You mailing a package to someone?" he teased.

Patience frowned. "Cookies. For you. They wedding cookies."

Of course. His special cousin didn't understand teasing or jokes, either.

"Gracie said." Patience held the bag out.

Zeke took it, but he wasn't hungry. He should've been, probably, but upon arrival, this whole mission had robbed him of his appetite, because of the menial tasks that drove home his personal incompetency. Because the pretty damsel in distress was so totally out of reach. Because he was paired with Vernon the overachiever and Zeke's biggest enemy.

This was a mission of failure. He should've stayed home. At least he had friends there. And some—a few—successes.

How much did it hurt Gracie to have her wedding...postponed...and to be giving away the food prepared for the singing following the ceremony? What about the wedding dinner?

His stomach lurched. He knew what they'd be having for the noon meal. The traditional Amish wedding dinner. Either fried or roasted chicken, mashed potatoes and gravy, and an assortment of vegetables. Of course, districts varied, so the meals did, too, but not by much.

And then the dessert table. The wedding cake...

His people were too frugal to throw perfectly good food out. So they'd be eating it for days to come. Sharing with neighbors and family.

Poor Gracie. Every bite would be like salt in the wound of her abandonment. She was alone instead of loved and married. While he was feeling the personal slight with every "job" and elbow jab by her brothers, she would feel rejection and maybe loneliness with every sandwich, cookie, or piece of chicken they ate.

Maybe the cake could be frozen. He didn't know. But he might've seen frozen cakes in grocery stores. Perhaps. He wasn't sure about that, either.

But the chances of her groom being found alive were slim to none. Gracie had to know that. On the other hand, she wasn't moping around. So maybe she didn't.

He wouldn't be the one who broke the bad news.

Hopefully.

Of course, since he was supposed to help her find him, he might be with her when she found out.

"Assuming he is ever found," Zeke muttered.

"Jesus calmed the storm." Patience beamed at him, and with a wave, she hurried toward the house.

Zeke grimaced. He'd forgotten Patience was beside him. Nevertheless, the storm had only just begun. But oh, to have faith and absolute trust like Patience.

His faith, his trust were sorely lacking.

He balled his fist, and paper crumpled. He looked down. Oh. He'd forgotten Patience's gift, too. He peeked in the bag.

Three cookies. Heart shaped. With pink icing. They were in a plastic baggie.

His stomach rebelled. He swallowed hard, forcing the bitterness back down.

He set the bag on the ground and finished fixing the mailbox, then removed the baggie from the paper bag. He set the baggie in the mailbox and raised the flag. The mail carrier would appreciate a treat.

He probably should pray for Gracie . . . and her groom.

What was his name? Tim? Timothy. That's right. And he should pray for the community as a whole.

Jesus calmed the storm. *Jah*, right.

* * *

Grace stared at the mounds of cold fried chicken.

Somehow, with the devastation of the tornado and the need to see Timothy, it never registered deep inside that with the wedding postponed—or cancelled—she would be eating her wedding meal today, after all.

Not all of it was there, though. Many women had helped prepare the wedding meal. *Aentie*s, her sisters-in-law, and more. They were to have brought the food over with them, but again, no one had. They'd be eating on their contribution for a while, too.

It'd be a reminder to pray for her and Timothy.

And since no one had come by to comfort her . . .

Not that she needed comforting. There were too many uncertainties. And it was a relief in a way. She loved Timothy. She did. But there were all the doubts, the fears, the unsettled feelings she'd wrestled with that he'd refused to even listen to. They'd courted for three years, after all. He was sure. She was the one with the commitment phobia. At least that's what he'd called it.

She wasn't afraid of commitment. She just wasn't sure.

Mamm had called it cold feet. Said it was normal. But Grace wasn't sure that was it, either.

She didn't know how to explain it, even to herself.

Timothy had gotten upset with her the last time they'd been together. He was sure, and she obviously needed to pray it through and align herself with *Gott*'s will, because *Gott* had told him she would be his wife, and they *were* getting married. It bothered her that *Gott* would tell Timothy that and not her. But she listened, went along with his plans, and prepared. And prayed. Sort of. Mostly that *Gott* would stop the wedding if He didn't want it to happen.

And He had.

Just not how she had expected or wanted. In fact, she hadn't expected Him to stop it at all.

Except, it had cost her family their barn and the church district their benches, and others their property or loved ones...

She hadn't wanted to hurt anyone. Couldn't *Gott* have stopped the wedding without sending tornados?

Now she felt relief and guilt. And also fear about what actually had happened to Timothy. She didn't want him hurt or killed. Plus she struggled with unwanted attraction to Zeke. Which greatly bothered her, because she *shouldn't* be so attracted to a stranger when she should be mourning the probable death of her groom.

Oh. And there was also fear that Timothy would be found alive and the wedding would still be on while her doubts remained.

She sighed.

Mamm turned from the stove where she'd just pulled the foil container of mashed potatoes out of the oven and patted Grace's arm. "It'll be okay, Gracie."

Jah, but she wasn't sure how.

"Trust and pray. Timothy will be found. You'll be married by this time next year."

Grace's stomach tumbled. Not pleasantly. "*Mamm*, is it wrong—?"

Mamm sighed heavily. "How many times do I have to tell you it's just cold feet, Gracie? Perfectly normal. Every bride gets a bad case of nerves—"

The backdoor opened and Zeke came in, carrying *Mamm*'s pink toolbox. "I fixed the mailbox." He gave them a crooked grin.

Grace's heart thudded.

His gaze went to the platter piled full of fried chicken. He winced, and the light in his eyes changed to something she couldn't identify.

Maybe pity. But she hoped not.

His fingers brushed the back of her hand as he passed and sparks shot up her arm. "I'm sorry, Gracie." His voice was soft. Caring.

Compassion, maybe.

Tears burned her eyes, pooled, and overflowed.

"Aw, honey. We'll find him," *Mamm* said.

A tear dripped from Grace's chin. She swung around and ran from the room.

* * *

Zeke's heart ached. He wanted—needed—to fix this, but how? When a little girl had gone missing in Shipshewana, the ones in charge had a map and graphed grids for rescuers to follow. But with eleven tornadoes, how would they even begin? Timothy could be miles and miles away. It wouldn't merely be tracking the potential path of a lost person; it would be tracking the path of destructive storms that crossed state lines.

Zeke didn't have the foggiest idea where to begin.

It was a good thing he wasn't in charge.

Gracie's *mamm* sighed and swiped a hand across her eyes.

Zeke supposed it must be hard for her, too. But he had nothing to say. Nothing.

He put the toolbox back where he found it and turned to head back outside.

"I just don't understand what got into her." Gracie's *mamm* slammed something down on the counter.

Zeke stopped. Turned. Opened his mouth…

"Three years they courted. Three years! And then as soon as they are published she wants to talk about whether she and Timothy are right for each other. Isn't that something she should've figured out sooner than two weeks before the wedding?" She looked at Zeke as if he had answers.

He didn't. Except, a tiny part of his heart latched on to the fact that she had doubts about her groom. Which meant her rush of emotion wasn't as much about loss as it might be about guilt or relief.

"Timothy is from a good family. His *mamm* and I are friends. It's cold feet, is all, because if it wasn't she would've broken it off with him long before. Ain't so?"

Zeke didn't know the answer to that, either. He shrugged. But if the *mamm*s were friends, maybe she'd felt pressured to go along with the wedding instead of forging her own path.

Maybe.

Gracie's *mamm* chuckled. "Just agree with me. I'm right."

He smiled. "Okay. If you say so."

"I say so. I'm Barbara. Everyone calls me Barbie."

"Ezekiel. Everyone calls me Zeke."

"Nice to meet you, Zeke. If you don't mind, ring the dinner bell, okay? We're ready to eat."

He nodded. "What about Gracie?"

"She knows better than to ignore the dinner bell. She may not eat much, but she'll join us."

His glance slid over the wedding feast they'd be enjoying. "Okay. But this particular meal might be a little hard on her."

Barbie looked at the food; then understanding dawned. "Ring the dinner bell; then take a sandwich up to her. I'll excuse her this time. But tell her that she needs to keep her strength up, and encourage her that Timothy will be found."

Zeke nodded, opened the backdoor, and clanged the bell. Rather pointless since everyone, except Vernon, was right there.

Wait. Vernon appeared at the back of the property. With a cow.

Zeke sagged. Well, he was happy the family had a cow again.

He quietly shut the door, trying to shut his inadequacies out with it.

"Take your bag up, too. You're upstairs. First door on the right."

He nodded, picked up his bag, and took the sandwich Barbie held out.

"Gracie is on the left. Last door. Tell Patience to come down."

"I will," he said quietly. He left the room, blowing out a puff of frustration, and went upstairs.

Vernon had already claimed the best bed in the room, the one nearest the window. Zeke put his bag on the other one, determined to make an effort to get along with Vernon. He left the room and found Gracie's room. She'd thrown herself across the bed, shoulders heaving.

Patience sat beside her, rubbing her back. "It okay, Gracie. Jesus calm the storm."

Zeke stopped in the doorway, laid the sandwich on the dresser, and backed out. He didn't take time to look around. Gracie needed Patience right now more than either of them needed food.

He dipped his head as he walked away. *Jesus, please calm the storm.*

But a sense of unrest persisted.

CHAPTER 7

Grace's head pounded and her throat hurt when she finally sat up, wiped her eyes, and hugged her sister. "*Danki*, Patience."

"You wash face now." Patience patted her back. "Feel better."

Not really. Grace wasn't sure she'd ever feel better. She wasn't even sure how to pray. *Gott* had answered her prayers—maybe. He'd stopped the wedding, but did that mean He didn't want her to marry Timothy? Or had *Gott* decided to give her a little more time to figure things out?

If it was the latter, how would she figure it out if no one listened to her?

If only she had someone to talk to at this very moment. Someone who cared. But she didn't. No one except Slush. And he might be a good, loving listener, but he never gave her any helpful advice.

"I hungry." Patience followed her to the bathroom and watched as Grace splashed cold water on her face.

"I heard the dinner bell a while ago. I'm surprised no one came to get us." Grace reached for a towel.

"Zeke did. He peeked in and left sandwich."

Grace spun around to face Patience, her face heating. "What?"

"Zeke did. He—"

"I heard you. Why didn't you say something?"

Patience's face screwed up. "To who?" She held her hands up.

Grace shut her eyes. "Never mind. Go on downstairs. I'll be there in a minute." She turned back to the sink and washed her face again, then tugged on her dress to make sure it wasn't clinging somewhere it shouldn't.

Satisfied that everything was in place, she returned to her bedroom. Patience was right. A sandwich waited on the edge of her dresser, right inside the door.

Her cheeks burned.

Zeke had been inside her bedroom and witnessed her lying on her bed crying like a big baby. How awful.

Not that anyone would judge her today. They would think she was in mourning due to the unconfirmed but extremely likely death of her groom.

And she was. Sort of.

Just mostly mourning that nobody cared enough to listen.

She grabbed the sandwich and carried it downstairs. She wasn't hungry anyway. *Mamm* would tell her she needed to eat to keep up her strength, but skipping one meal wouldn't hurt, would it?

The table was pulled out to full capacity, and her family plus Zeke and Vernon filled all the chairs except one. Everyone's head was bowed.

Oh, they were praying. Maybe she could escape out the front door. Or return to her room.

"Amen," *Daed* said.

So much for escaping.

She slipped into the empty seat between Patience and Jon and kept her head bowed. Hopefully, no one would notice any remaining tearstains.

"Glad you joined us, Gracie. Zeke didn't think you would," *Mamm* said. "You need to keep up your strength."

Grace nodded and tried hard not to roll her eyes at how predictable *Mamm* was about "needing to keep up her strength." Despite herself, her gaze rose to meet Zeke's. His mouth quirked in a half smile, but his eyes remained serious. Caring.

As if he might be the one person in the world who'd listen to her selfish concerns.

Not that they mattered. Timothy was still missing.

And it was her fault, because she'd asked *Gott* to stop the wedding.

* * *

After dinner, Zeke went outside, retrieved the dog brush, and called Slush over. Vernon retreated into the woods as Zeke sat on the bottom step, the husky leaning against his legs. Dishes clattered inside as the three women cleaned the kitchen.

The Lantz men all scattered in different directions. At the noon meal, Seth had said something about him and Jon getting tarp or plastic to cover the broken windows, and shingles to repair the roof, as well as ordering supplies for a new barn. One of the brothers went for a wagon to collect the wood stacked on the side of the road. The others went to their homes to take care of things and inventory damages there. Seth had also mentioned something about a planned schedule for tomorrow.

Left alone with the dog, Zeke rubbed the animal's ears with one hand and pulled his phone out of his pocket with his other. No new messages, no missed calls. Hadn't Daniel Zook checked his phone yet? Or did he already know about the three missing men? Seth Lantz had mentioned that *Englisch* experts would be in charge. Zeke would wait until evening and try to call him again.

The backdoor opened. Gracie emerged and sat on the opposite side of the wide steps. She twisted to face him. "The dog isn't going to get brushed at this rate," she teased.

He glanced at Slush leaning into his touch. "Guess not." He patted the dog's head. "Time to get to work, boy."

Slush gave him a mournful look and shifted away.

Zeke ran the brush through the dog's fur but glanced at Gracie. Maybe she'd have some idea where Timothy might've taken refuge. "Tell me about Timmy."

She hesitated. "He's confident. Overly so, sometimes to the point of being arrogant. He never asked me to do something—just stated it, and I jumped. I don't know why. Maybe because *Mamm* bends over backward to do what *Daed* wants, but their relationship is different somehow. *Daed* tries to please *Mamm*, too."

Zeke frowned. He'd meant what Timmy liked to do or where he liked to go so they'd know where to begin looking, but Gracie's comments concerned him. "You like the bossy type?" Not that it was his business.

She shook her head. "At first it was flattering. That first Sunday evening I was old enough to go to a singing he came up to me and said, 'I'll take you home.' Then he walked off. My friends and I giggled about how he knew what he wanted. But then I witnessed guys asking—*asking*—my friends to ride home with them, and that seemed kind of sweet, you know? As if they had value and were respected."

"Mm-hmm." *Note to self: Ask her what she wants.* Zeke looked away and continued brushing Slush. He'd always asked girls—hands damp with sweat, a quiver in his voice, and knees knocking, worried about the chance of a refusal that implied he wasn't good enough.

"His *mamm* and mine are friends, so *Mamm* was excited when she learned Timothy had started courting me. I was still flattered, but he acted possessive sometimes. If I talked to another guy, he would come over, interrupt, and pull me away to talk to someone else. When we were alone, he'd speak to me about being unfaithful. I'd really be in trouble if he saw me sitting here next to you, talking."

Zeke glanced at the wide space between them. Big enough for both Eli and Kiah to sit without any of them touching. He grunted.

"If I made plans with a girlfriend, he wanted me to clear them with him first."

His fist tightened around the brush. "And you agreed to marry him when he asked?"

"He didn't ask. *Gott* told him that we were going to marry. And who am I to question *Gott*?"

"How did your *daed* like this?" Zeke glanced at her. How many times had he questioned *Gott*?

Gracie played with her *kapp* ribbons, twirling them around her fingers. "I didn't tell him. Maybe it's normal, you know? *Mamm* tells *Daed* everything like that. Then I tried to talk to *Mamm*, but she told me I have cold feet and said it was normal."

Zeke nudged the dog into a different position. "I'm not sure if it is or not. You should've talked to your *daed*."

"It's my fault Timothy's missing."

Zeke's hand fumbled the brush. He jerked away from Slush and stared at her. "How so?"

"I prayed that *Gott* would stop the wedding." Her voice broke.

He shook his head. "I hardly think you are to blame for a tornado. That is caused by barometric pressure, I believe. Warm fronts mixing with cold fronts. Something like that."

Slush got up and nosed Gracie's hand. She petted him. "*Jah*, but..."

He waited, but she didn't continue. "Why do you want to find him so badly? If you didn't want to marry him, then..."

She was silent for what seemed an eternity. "I love him. We grew up together. We had fun sometimes. He can be really sweet. I just wasn't sure I wanted to marry him."

"And now you are?" Wow, absence really did make the heart grow fonder.

She snorted. "*Nein*. I'm not at all sure. I just don't understand why *Gott* would tell him it was His will for us to marry, but He wouldn't tell me. Is it because I'm a woman?"

It was true that the Amish teaching said one thing, but Zeke had found women like Gracie have brains of their own. And why wouldn't *Gott* speak to them about something so important as marriage, too?

"Besides, do I really want to have to explain every move I make and clear every friendship with Timothy for the rest of my life?" She glanced at him. "And why did *Gott* stop the wedding if it was His will for Timothy and me to marry?"

She asked tough questions. He tried to think of a good response. Nothing came to mind. Especially when Slush's earlier grin made him wonder if *Gott* had stopped the wedding so Zeke had the chance to meet Gracie. Not to mention Patience's words about Zeke marrying Gracie. His cheeks burned. Not going there. He puffed out a breath and clasped his hands over his knees. "So do you want to find him?"

"Of course. Why wouldn't I? His family is worried about him, and I am, too. Besides, I need to have some closure. And if he used the tornado as an excuse to run away, I need to know, right?" Gracie shifted and the step creaked. "I refuse to be jilted. That is like the ultimate shame."

"Why would Timmy run away if he believes it is *Gott*'s will for you to marry?" Zeke grimaced. He shouldn't have asked that. Besides, it seemed to him it'd be better to be jilted than married to the wrong person. "You know, never mind. Where should we start looking for him?"

Gracie bounced to her feet. "His two best friends'

homes. Grab the chain saw and harness the horse. His name is Charlie, by the way. My *grossdaadi* named him. Charlie Horse."

He forced a chuckle. Stood. Something didn't feel right about this at all. He wanted to find Seth and talk to him about Gracie and Timothy. But it was none of his business.

"I'll tell *Mamm* and see if she wants me to take Patience with us." She grabbed the dog brush, dashed up the stairs, and disappeared inside the house.

Slush moved to lean against Zeke's legs again and looked up at him with a sad puppy dog expression.

"Do you want to come?" Zeke ran his hand over Slush's head.

The dog tucked his tail, plopped down on the ground, and sighed.

Funny how well Slush communicated. Zeke grinned. "Okay. Let me know if you change your mind."

"*Nein*! You not find Timmy. Marry Zeke!" Patience wailed from inside. A thump followed.

Zeke jerked to attention and glanced toward the *haus*. Leave it to Patience to state her desires so clearly. He liked Gracie, but they were barely acquaintances. Hardly ready to marry.

He headed for the pasture and Charlie Horse. He didn't even know Gracie's *grossdaadi* and he already liked his sense of humor.

Since he wasn't even an opponent running some race against the confident Timmy, he needed to stay far away from the marriage drama.

Not his business.

Even if he wanted it to be.

* * *

Grace tried not to glare at Patience, but really, she wanted to. Patience wouldn't understand, though. Especially since she'd connected faster with Zeke in a few hours than she had with Timothy in over three years. She'd heartily disliked Timothy. And he'd barely tolerated her.

Grace really shouldn't focus on the negative aspects of her groom. But wow, it was so nice to have someone listen to her and show some concern like Zeke had. He hadn't offered any advice, though, other than to talk to *Daed*. And maybe she should, but with Timothy missing it hardly seemed appropriate.

And then Zeke had to ask why she was so determined to find Timothy. Maybe part of the reason she wanted to find him was so this time she could tell him no—even if it was just to see how he'd react so she'd know what the rest of her married life might involve. Or maybe to suggest they wait another year. To make sure she was certain.

"Hush now, Patience," *Mamm* said. "She hardly knows Zeke. Besides, he doesn't even live here. Timmy is a sweet young man and will be a fine husband for our Gracie." She looked away from Patience and turned her attention to the piecrust she was making. "Patience can stay home with me. It might be better if she did, given her infatuation with a certain Indiana guest."

What would *Mamm* think if she knew Grace was infatuated with him, too?

Grace shook that off. "Okay. I'm going to visit Timothy's friends and see whether they made it home and if they know where Timothy might be."

"I do hope you find him safe and sound. Take another few bags of sandwiches and cookies with you. I sent some home with your brothers, too. They'll go stale by the time Jon and Aubrey marry, and even if we have them for supper the next five nights, we have plenty."

Jah, it took a lot of sandwiches to feed a barn full of guests.

Grace went downstairs for the picnic basket again to refill it with sandwiches and cookies. She carried it up, filled it, and took it out to the waiting buggy. Zeke held Charlie's reins in one hand and reached for the basket with the other.

"Feeding the electrical workers again?"

She smiled, handed him the basket, and then climbed into the buggy. "I'm driving."

He lifted the picnic basket into the back and climbed in next to her. "Lead on, my lady."

When had anyone ever called her a lady?

Grace steepled her hands and pressed her fingers to her lips as she closed her eyes. *Lord* Gott—

"So, Timothy's friends—"

She opened her eyes, unsteepled her hands, and pressed one finger to her lips.

His gaze dipped.

"Shhh." She'd barely made the noise when his fingers gently closed around hers.

Sparks shot through her. Her eyes widened as his eyes rose to hers.

"I was praying," she whispered.

He kept his hand against hers. "We'll both pray. *Gott* knows where Timmy is. We'll see you married, Lord willing, and if he's who you want."

"What if he's not?" She whispered that, too.

Zeke's jaw worked. "Then you have the right to say no."

She moistened her lips, let her gaze trail over the firm planes and angles of his face, then pulled her hand from his.

It was so nice to have someone listen to her and, more importantly, hear her.

Someday, she'd thank him.

Someday.

Somehow.

Someway.

CHAPTER 8

Zeke should pray. He should. Instead, he dipped his head and watched Gracie out of the corner of his eye.

She resteepled her hands and closed her eyes again. Her light-brown hair and *kapp* had been straightened sometime, but she still had wood chips clinging stubbornly to her blue dress. It wasn't light like the sky, or dark like navy blue, but a shade that fell somewhere in the middle of the color spectrum. Whatever color it was officially known as in the artist world, it was a color that, with the light and shadows, complemented her eyes. Reflecting blue in some parts, gray in others.

Beautiful eyes. A beautiful girl. Someone he would've considered working up the courage to ask out on a buggy ride, if she lived in or near Shipshewana and he could easily date her.

But distance between their homes aside, she loved Timothy. He needed to remember that. Even though she had issues with Timothy's controlling nature, she loved him.

Zeke had to admire the man's courage, though. He'd never have the self-confidence to march up to a pretty girl and tell her that he was taking her home. But then Zeke stopped himself. Gracie didn't appreciate not being asked. And...

Timothy was controlling her friendships. That bothered Zeke more. He wasn't sure, but he thought he might've heard something sometime about men who did that being abusive. Zeke wouldn't testify to that, though. Maybe he imagined it.

But at the end of the day, Gracie loved Timothy.

If she and Zeke ever became anything more than acquaintances, they'd be temporary friends at best. Just until Timothy was found—alive—and Zeke turned and walked away content in the knowledge that she was reunited with her one true love.

The stuff romance novels were made of. He could almost imagine his sixteen-year-old sister, Elizabeth, sighing over that ending in one of those endless Christian romance novels she was eternally checking out of the library, four or five at a time. He teased her about it, but there were worse vices to have than being a romance-loving bookworm.

Like buggy racing the night before a wedding, during a tornado. And what—had the guys stopped to go skinny-dipping? In November? Is that how Timmy lost his pants?

Gracie made a clicking sound and Charlie Horse trotted toward the road.

Zeke shook his runaway thoughts back on course.

Checking with Timothy's friends was a good place to begin. Because beyond that, Zeke didn't have the vaguest idea where to start. Maybe checking storm shelters . . . but it seemed the owners would've noticed a random Amish man joining their family in the shelter. Unless the homeowners weren't home, and he somehow got pinned in by a fallen tree or something.

That'd be something to mention to Daniel Zook, too, whenever Zeke succeeded in reaching him.

He shifted in his seat as the buggy zoomed too fast for his comfort onto the road without so much as a pause at the mailbox. He pinned his gaze on Gracie. "You're dangerous. What if there was a car coming?"

"There wasn't."

"But what if there was?"

"I looked both ways as I neared the road. We're fine." She had a weird tone in her voice, as if she were trying to pacify an overly worried toddler or something. It was the smiley voice that preachers' wives used with difficult church members.

He wasn't pacified. "Admittedly, I live in Shipshewana where there are a lot more cars and tourists around, but even here vehicles move a lot faster than horses and you should be a little more cautious." Or a lot more.

"I could beat Timothy in a buggy race," Gracie stated. "Not with this horse, but with Author Itis."

Zeke's breath lodged in his throat. This woman was reckless and lived dangerously. Timothy's overprotectiveness suddenly made sense. When you loved someone, you wanted to make sure they were safe. Zeke would withhold any further judgment on Timothy.

"Well, I'd like to live long enough to get back home

and see my family again, so if you don't mind slowing down some and being a little more careful, I'd appreciate it." Then the horse's name sunk in. He barked a laugh. "Author Itis? Another horse your *grossdaadi* named?"

She flashed a quick grin in his direction. "*Jah*. And Ben Gay."

"Charlie Horse, Author Itis, and Ben Gay." Zeke would love to meet her *grossdaadi*. Not that it would happen. He was here for cleanup and rescue, among other things, not to meet extended family members of his host family.

She took another turn at breakneck speed, bumping over rubble in the road, and swerving around a tree. If a vehicle had been on the other side, she wouldn't have seen it until it was too late.

Zeke fought the temptation to fall to his knees and beg the Almighty *Gott* for his life. Instead, he gasped for air and gripped the edge of the seat. "Please. Slow. Down."

"Sure. We're at Toby's *haus* anyway. His real name is Tobias, but everyone calls him Toby." She guided the horse into a narrow drive with deep ditches on both sides so fast Zeke could've sworn the buggy tilted on two wheels. Whether or not it did was debatable.

"I'm driving to the next place," he stated.

"You like to take it slow and easy, do you?" she said, turning to look at him as Charlie Horse stopped in front of a barn.

Well, actually, he'd never thought so, but...He nodded. "*Jah*. *Jah*, I do." And compared to her, he definitely did.

She reached over and patted his hand. "There, there.

That was nothing. When Author Itis is found, I'll show you what fast looks like."

He was hunting for some sarcastic remark when an older, sober-faced man with red-rimmed eyes emerged from the barn.

And Zeke knew.

Tobias was no more.

*   *   *

Grace's heart sank. Without a word, she climbed out of the buggy and wrapped Toby's *daed* in a brief hug. "I'm so sorry."

He cleared his throat a couple of times, then nodded toward the *haus*. "My wife..." He coughed and turned away, shoulders heaving as he walked toward the barn.

"Of course." Grace grabbed the picnic basket from the back seat and glanced at Zeke. "You might want to help Toby's *daed*—his name is Luke—in the barn."

She entered the not-quite-quiet farmhouse and found Toby's body lying on a quilt on the dining room table. His clothes were soaked, one shoe on, one off, and the foot with the missing shoe had a sock dangling from it. His *mamm*, Tabitha, huddled on a chair, bent double, sobbing into her apron.

She looked up as Grace entered.

"Oh, Gracie." Her name came out on a teary sigh. "My Luke just found his body in the backfield. He said he was going to call the police and told me not to disturb anything. I mean, my son died in a tornado, but they might investigate it? Isn't that just adding insult to injury?"

Grace didn't know. Her heart hurt. She hadn't wished anyone dead. She'd only wanted the wedding stopped. "You're here alone?" She gave her a hug, then glanced around as if Timothy would walk into the kitchen as he had so many times before. Pure foolishness, considering if Toby was gone, then chances were good that Timothy...

She choked on a sob.

Tabitha pulled her back into her arms and returned her hug. "So much loss. So much destruction. We haven't notified family yet. I just want to be alone with my baby one last time. At least until the police come."

"I'm sorry for intruding. I brought sandwiches and cookies."

Tabitha exhaled. "You're a sweet girl, Gracie. They'll certainly come in handy in the days ahead. I'm really sorry about Timmy." She wiped her eyes with an already soggy tissue.

"Was Timothy found with Toby?" Grace asked without thinking.

"No. Not in our field, at least. But the boys were spending the evening together doing crazy stuff like racing buggies. During a storm, no less." Tabitha shook her head. "And if Toby didn't survive it, I daresay Timmy might not have."

Jah. It was what she feared. Tears pricked her eyes.

"Is there any way I can help?" Grace glanced at the sock dangling half off Toby's foot.

Tabitha sighed. "I want to be alone. But maybe call the bishop and leave a message on his phone if no one answers. We'll need his help planning the visitation and funeral."

"I'll do that." She wanted to call home and tell *Mamm*, too, but the phone was gone along with their barn.

Grace gave Tabitha one last hug. "I'll sure be praying. And I'll get the word out."

She emptied half of the sandwiches and cookies out of the picnic basket and went out to the small phone shanty just beside the barn. She lifted the receiver, but there was no dial tone. Of course. She should've thought of that. If electrical lines were down, then phone lines would be as well. She'd stop by and tell the bishop in person, but he might not even be home. Not if he lost his roof.

Grace hung up the receiver and picked up the picnic basket she'd set at her feet while she attempted to make the call. She carried it out to the buggy, then went to find Zeke. His head was bowed as he apparently prayed with Luke.

A half-finished casket was on the worktable. Toby and his *daed* were furniture makers, but they also made caskets for the community and the local funeral home. Grace's heart hiccupped. Toby had likely worked on his own casket.

The men looked up as she started to back out of the room. Luke scrubbed at his eyes with his fist. "I couldn't even call the police. Another way I failed my wife. Phone's dead."

"I can do that for you." Zeke stood and pulled his cell phone out of his pocket. He pressed something.

"Nine-one-one, what's your emergency?" a female voice said from the speaker.

Zeke handed the phone to Luke, reached for Grace's elbow, and led her from the room. "He needs his privacy for this call," he said quietly. "I don't think they should be alone while they wait for the police and the coroner, but I don't know who to contact to come help them."

"The bishop's phone number is posted on the wall in the phone shanty. Not that it'd do much good since the lines are down. I'll run to the *haus* next door and tell them. They'll come if they can."

Zeke raised his hand and his thumb brushed against her cheek. His blue eyes gazed into hers. "You're sweet, Gracie. A true angel of mercy as Timothy's *mamm* said."

For a second, she was tempted to lean into the comfort of his touch, maybe even step into his embrace and cry on his broad shoulders, but it would be ever so wrong. She tried to find a smile. Hopefully, she succeeded.

His mouth flexed, a dimple flashed, and he pulled away.

"You're dangerous, Gracie Lou. Dangerous."

Her smile faltered. "It's Grace Lynn. And you aren't exactly safe, either."

At least not to her wounded heart.

* * *

Zeke watched as Gracie ran up the driveway and turned right on the road. He stood there, not moving, until she was out of sight, then he turned to go back inside the barn. Hopefully, he'd be able to talk Luke into going into the *haus* and sitting with his wife. Zeke didn't have a whole lot of experience with this type of thing, but it seemed to him that neither should be alone. They needed each other.

And maybe to be reminded that *Gott* is still *Gott* in the bad times.

The sign in front of the destroyed church that said something about God calming the storm flashed in Zeke's memory, and he snorted. The physical storm might be over and past, but the emotional storm was still ongoing. And he didn't see any effort on the part of the Almighty *Gott* to calm either one of them.

Although it could be because his focus was on the storm and not on *Gott*.

One of the preachers—Kiah's *daed*—had said something about that last Sunday in Shipshewana. He'd spoken about Peter seeing Jesus walking on the water during a storm and how Jesus had beckoned Peter to come ahead and walk on the water to Him. But when Peter stepped out of the boat, the waves swelled around him, he took his focus off Christ, and he began to sink.

Zeke's focus wasn't on Christ, either. It was on the destruction. The death. The despair. And maybe—though he'd never admit it to anyone but himself—on the very pretty and very appealing Gracie.

He really should've prayed when Gracie did instead of thinking about her dress shade and how her eye colors changed and whether or not they'd be temporary friends. None of that was important.

Focusing on *Gott* during this storm was.

It wasn't too late to pray now.

Zeke changed directions, stepped into the built-into-the-barn phone shanty, and lowered himself to his knees on the dusty floor. He bowed his head, his thoughts still on the sermon. What had Jesus said when Peter began sinking? Zeke pressed his fingers against the bridge of his nose and tried to remember.

And immediately Jesus stretched forth his hand, and

caught him, and said unto him, O thou of little faith, wherefore didst thou doubt?

Zeke closed his eyes. He doubted. That was for sure. And his faith was indeed small. *Lord, help my faith to grow. Help me not to doubt. Help me to help this hurting community.* And maybe prove to *Daed* that he wasn't a big goof-off, after all, and was worthy of someday...

Nein. That was turning the prayer selfish. Whether or not *Daed* ever trusted him should have nothing to do with Zeke's prayer life. His faith. His trust.

The door opened with a whoosh.

Zeke looked up.

Luke shuffled into the room, his shoulders hunched like an old man's. He handed Zeke his cell phone and lowered himself to the stool beside the nonworking landline. "No point wasting your time, boy. Prayer isn't going to change a thing." There was a curse word inserted in the last sentence.

Zeke jerked in reaction.

The doubt, the despair filled the room—again—with the rapidness of a flash flood. And just like that he was sinking in the turbulent waves again.

Lord, help my faith.

And immediately Jesus stretched forth his hand, and caught him, and said unto him, O thou of little faith, wherefore didst thou doubt?

The verse replayed but did little to combat the hopelessness and anguish filling the atmosphere.

Gott, *give me words. Catch me, Jesus.*

Peace filled him, along with the certainty that *Gott* did have the storm under control. Somehow.

But the words to comfort the grieving man didn't come. There was no comfort in "It was Toby's time." There was no comfort in "He can cause the dead to live." There was no comfort in any of the other platitudes that came to mind.

"We can't choose whether or not storms come. But we can choose where we stare during a storm." The words burst from Zeke, startling him, because he couldn't remember even thinking them.

Luke grunted.

Right. Maybe there was no comfort there, either.

But somehow, it filled Zeke's soul with courage. Peace.

He stood, started to pocket the cell phone, and then noticed he had a missed call.

He slid his finger over it. It was from Daniel Zook. No message.

"Police are on the way. Suppose I'd best get to the *haus*." Luke stood, too.

"Gracie went to notify the neighbors." Maybe someone else would have the words of comfort that Zeke couldn't find.

Luke grunted again and left the room.

Zeke pushed the button to return the call. It went straight to voicemail.

He stepped outside as a closed buggy, carrying two strangers and Gracie, stopped behind the Lantzes' buggy. A woman emerged with a casserole dish, wrapped in towels. She raced toward the *haus* without so much as a glance in his direction.

The man followed, much slower.

Gracie grabbed the reins and climbed into her buggy.

"Let's go. They've got this, and I'll tell the preacher or bishop when we pass one of their homes."

Zeke stopped beside her. "Scoot over, Gracie. I'm driving."

"You have serious trust issues." Her tone was teasing, and she said it with a wobbly smile, but he nodded.

"*Jah*. I do. More than you know." Should he tell her about it? Probably. Or at least ask if she wanted to hear. "Do you want to know the story?"

She scooted over. Her smile faded. "*Jah*. Tell me about it."

He wasn't sure if she seriously wanted to know or if she was agreeing and saying she had trust issues, too. But he decided to take her at face value. He'd tell her once they were on the way.

He unlocked the brakes, clicked to Charlie Horse, and set off toward the road. "Which direction?"

She pointed left.

He carefully navigated the end of the driveway, mindful of the deep drainage ditches still filled with muddy water from the rain the previous night.

"Tell me." She edged closer and angled herself to face him.

"You know the story of Jesus walking on the water..."

CHAPTER 9

Grace nodded when Zeke finished his story about feeling as if the waves crashed over him and how he needed to learn to always keep his focus on *Gott* and not on his circumstances. "Something I struggle with." She could relate. Especially to his closing statement: "We can't choose whether or not storms come. But we can choose where we stare during a storm."

Oh, to feel the peace and calm that was reflected on his face.

She swallowed. "It's easier to think of the problem and worry about that than it is to keep looking at an unseen *Gott* and trusting Him to take care of it. But you know what catches my attention most?" She hesitated. "Turn right at the upcoming intersection."

"Okay." Zeke glanced at her. "What catches your attention most?" His forearm muscles rippled as he signaled to the horse.

"Jesus knew the storm was coming, but He went up on the mountain alone to pray."

Zeke's eyebrows rose. "So?" He pulled to a stop at the crossroads and looked both ways.

"So, what do you think He prayed about?"

"It doesn't really matter. We don't know. And what we think would just be a guess."

True. But... "What if He was praying for His disciples out on that boat during the storm, that they wouldn't be afraid and would trust Him?"

Zeke shrugged, and his gaze narrowed. He made the turn, then glanced at her, his expression thoughtful. "I don't understand."

"Fifth *haus* on the left," Grace directed. "What if Jesus is talking to *Gott* right now about our faith, our trust? I don't know. He knows where Timothy is and whether he's alive or not and if he is, when the wedding will be. And yet, I'm scared and worried."

"You don't act scared or worried."

Grace eyed him. "Of course not. I have a lot of practice in not scaring or upsetting Patience."

"I guess that's true." Zeke slowed in front of the fifth mailbox. "Whose *haus* is this? It's missing the roof and maybe the second floor. At least, part of it."

"Bishop Nathan's *haus*. It looks like someone's there, so go ahead and turn in. I need to tell him about Toby."

Zeke slowed, turned into the muddy, litter-strewn drive, and parked next to a wagon already piled full of debris.

A gray-haired man with a long beard emerged from the *haus* carrying another load of trash. He deposited it in the overflowing wagon, then came to meet them.

Grace climbed out her side of the open buggy, the side closest to the bishop's wagon.

"Grace Lynn. I hope your family is all right—despite the circumstances." Bishop Nathan's gaze slid from her to Zeke. "And you are?"

"Ezekiel Bontrager. From Shipshewana."

"Ah. The infamous Zeke."

Zeke's eyes darkened, his lips turned down, and he slumped. He aimed his gaze toward the ground.

"You heard of him?" Grace's mouth dropped open. And what was with Zeke's reaction?

The bishop glanced at her. "Your grandfather mentioned him." He turned his attention to Zeke. "Grace's grandfather is assisting with organizing the helpers at the school coordinating relief efforts. You likely met him. I'm Bishop Nathan Fisher. Nice to meet you."

"Likewise. Though it's rather disturbing to know my reputation precedes me." Zeke didn't smile. His gaze slid to Grace. "So I met your *grossdaadi* at the school, then."

Bishop Nathan chuckled. His attention swung back to Grace and he sobered. "I'm sorry about the wedding. Any sign of Timothy yet? We're still trying to figure out how to get his buggy out of my *haus*." He grunted. "Actually, we're waiting on the buggy repairman to come and help us disassemble it in a way that won't leave it unserviceable."

Grace glanced that way but didn't see the buggy.

The bishop tugged on his beard. "The tornado lifted off half the second floor, set it down in the cornfield, and set Timothy's buggy down through the hole in the floor, just as neat as you please." He shook his head. "I'll probably use this in a sermon someday. Somehow."

"I have news to share with you, Bishop. Toby's body was found in his family's cornfield." Grace's voice caught. Broke. "We're on our way to Peter's." She glanced at Zeke. "He is—was—Timothy's other best friend."

The bishop shifted. "Peter was found about an hour ago. He's alive but unconscious. Near as his parents can tell, he has two badly broken bones in one leg, and the opposite arm is broken. Not sure about internal injuries. He's on his way to the hospital. His family stopped by to let us know."

Grace swallowed the lump in her throat. "Good. I'm glad he's alive." But her breath caught again.

"We'll reschedule your wedding for the first available Thursday after Timothy is found. If he's able."

Grace forced a smile. "*Danki*."

Zeke frowned and gave her a look. She shook her head. She couldn't talk about her doubts to the bishop when it might not even matter.

Bishop Nathan studied Zeke. "You looked like you had a question. Is it something I can help you with?"

Grace cringed. Now Zeke would share her concerns about Timothy with the bishop, and they'd be forced to talk it through. She shifted.

Zeke hesitated and his frown deepened. "On the way here, Gracie and I were discussing Jesus walking on the water, and how the waves overwhelmed the disciple Peter and he took his focus off Christ. And—"

"Ah. *Jah*. The disciples thought He was a ghost. It's funny, but we never expect to see Him in a storm. But that's where He does His finest work. It's in the storms that He has our keenest attention."

Grace blinked.

"I never thought of that," Zeke said.

"But it's true, ain't so?"

"Patience kept praying for Jesus to calm the storm." Grace shifted again. She'd have to thank Zeke for not giving her secrets away.

"I think, if we're honest, we're all praying that." The bishop looked at what remained of his *haus*, took his hat off, slapped it against his leg, then replaced it with a long, drawn-out sigh. "*Jah*, indeed. It truly is hard to keep our focus on Him when the waves crash over us."

Zeke tilted his head toward Grace. "And we were wondering what Jesus was praying for up on that mountain when His disciples were tossed at sea."

Bishop Nathan blinked. Twice. "You ask the hard questions, do you?"

"Actually, Gracie asked me. I wasn't sure." Zeke grimaced.

"I'm not sure, either." The bishop tugged on his beard. "I never actually thought about it. But I think that, possibly, He might've been praying for His ministry and *Gott*'s will for the next day. I don't know. Scripture doesn't say. However, if I'm reading your question right"—he looked at Grace—"the Bible does say that Jesus is sitting at the right hand of the Father, interceding on our behalf."

Grace smiled. That made her feel better. Maybe Jesus was telling *Gott* all about her worries, her guilt, and her shame so she wouldn't have to. Though she did need to voice them in her prayers at some point. The Bible was clear about the need to confess sins.

The bishop exhaled noisily. "As much as I love to discuss the scriptures, I have to cut this short, because I have much to do. I'll tell my wife about Toby. She'll organize the women to bring meals and clean the *haus* for the viewing and funeral. I'll stop by there later this afternoon or evening."

"I hope the buggy repairman can help you figure out how to get the buggy out of your *haus*." Zeke climbed back into the buggy.

Bishop Nathan frowned. "*Danki*. Let me know if you have a brilliant suggestion. I expect to see you around at some of the work frolics, Zeke."

"Wherever they need me," Zeke replied.

"*Daed* asked him to help me find Timothy," Grace said. Though she couldn't remember exactly what he'd said. It seemed her thoughts whirled about as out of control as the tornado last *nacht*. For better or for worse, she was supposed to be a married woman right now. Not traipsing around the countryside looking for her groom while sitting beside a man who made her pulse race. She climbed into the buggy and plopped down on the seat.

The buggy shifted under the pressure.

Zeke glanced at her, concern in his eyes. "Where to?" He'd probably edited the question due to the bishop being within hearing still.

"I don't know where to look now. We've been to his home. His friends are accounted for in one way or another, and... well." She shrugged. "I could check on my friends."

"It seems someone should be checking on you." His voice was quiet, barely above a whisper.

"*Jah*, but..." How many times had she heard those words that day? Twice at least, maybe three or four times. But…"Nobody ever checks on me. I am the strong one. I have to stay calm for Patience. I—"

Zeke clicked to the horse and drove toward the road. "There's a song that plays on the oldies radio station, and *jah*, I know I'm not supposed to listen to a radio, but that's our secret, okay?" He raised an eyebrow.

She swallowed the rest of her argument. "O-kay." She winced at the doubt filling that one drawn-out word. But he didn't visibly react.

He paused at the end of the driveway. She pointed west. He nodded and checked for vehicles before turning. "I'm not exactly sure of the whole song, but some of the words are, 'If everybody wants you, why isn't anybody calling?'"

Ouch. The words hit her like a slap across the face, and she recoiled. "That's mean."

"I don't mean to be unkind. Really. But you need to step back and slow down before you have a breakdown."

"I won't have a breakdown."

"Patience isn't here right now, Grace. It's okay to cry. You've had your plans destroyed, even if you did pray for *Gott* to stop the wedding. You didn't expect the destruction, death, or injury to follow in *Gott*'s answer to your prayer. Not that you're responsible for the tornado…" He half chuckled, then grimaced. "I'm making a mess out of this. But don't you need to mourn and pray for peace, too?"

She wasn't sure what to do or say. So…she'd ignore it.

"Turn into the first driveway on the left." She shifted away from him. Because really, she didn't have time for dramatics. She needed to focus on the here and now, and not on her feelings.

She should've told herself that from the beginning. That, and love is a decision. She shouldn't have prayed for *Gott* to stop the wedding. Then the tornado wouldn't have come, Toby would be alive, Timothy would be by her side, and this dangerous, gorgeous hunk of mankind would be safely back in Indiana and not messing with the tattered remnants of her shredded heart.

She shook her head violently. She would not—could not—think like this.

"If I get into the habit of venting when Patience isn't with me, it might accidentally slip into my behavior when she is. And that would be bad." Though she did cry right before the noon meal, and Patience tried to comfort her. And her sister hadn't gone off the deep end. Hmm...

Zeke let go of the reins with one hand and reached for her. "Gracie..."

No, she couldn't let him touch her again. She was still promised to Timothy, and Zeke was way too appealing. She moved her hand out of his reach. His hand landed on her knee.

Her whole body reacted to his touch. Burning. Tingling. She shoved his hand away.

He white-knuckled the reins. "Sorry. I didn't mean to touch you like that." His mouth worked a second. "I just wanted to remind you to breathe. Just breathe."

* * *

Zeke clenched the reins tighter. He probably needed to shut his mouth and just let her be, but she seriously needed to take a quiet moment and mourn. At least he thought she should. But he did understand the need to be strong for Patience. He had to be careful around his special cousin, too.

He directed Charlie Horse to turn where Grace indicated and parked between the barn and the *haus*. "Who lives here?"

"One of my best friends. Elsie Miller. My other best friend, Hallie, works at the restaurant in Arthur. She took the day off for my wedding, but I'm sure she was called in to work with all the rescue workers coming to town. And tourists checking out the damage. That would be the place to be. Local hot spot for gossip."

"I guess." He shifted. "They're using the public school gymnasium to house those left homeless."

"The *Englisch*, you mean? I don't think the bishop or any of the Amish would go there. We take care of our own."

"Some of the *Englisch* do, too. But what if they have no family in the area and no place else to go?"

Gracie shrugged.

"They had several cots set up already when we checked in this morning. A janitor was on duty. I heard a baby crying. And that's where I found your dog."

She glanced at him, eyes wide. "You mentioned that earlier. But really? He went that far?"

It wasn't so far. Maybe five miles, give or take. He shrugged.

Nobody came out of the Miller *haus*. Zeke didn't notice any damage, though, other than several uprooted trees. No one was working on them. The place had an abandoned feel.

Gracie climbed out of the buggy and went into the *haus*.

Charlie Horse snorted and stomped his foot.

"Help!" A faint cry, followed by pounding, came from somewhere.

Zeke climbed out of the buggy, let the reins drop to the ground, and ran toward the *haus*. "Gracie?"

More yells and thumps.

He jogged up the steps to the porch and opened the door. "Gracie? Are you okay?"

"Help!"

The shout didn't seem to come from the *haus*. Zeke turned and surveyed the yard. The uprooted trees. "Where are you?"

"Storm shelter!" the answering shout came.

Gracie ran out of the *haus*, almost running into him. She skidded to a stop. "No one is home, but the beds are unmade."

"Where's the storm shelter?"

"The storm— Oh." She pointed. "Over there. Where the trees are down. Do you think they're in there?"

"I'm almost positive." Almost, because there was always room for doubt. Though, unless trees had started talking . . . He shook his head. That was plain foolishness. "Did you put the chain saw in the buggy?"

"*Nein*. I asked you to do it."

He frowned. If she had, he'd forgotten. Another failure on his part. "Do you think they might have one in the barn?"

She shrugged. "They don't. Because they don't have a woodstove or a fireplace. Propane."

"No chain saw." A voice said from the shelter. "We have a handsaw."

"Would the bishop have one?"

"I'll find one."

"I never thought I'd say this to you, but hurry." He grinned. "I'll go see if I can find the handsaw."

She scampered into the buggy and drove off.

Zeke went into the barn. She was right, they didn't have a chain saw, but he did find the handsaw. That'd be a start.

He carried it out and walked over to the uprooted tree. "We're working on getting you out. Hang tight."

"*Danki*," the tree answered.

Zeke couldn't see the storm shelter at all, underneath the colorful leafiness of the fallen trees. He guessed where the door probably would be and went to work.

"Okay, I'm beginning to saw the smaller branches off. This might sting a bit." He was trying to be funny but at the same time keep the unknown occupants of the storm shelter up-to-date with his progress.

"I'm a big, strong tree," a male voice said with a chuckle. "I think I can handle it."

"Ah. A male tree. Well, I'm going to cut off the leafy twigs first so I can better see what I'm doing."

"I was overdue for a good trimming anyway," the tree said.

Zeke laughed. "Indeed you were."

"There's a tree trimmer in the barn—should be hanging on a pegboard near where you found the saw," a female said.

Zeke grinned. "I'll see if I can find it and come right back." He put the handsaw down and ran back to the barn. The tree trimmer was tucked off in a dark corner, not easily visible, but he found it and carried it out to the tree. "Okay, I found it, and I'm back. Might want to close your eyes."

"So we don't point out your mistakes?"

"That, and so I don't get leaves in your eyes."

A chuckle.

"Okay, I like to get to know my victims before I cut them up, so tell me about you."

Silence for a beat. Then a short laugh. "That's rather disturbing, but since I'm doomed for someone's fireplace anyway, I'll share my tale. I was born a poor seedling purchased to be a windbreak on these windy plains..."

Sometime later, the tree's detailed story almost complete and a significant dent made in a portion of the tree, Gracie drove the horse and buggy back into the drive, followed by a small bulldozer.

Where on earth did she find one? The girl—woman—was brilliant.

Zeke climbed out of the mess of disconnected branches and got out of the way. At least the storm shelter was visible now, even if he hadn't cleared quite enough to get the door open.

The bulldozer operator scraped the trees to one side, making short work of freeing the rather dented shelter door.

As the noisy machine rumbled out of the way, Zeke ran over, gave the door handle a good yank, and threw the hatchway wide open.

A gray tabby cat, fur standing on end and tail flicking, flew out as if it were launched. It was followed by ten Amish people of assorted ages and sizes. Two of them were older, likely the grandparents. Two middle-aged. The parents? Two were unmarried young men. One school-age boy and three females—girls of assorted ages. They were all chuckling over the "talking tree."

He glanced at Gracie, almost expecting her to dash to one of the men, embrace him, and introduce him as her Timothy. Zeke stiffened, waiting for the inevitable happy reunion.

But if one was Timothy, he went unheralded. And none of the men looked at her as he should his bride.

A young woman with strawberry-blond hair, maybe the same age as Gracie, ran to her and embraced her. That must be her friend Elsie.

Zeke approached the *Englisch* man with the bulldozer. "*Danki*." Oops, he'd meant to say it in *Englisch*.

The man seemed to understand anyway. "No problem." He slapped Zeke on the arm.

The oldest Amish man stepped forward. "Thank you for rescuing us, young man." He shook the *Englischer*'s hand.

Zeke tried not to slump. But if he'd harbored any hopes of being the hero in this situation, they'd been firmly trampled in the mud. He wasn't the hero. He'd never be the hero. The sooner he got that thought rooted in his head, the better.

Why did he even try?

He turned to ask Gracie if she was ready to go since their "good deed" was done here, but she'd managed to disappear when he wasn't watching. She, the woman who was hugging her, and all the other females who'd come out of the shelter. The men began stalking around the property surveying everything, probably checking for damage.

Zeke didn't see any, but then he was unfamiliar with

the property, so he wouldn't notice a minute, little something.

The guy with the bulldozer drove off, the machine rumbling.

Was it too much to ask to be a hero in somebody's eyes? Especially if that somebody had enough clout to talk to his *daed* and tell him what Zeke had accomplished? Not that it'd make much difference. *Daed* would only see what he wanted.

The *grossdaadi* waited quietly beside Zeke. When Zeke turned to look at him, the *grossdaadi* grasped Zeke's shoulders with both hands and gave him a brotherly kiss on both cheeks. "*Danki* for what you did to rescue us. Really appreciate you coming by as you did, *sohn*. It also helped to have a running commentary on your progress, especially since you lightened it up so much."

"No problem." Zeke adjusted his hat, blinked the sting from his eyes as he turned toward the barn and returned the handsaw and the tree trimmer. Perhaps Zeke was a hero to someone after all. When he had his emotions under control, he walked toward the *haus* and went to the now open door. The women were in the kitchen—at least most of them were—putting coffee on and emptying the contents of the picnic basket Gracie had brought onto the table.

Food. Really? But then these people had been stuck in the storm shelter for over twelve hours. They were likely starving.

Gracie smiled at him, and for some weird reason, his heart pounded and his hands grew sweaty.

He angled his steps in her direction and leaned close

to her ear. "It's a good thing you wanted to check on these people. I shouldn't havc tried to talk you out of it."

* * *

Grace tried not to shiver as Zeke's whisper tickled her ear and stirred the loose strands of hair that were too short to put into her bun. As he walked past, going toward the sink as if he intended to wash up, she tried not to notice his confident stride or the way his pants hung on his hips. Face heating, she turned to see how she could help.

Well, at least until she met Elsie's wide-eyed, totally shocked gaze.

Grace looked away, face heating.

Elsie grasped her elbow and pulled her from the room. "You can help me upstairs."

Grace stumbled, trying to keep up with Elsie's fast pace. Or maybe she was dragging her feet.

Elsie waited until they were in the room she shared with her two sisters before she faced Grace. "Who is he? What are you doing?" she hissed. "And where's Timothy?"

Grace's eyes stung. "I don't know. We're looking for him. Timothy, Toby, and Peter went buggy racing last night. Now Toby's…gone, Peter's in the hospital with multiple injuries, and Timothy's missing."

"Toby is…" Elsie swallowed. Blinked hard. "Oh no. That's terrible. Hallie is going to be crushed." She dropped onto the bed and buried her face in her hands.

"*Jah*, I don't think she knows yet." Grace's voice caught. "I dread telling her."

Elsie sniffed and looked up. Tears beaded on her lashes. "But who is the guy in our kitchen, and why were you looking at him like..." Elsie waved her hand in front of her face like a fan.

"Seriously? Did you even *look* at him?" Grace flapped her own hand. "I know I shouldn't notice, but well, he is nice looking."

"I suppose he's a great distraction, but who is he? Is he one of Timothy's cousins here for the wedding?"

"His name's Zeke, and he's from Shipshewana. He came with a crew to help with the tornado cleanup."

"So he's cleaning up your broken heart?"

Grace huffed and turned away to hide her expression. Her heart wasn't exactly broken. Not yet, anyway. Elsie knew Grace's doubts and fears but was one of the members of the you-just-have-cold-feet club. She'd never understand. Grace gave the sheet a good tug on one of the twin beds and straightened the covers.

Elsie grabbed the pillow and fluffed it. "Don't flirt with trouble, Gracie. He's cute and he knows it. Besides, he's not from here. Long-distance relationships never work, and I don't want you moving to Shipshewana. Besides, Lord willing, Timothy will be found safe and sound, and you'll be happily married in a week or two."

"Jon and Aubrey will be getting married in two weeks."

"*Jah*, and I'm sure they won't mind sharing their special day and having a double wedding with you and Timothy, all things considered." Elsie moved to the next bed, the bottom bunk, and straightened the sheets.

Grace climbed partially up the ladder to make the top bunk. "I'm sure you're right." Sometimes it was just easier to agree with Elsie. While Grace believed Aubrey would agree if she were asked, there would still be this awkwardness of sharing such a special day in an un-planned manner. Besides, even if Timothy was found alive, he might've sustained injuries that would make a wedding during this season unfeasible.

Lord, please let Timothy be alive. And help me to work through my fears and commitment issues.

"Do you think Zeke's seeing anyone?" Elsie wiped her eyes with her apron, straightened, and peered up at Grace.

Grace giggled. "He's still from Shipshewana and it'd still be a long-distance relationship." She grinned at her friend. "But I don't know. I never asked. But as you said, a guy like that..."

"We ought to ask. Pretend we want to set him up with a friend." Elsie threw herself backward on the first bed they made. "But you'll have to do it. Since you're taken and all."

"And since you're not?"

"It's the kind thing to do. And of course, I'll be the girl you set him up with."

"Of course," Grace agreed. Sort of. Because kind or not, she didn't want to set Zeke up with anyone. "He's probably not allowed to date while he's here, seeing how he's on a service-oriented mission trip of sorts."

Elsie sat up. "That's probably true. There's no use dreaming of what-ifs. Let's finish up here and go down to see how we can help."

"I'll need to go soon, actually. I'm supposed to be looking for Timothy. But I don't know where to look next. His buggy was found in the bishop's living room.

Toby was found in his father's fields. I don't know where they found Peter."

"Well, I'm sure he'll be found soon." Elsie grabbed some fake flowers off the nightstand and clasped them in her hands as she hummed the *Englisch* wedding march.

CHAPTER 10

Zeke shifted uncomfortably in the roomful of unknown females setting the table for a late noon meal. He was underfoot in here, and they were staring at him. He glanced toward the doorway where Gracie had disappeared with her friend, willing them to return.

The youngest girl, maybe about twelve or thirteen, held up a plate piled full of Gracie's wedding sandwiches. "You hungry, mister?"

He shook his head. *"Danki, nein."* And he wasn't. They'd just had the wedding dinner of fried chicken, mashed potatoes and gravy, and all the extras less than two hours ago.

Should he go outside and trail the men who were assessing damages? That'd be just as awkward, but he'd be among his own gender instead of sticking out like a sore thumb in the roomful of women. At least the scene was complemented by the eye-opening, mouthwatering aroma of coffee. He could use a mugful of the strong brew, but water would be healthier, and Gracie had a couple of water bottles in her buggy.

He turned to go back outside. He could do more work on the tree. He actually should've thought of that instead of putting the tools away when the people—and the gray tabby—were released from their storm cellar.

Before he reached the door, the *grossmammi* stepped in front of him and peered up. The top of her head barely reached his chest. "*Danki* for rescuing us, young man. You are a gift sent straight from the hands of *Gott*." She stood on tiptoe, stretched to put her wrinkled hands on his upper arms, and leaned in to kiss his cheek. Not that she quite reached. It landed on his jaw, but it was the thought that counted. And the gesture. His eyes burned, and he bent to engulf the *grossmammi* in a hug. It was nice to be appreciated.

"*Danki*." The word was rather hoarse. He cleared his throat and tried again. "*Danki*."

The *grossmammi* released him from her surprisingly tight embrace and he straightened.

He was still in the way, though, so since Gracie hadn't yet returned, he went to the barn, retrieved the saw and trimmer, and went back to work cutting up the tree. The Miller family would likely want to sell it for firewood, especially since whoever he chatted with in the shelter initially indicated it was destined for someone's fireplace.

The handsaw was a lot slower going than a chain saw, but he'd still made progress when the *grossmammi* approached, carrying a mug of coffee. She was followed by Gracie and Elsie.

"Coffee?" The *grossmammi* stopped beside him, one hand resting on his sleeve. "We appreciate your hard work."

"Sounds wonderful. *Danki* so much." Zeke accepted the mug and drank the brew as she brought it, apparently with a spoonful of sugar and a spot of cream, since it tasted sweeter and was lighter than the plain black coffee he usually drank. He wouldn't complain, though. He downed the coffee in a couple of gulps and handed the mug back to the *grossmammi*.

"Ready to go, Zeke? We probably should check on a few more people before heading home." Gracie tilted her head toward the buggy.

The *grossmammi* turned her attention to Gracie. "This one is a keeper, Gracie. If you don't want him, maybe Elsie does."

Elsie giggled, her face flaming pink. "*Mammi*, Gracie is marrying Timothy." But the glance she sent his way wasn't dismissive.

Zeke squirmed. "Not here to date." Actually, he wasn't allowed to date. The Mennonite missionary Daniel Zook had rather sternly and very publicly made that clear after Zeke's not-so-joking question about whether Seth Lantz had any unmarried daughters. And the missionary had added that the line was drawn in quicksand. Immediate punishment.

"You probably have a girl back in Shipshewana anyway." Elsie turned away.

Did he need to bother acknowledging that dismissal with a reply?

He'd ignore her. None of her business anyway. "Nice to meet you all," he said as he headed toward the barn with the tools. "I'm glad you are all safe and the damage is minimal." As far as he knew.

Once back at the buggy, he untied the reins from a pole, though he was pretty sure he hadn't thought to secure the horse, and climbed into the buggy.

Gracie settled in beside him.

Gracie, who had taken the horse out and returned with a bulldozer. She would've tied the horse to keep him from bolting with that noisy machine nearby.

"Where to?" He didn't mean to sound so curt. He clicked his tongue and Charlie Horse pulled the buggy toward the road.

"Elsie wanted me to ask if you were seeing someone and maybe fix her up with you. I told her you probably weren't allowed to date."

He'd said something similar to that, too, to the matchmaking *grossmammi*. Though the other women likely overheard. But was it his imagination, or was there something in Gracie's voice—a wistfulness—as if she wished things were different?

It was a rule he'd break in a heartbeat if he figured he could get away with it. But not with Elsie. She was pretty but not as intriguing as the woman sitting next to him. He stopped at the mailbox and waited for directions as well as several vehicles to pass.

"This is as close to dating as I'm going to get." He flashed a quick grin in her direction. "Seriously, I was not-so-gently reminded that's not what I'm here for."

"So no girlfriend in Shipshewana?"

Charlie Horse stomped his foot and tossed his head.

"Fishing, Gracie?" he teased.

The last vehicle, a police cruiser, drove by. Probably headed to Toby's *haus*.

And just like that the mood sobered.

Gracie crossed her arms and looked away, but what he could see of her profile was bright red.

Zeke turned the direction they'd been going. Opposite from the way the police cruiser went.

Or should he have followed it to see if someone had found Timothy?

She sighed. Heavily.

Not speaking was also communicating.

"I'm not courting anyone in Shipshe," he said quietly.

* * *

Gracie pointed to a gravel-filled area just ahead. "Pull off there."

"Do you want me to turn around?" Zeke directed Charlie Horse to the side of the road. "Maybe see if we can find where the police went?"

Startled, she glanced at him. "*Nein*. I just need to think. I'm not sure where to go next."

"What are our options?" He shifted to face her.

"I thought I'd check on my other best friend, Hallie, but I'm pretty sure she was called into work at the diner with all the extra volunteers in town. But then again, she might be stuck in her storm shelter, too, and it'd hardly be feasible to stop at every *haus* between here and there to make sure everyone is safe. Besides, *Mamm* will be expecting me home to help with supper, and..." She peered up at the sky and squinted at the sun. She'd never been very good at telling time this way, but *Daed* could.

Her attention shifted from the sun to a large piece of metal siding hanging precariously from a tree. The sun reflected off of it, making it almost blinding. How would someone get that down?

A beat passed. Two. Zeke cleared his throat, pulling her focus away from the siding. "What's for supper?"

Typical male. Always hungry. She snorted. "Sandwiches. *Mamm* kept enough back for our meal. A few of them, actually. That and raw vegetables, deviled eggs—stuff like that." She shrugged.

"So, it won't take long to get it ready. How about we head toward your friend's home and we glance at the residences we pass on the way? If we see people, we'll know they don't need rescuing. If we don't, we'll double-check."

"Except some of the people work and might not be home. Or they might be out and about like we are, trying to check on loved ones and trying to help."

Zeke shrugged. "We could still check."

"Don't you have better things to do than hang around with me?" As soon as the words left her mouth, she cringed. They sounded rude.

Zeke shook his head. "Not really. Your *daed* said to help you find Timothy. He assigned Vernon to finding missing farm animals. I hope he's having better luck. I don't have a clue where to look for Timothy, other than what we're doing."

"Jon said Timothy probably took advantage of the tornado to get out of marrying me."

"Ouch. Who's Jon? I remember that name..." His brow furrowed. "Your brother?"

"*Jah*. My brother. The unmarried one. He's getting married in two weeks."

Zeke grunted. "Only a brother would say something like that. But if it's any consolation, I don't think any man in his right mind would want to escape marriage to you."

"Says a man who doesn't know me." Grace rolled her eyes.

"I know enough, Gracie. I know enough," he said softly.

Grace blinked and stared at him. "You actually sound like you mean it."

His dimples flashed. "I do."

Grace sighed a happy sort of sigh that left a smile on her face. "I could kiss you for that."

His blue eyes collided with hers. Held.

Grace was afraid to breathe. Afraid to move.

His gaze lowered.

Her lips tingled in response.

Another long, breathless moment.

Then he looked away.

She lowered her gaze to her lap, face heating.

The moment passed.

Gone.

* * *

Zeke stared at the long gray stretch of road, broken yellow lines marking the center, and at the fields, houses, and trees lining this particular street. It wasn't dirt, like some of the others; this one was much more main. Did it lead to town?

And if it did, did it even matter?

Assuming they even had an old-fashioned soda shop

in Hidden Springs, he could hardly take Gracie in and buy her—them—a malted milk to share, as it had been depicted in the old picture he'd seen at a flea market in Shipshewana. A boy and a girl at a tiny round table, both of them leaning into a malted milk with two straws. Heads almost touching. He'd heard girls giggling about the romanticalness of the painting.

Didn't matter anyway. It'd be construed as a date, and that was forbidden.

In more ways than one.

He shifted as the silence grew and lengthened, becoming stifling. The expanse of road remained void of traffic; only the distant clip-clop, clip-clop of a horse's hoofs against the pavement broke the silence.

Not even a bird dared to tweet.

It was as if nature held its breath, waiting to see what he would do.

What could he do?

Simply nothing, as far as he knew. He could hardly sweep her into his arms, kiss her full lips, and declare he'd been waiting for her his entire life. Which might sort of be true. He'd been waiting for someone who piqued his interest like she did. But not her, particularly. She was engaged, and her groom was out there somewhere.

Because wouldn't she know, internally or something, if Timothy was dead?

A dog barked, breaking the unnatural stillness.

Charlie Horse tossed his head and snorted.

The buggy creaked and swayed as Gracie shifted. "I suppose we should go."

"*Jah*," he agreed, but he didn't click at the horse.

He just sat there. Staring. Lost in a world of confusion.

Maybe it would've been better if she had kissed him, because then they would have the shocked awkwardness and tension to work through. That would've beaten this uncertainty that left him breathless and wondering.

"Go west, young man, go west," she quoted, with a slight touch of humor in her voice.

He swallowed hard. Looked at her. "Which way is west?"

His voice was husky, as if he had a cold. Or as if he'd been thinking of actually being kissed by her.

Which he was.

Most definitely.

CHAPTER 11

Grace silently cursed her runaway tongue as she replayed her words. *I could kiss you for that.* How could she say something like that to Zeke? She couldn't imagine what he must think. Probably that she was a very forward girl. She wasn't, really, but something about Zeke brought out the flirt in her.

Without looking at her, Zeke clicked at Charlie Horse and started driving down the pavement. He kept the buggy much closer to the side of the road than she did. She figured the SHARE THE ROAD signs were posted for a reason, and it wasn't so the buggies would drive half off the road, but so the *Englisch* drivers would watch for them. That was how her brothers taught her when they took her out driving the horse and buggy.

Should she mention that he drove too close to the edge of the road? Or would he take offense at it? Maybe driving in Shipshewana was different. He did say they had a lot more traffic there. She couldn't imagine more traffic. Especially when some of the vehicles were driven at top speeds.

She dragged her focus from the grassy embankment and looked at him, taking a moment to enjoy the view. But then the buggy wheel bumped over something, jarring her attention back to the roadside. He was definitely "off-roading" with the right-side buggy wheels. She glanced at him again. "You don't need to hug the edge of the road quite so close."

His shoulders jerked. "Hug? What?" He glanced at her, eyes wide. "I didn't hug anyone. Except for your friend's *mammi*." His kissable lips quirked.

She stared a moment. Was he being deliberately obtuse? But if he was, he hid the deception well. She'd give him the benefit of the doubt. "I think you missed a few words."

His cheeks reddened. "Sorry, Gracie. I was thinking about..." His eyes dipped to her lips before they shot up, then jerked back to the road. "Uh. Um. Well, other stuff."

Like her *I could kiss you* words? Was he thinking about that? Oh, she hoped so. Her face heated.

"That might've involved close encounters of the hugging kind?" She deliberately widened her eyes, hopefully appearing innocent while quoting *Englisch* friends.

"Were you this flirty with Timothy?" He didn't look at her. His hands tightened around the reins.

Apparently the feigned innocence failed. Her breath lodged. "What do you mean?" she whispered.

His Adam's apple bobbed. But other than an assessing glance her way, he didn't answer.

She slumped. Zeke had sent her a deliberate message

telling her in no uncertain terms that she was wrong, wrong, wrong to flirt with him on her no-longer-wedding-day. She should... she should...

She didn't know what she should do.

She definitely shouldn't tell him about her unanticipated strong physical attraction to him. A stranger. Of course he knew, thanks to her flirting, and that was the point of his assessing look.

And maybe the stranger part was what made him safe: He wasn't from here. She could be real with him and never see him again.

"Sorry," she muttered. She slid down farther in the seat. If she were lucky, a hole would open up in the buggy floor, and she'd tumble right through it.

"I don't mind." He might've looked at her, but she was too busy staring at her dress to notice. "I like you, too. But I'm not allowed to date while I'm here, and, well, you've got twelve brothers."

The number of her brothers had absolutely nothing to do with anything as far as she could see. Except, she had seen their protective nature before. She squeezed her eyes shut, but even so her cheeks burned hotter than she could ever remember.

"Not to mention you love Timothy—you said so yourself. Today is your wedding day, and I'm not some bachelorette boy toy."

She gasped, her eyes flew open, and her head jerked in his direction. "Some... some... *what*?"

He winked.

Never mind hot. Her cheeks were on fire.

"Okay, kissing, hugging, and flirting aside, we just passed three houses, but I saw people in the yards, so we'll assume they're fine. There's an intersection up ahead. Fill in the blank. I go..." He raised his eyebrows, his voice calm as he deliberately changed the topic.

Oh. So they were going to pretend the previous conversation never happened. That was best. Definitely best. Especially since she'd been propelled way out of her comfort zone. "Straight." Her voice squeaked.

"*Danki*." He stopped at the intersection even though there wasn't a stop sign on any of the corners.

She couldn't adjust her focus so easily. She cleared her throat but didn't know what to say. Except, "I'm sorry."

"Don't be." His grin was quick. "Like I said, I like you, too. But let's just concentrate on being friends for now."

For now. Because that would end when Timothy was found.

Or when Zeke returned to Indiana.

"Where does your friend live?" He drove through the intersection.

"Tenth driveway on the right. I think. I never actually counted."

"Okay. Let me know when we get near."

She nodded as they passed a formerly big, beautiful tree uprooted on the side of the road. "Elsie told me that her *daadi* told you the history of the tree you sawed up."

"I asked. I also kept them updated on what I was doing. I think it gave them a sense of security to know someone was out there, working to free them."

"They loved it." And Grace appreciated his sense of humor in the face of a bad, tragic situation. It made her glad there were men in the world like him and glad he had come here. "So. What made you decide to come to Illinois to help out?"

He frowned. "It happened so fast I actually didn't give it a lot of thought. My brother and best friend and I were assisting in the birth of a horse. Animals always like to give birth during severe storms, I think. We turned Kiah's radio on to listen to the weather alerts and mentioned that we'd like to help. Kiah—his real name is Hezekiah— his *daed* overhead, and he'd somehow already gotten the news and knew about the Mennonites leaving in the wee hours of this morning, and he said Kiah and I could go."

She looked at him. "Kiah. I thought he said his name was Vernon."

"*Jah*, Vernon is... Vernon. He's from my district, too." A sigh, as if he didn't quite measure up to Vernon. "They separated Kiah and me. Probably so we wouldn't race buggies." He grimaced. "Sorry, that was insensitive. But Kiah and I do tend to goof off sometimes."

"That's normal. My brothers act immature some- times." Why would he think that's a bad thing? But in light of the tornado, maybe it was. "So tell me something else about you."

Zeke shrugged. "Not much to tell. I have two brothers—Ezra, who is older and married, and Eli, who is three years younger than me—and one sister, Eliza- beth, who is sixteen. My *mamm* works in a cheese store, in the back, but there's a window so tourists can watch her make cheese. My *daed* and my older brother both work at an RV factory. Eli does, too, but he's kind of treading on thin ice there. He misses a lot of work. I understand. It's kind of monotonous work. I didn't last there six months. They let me go, and now *Daed* believes

I'm lazy and unmotivated, but really, I just have different goals." He sounded bitter. "I'm sorry. I didn't mean to vent." He cringed and glanced at Grace.

"You're fine," she said, but she shifted away. Did he work at all, other than watching horses deliver in the wee hours of the morning and hanging out with Mennonite missionaries? But then he had muscles, and he knew how to cut fallen trees, so he wasn't completely lazy. She glanced at the house they passed. A woman was hanging out laundry on the line. A bit late in the day, but maybe other jobs took priority. She waved.

Zeke glanced at the woman. "Is that where your friend lives?"

"*Nein*. Two more mailboxes. It's the one shaped like a largemouth bass."

"The fish. Right. I see it." He nodded. "I don't want you to think badly of me. I work at an Amish-owned construction company. My *daed* doesn't understand, but he does piecework while I have my hands in the whole building project. Not to mention my boss likes to take time to have fun, so we work as guides on white-water rafting trips, volunteer at a camp for special-needs children, or teach skills at a boys' ranch during the summer."

Grace relaxed. That sounded a lot more positive. No wonder he was so good with Patience. Why would his *daed* think that was lazy and unmotivated? She'd have to pray that Zeke and his *daed* could heal their differences.

Zeke signaled Charlie Horse to turn in at the fish mailbox, and Grace glanced around. Laundry hung on the line, but someone was folding it. Hallie or one of her sisters. They all had the same build. Hopefully, it wasn't Hallie. Grace wanted to see her friend but didn't want to share the news about Toby. But maybe she'd already heard if she'd been in town at the restaurant.

Hallie's *daed* was up on the roof with a tarp.

"Halt." Zeke tugged the reins and Charlie Horse stopped.

The woman at the clothesline turned. It was Hallie. She smiled and came toward them, but then her gaze narrowed on Zeke in curious speculation.

Grace slumped. Her friend looked happy, so that meant she hadn't heard. Why did the Amish grapevine have to fail now?

"I'm so sorry about your wedding, Gracie. I was happy when I thought I saw you and Timothy turning in, but now I'm confused," Hallie said, glancing at Zeke as Grace climbed out of the buggy.

"This is Zeke Bontrager. He's here from Indiana to help with cleanup. Zeke, this is my friend Hallie."

"Nice to meet you." Zeke exited the buggy and tied the horse to a post.

"Nice to meet you," Hallie echoed.

"I'm surprised to see you home. I thought for sure you'd be called in to work." Grace hugged her friend.

Hallie returned her hug. "I was. I heard your wedding was postponed due to the tornados, so I worked the breakfast shift. I walked since the roads were blocked this morning. What brings you by?"

Grace took a deep breath. She'd avoid the news about Toby for a bit. "We're out looking for Timothy. He's gone missing."

Hallie's eyes widened. "I saw Timothy in the crowd at the restaurant."

Zeke's mouth flatlined. His eyes met Grace's. Something she couldn't identify shimmered in the depths of his blue eyes.

Grace's heart lurched and struggled to find a rhythm when it restarted. Pain knifed through her. Her eyes burned. And for a moment, she might have forgotten to breathe. Timothy was in town? His *mamm*'s worried expression from this morning flashed in her memory. Then why hadn't he gone home? Checked on her?

Why hadn't he...?

Why, why, why...?

Her stomach cramped with rejection. Didn't he care?

So many questions, but there weren't any answers.

Yet.

Not that she was sure she wanted to find them.

Not when she could be lost forever in Zeke's eyes.

She sucked in a breath and looked away at the lonely row of clothes on the line left hanging and forgotten and flapping in the wind. Just like she was.

Timothy was alive and somewhere in town.

Timothy. Was. Alive.

And the comforting blueness of Zeke's eyes was not hers to get lost in.

* * *

Zeke stilled, his focus on Gracie. Timothy—in town. Would she want to go right away, or would she want to update her friend about the tornado damage and Timothy's friends first? And why wasn't she smiling? He understood that she had doubts, but...her groom was alive.

Instead, she appeared...confused. Hurt. And worse,

her eyes filled with tears. Big, shimmery drops that beaded on her lashes.

And Zeke, selfishly, wished Timothy hadn't been found. He wasn't ready to end his friendship—acquaintance—with Gracie. Not yet. Even though he was supposed to turn around and walk away, content in the knowledge she was with her one true love, he wasn't ready to do it.

Not yet? That was almost laughable. He might never be ready.

But that didn't change a thing.

"Timothy's alive?" Gracie whispered. And one of the tears clinging to her lashes escaped and rolled over the curve of her cheek. She swiped it away.

Zeke wanted to pull her into his arms and hold her. Just to comfort her. Of course.

"I think. Maybe. Or not." Hallie shook her head. "I don't know. I thought it was him. But I might've been mistaken, because I said hi to him, but he didn't respond. He stared at me like he didn't know who I was. So I moved on with my work. We were very busy."

Gracie was silent. She just stared.

Wait, no. Another tear escaped. And, wow, it hurt Zeke to see her cry.

"They say everyone has a twin," Zeke commented rather inanely, backing away. Because he didn't know what else to say or how to react or even what she was thinking. Besides, he didn't do well with tears, and she probably needed privacy to vent with her friend. And even if she didn't need privacy, it wouldn't be right for him to pull her into his arms and let her cry on his shoulders while he just held her. And prayed. And probably enjoyed the experience way too much.

It was definitely time to turn and walk away.

He glanced at Hallie and tilted his head toward Gracie. "I'll leave you alone to talk. Do you think your *daed* needs help on the roof?"

Hallie looked up. "I don't think he'd refuse. Especially with the breeze."

Zeke nodded, turned, and tried very hard not to flee from the two friends as he speed walked around the *haus* to the side where a tall ladder leaned against the building. The ladder wobbled a bit, but he'd climbed less-secure ones, so he ascended it.

Hallie's *daed* raised his head as Zeke stepped onto the roof.

Zeke smiled. "Hi. I'm Zeke from Indiana, and I've come to help you."

The older man's eyes twinkled. "Hi, Zeke from Indiana. I'm Ted from Illinois, and I would appreciate your help. Can you grab that end of the tarp over there and see if you can help me pull it tight? The breeze is not being so cooperative."

"Sure." Zeke strode to the other end of the tarp and knelt on it long enough to get a grip; then he shifted off.

"This is a temporary fix, obviously, but I heard the Lantzes lost their barn, and there will be a work frolic there tomorrow. Barns are quite important, you know. More so than leaky roofs." Ted secured one corner of the tarp, pounding nails in with a hammer. "What brings you by with our Gracie?"

How was it that news of dismantled barns traveled faster than news of three missing young men? Zeke pushed his hat tighter against his head as another gust of wind threatened to send it flying.

And why did wind blow stronger on rooftops?

"Gracie's groom went buggy racing last night," he began, maybe a bit too cautiously.

Ted raised his head, his lips turning down and his brow furrowing. "I heard his buggy was found in the bishop's living room. Are you saying—"

"*Nein*! Not Toby!" A horrible wail came from one of the two women on the ground. It didn't sound like Gracie.

Zeke sucked in a breath, realizing too late that Hallie was reacting with the grief over Toby...

Grief that was totally missing from Grace today.

Ted paled and bolted to his feet. He dashed for the ladder.

"Easy now," Zeke said.

The wind gusted. The ladder lost its footing as Ted bumped against it. His arms flailed.

Oh no, no, no, no, no...

Zeke dropped the tarp and ran, but before he got there, Ted fell. He caught himself on the edge of the roof. Zeke's hat blew off and soared over the edge.

And the ladder clattered to the ground.

Zeke grabbed Ted's hands and hauled him back up onto the roof. Ted lay there a moment. Panting.

"You okay?" Zeke stayed beside him, trying hard not to fixate on the now silent ladder, flat on the ground, two stories below.

"Just had about ten years scared off my life." Ted sat and scooted away from the edge. "*Danki*."

The women hadn't noticed either the clattering ladder or the flying hat. Somewhere in the midst of the tears and clinging, they'd disappeared. Into the *haus*, probably.

That was just fine with Zeke. Women and tears... some things just don't mix. They could finish securing the tarp on the damaged roof while the women mourned for...Toby? Timothy? Both?

Ted slumped where he sat on the roof. "Toby and Hallie just started courting. Maybe three, four times as a serious couple."

Zeke glanced at him, but he had nothing. Nothing. Maybe the best thing he could do was listen. And pray. He stood, walked across the tarp, and grabbed the hammer and button-top nails, then made sure the corner Ted had started was secured. It was sloppily done. He fixed it and added another nail.

"He was a good, solid young man. Planned to join the church this summer. In preparation for marriage, you know." Ted gulped and then a sob broke loose. A terrible sound.

Zeke secured the opposite corner of the tarp. He still didn't have any words, but his heart hurt. For Toby. For his parents. For Hallie. For everyone affected by his death. By the tornados.

His eyes blurred. He blinked the moisture back and whispered a prayer that *Gott* would bring them comfort in this time of loss.

And oh, he blinked. "I'm sorry for your loss." He meant it, really.

Ted nodded in thanks. "He and Hallie had been friends for years. Years. But there comes a time when a man and a woman can't be friends. They just can't. Keep that in mind. At your age there is no such thing as simple friendships between men and women."

Zeke didn't have any friends that were girls. Except

Gracie. But she didn't count since she fell in the temporary-friends category. He grunted in response as he moved to the third corner.

Ted released a heavy sigh, swiped his hands across his eyes, and stood. "I suppose Timothy's gone, too?"

"We don't know. That's what we're doing. Looking for him. For answers." Zeke moved to the fourth corner.

"You know what you're doing," Ted said.

Huh? Zeke looked up. Raised an eyebrow. If he knew what he was doing in the search for answers, he'd already have a good relationship with *Daed* and know what box to put Grace in...

Ted motioned at the roof.

Oh. The roof. At least here he knew what to do. "I work construction."

"Hmm. Too bad I didn't think to grab two hammers."

Fourth corner secured, Zeke hammered button-top nails in around the edge approximately every six inches, and finished up with a batten strip diagonally across the middle.

Ted stalked across the roof, checking the rest of the shingles and pointing out the ones that needed extra help. Zeke secured some, but lacking another tarp, that was the best he could do.

"I hope Hallie thinks to check on us before she rushes to Toby's *haus*." With the job done, Ted sat on the roof, facing the barn so he could see anyone leaving.

"Is Hallie the only family member home?" Zeke sat beside him.

"*Jah*. She just got home from work about an hour ago. My wife and my two other daughters went to be with my son's wife. She went into labor in the wee hours of the morning, just before the tornado hit."

Zeke snorted. "Horses and women."

Ted acknowledged that with a slight nod. "And cows. The worse the weather, the more likely someone or something will give birth. My wife is a midwife. Oldest daughter is apprenticing. Youngest went along to help however needed."

Zeke had nothing to say. And the *haus* remained quiet. No one emerged.

Should they shout?

Charlie Horse snorted.

The horse was probably thirsty. Zeke would need to water him when he was rescued.

If he was rescued.

No. He wouldn't think like that. Nobody was ever permanently stuck on a roof and forgotten. He didn't think.

"*Daed*?" A door shut and Hallie and Gracie came into view. "I'm going to...Toby's." Hallie's voice broke.

Ted stood. Puffed out air. "Can you put the ladder back up before you go?"

Gracie stared up at them, her fingers over her lips, eyes wide. Then she ran around the side of the *haus*. A second later, Hallie followed.

The ladder banged.

Ted headed in that direction.

Zeke looked toward the sky. Danki, *Lord, for not forgetting us. For sending hope. Uh, help. Well, hope, too.*

Though maybe the hope part was a bit premature.

Then Zeke stood, grabbed the hammer, and followed Ted.

Hallie and Gracie both held on to the ladder while Ted descended. At the bottom, he turned in Hallie's direction and held out his arms. She flew into his embrace. Crying.

"I'm sorry, baby. So sorry. I'll go with you. Perhaps I could help in some way."

Whatever Hallie said was muffled by her mouth pressed against her *daed*'s chest. And by the wind gusting past Zeke's ears as he started his descent.

Gracie's eyes were red rimmed when he glanced into them. It was good that she'd cried with her friend. It probably did her good.

He reached for her hand and gave it a light squeeze. "I'll hitch up their horse and buggy for them."

"You're a good man, Zeke." Gracie's voice broke.

He managed a tight smile as he grabbed the ladder, collapsed it, and carried that and the hammer to the barn.

He just wished he could do more.

* * *

Grace went back into the *haus* and left a note for Hallie's *mamm* and sisters, then returned to the buggy. Zeke—or someone—had given Charlie Horse a pail of water.

"Hallie and Ted just left." Zeke gestured toward the road when he came out of the barn. "I took care of their tools as best as I could." He sighed heavily and shuffled his feet a bit. "Did, uh, you want to head to town and see if we can find Timothy?"

Grace pursed her lips. "Why?"

Zeke frowned. "Because Hallie said she saw him?"

"She thought about it and decided it wasn't him. There's no point in going to town to search for Timothy's look-alike. What good would it do?"

Zeke's brow furrowed. "But…well, wouldn't it be best to be sure?"

Grace wasn't sure she wanted to know. If it was Timothy and he was playing dumb with Hallie, Grace wasn't sure she would be able to keep from telling him off. And maybe telling him that very firm NO and actually meaning it. Because any guy who worried his *mamm* and didn't check on his bride on their wedding day just wasn't the type of man she wanted to be married to.

She forced her temper under control, tried for a calm exterior—though she probably failed—and shrugged. "Where would we start to look? I doubt he hung out at the restaurant all day. Besides, we should probably get home."

Zeke didn't look too certain. He opened and shut his mouth a few times, then shrugged. "Your wish is my command."

As if what she wanted actually mattered.

As if he'd move mountains if she asked him to.

Or maybe even uproot himself and relocate to Hidden Springs, just to be near her.

If she wanted.

If she found the courage to hope. To believe.

To ask.

CHAPTER 12

A half hour later, the Lantz farm came into view, bordered on the sides by a swollen drainage ditch. A disheveled, mud-covered figure hovered near the edge. The figure locked gazes with Zeke a moment before recognition sparked in his eyes. "Ezekiel. Wait."

"Vernon?" Zeke pulled on the reins. "Halt."

Vernon took a giant step over the ditch and slipped. His knees sank into the mud.

Zeke jumped from the buggy and offered a hand, helping him scramble up to the road. Why was he out here by himself? Was he hurt? "Are you all right?"

"*Jah*, I'm fine. *Danki*." Vernon glanced at Gracie. "Did you find Timothy?"

"Not yet," she answered.

Vernon glanced at Zeke, his brown eyes serious. *Jah*, Zeke agreed with Vernon's unspoken assessment. If Timothy wasn't the man Hallie thought she'd recognized in town, then *Gott* alone knew if Timothy was still alive or where the tornado set Timothy down. The next town, the next county, the next state. They really needed to track the system and form a detailed search grid—

"I found another cow."

Huh? Zeke glanced at Vernon, then at the cornfield behind him. No bovine appeared behind him in the almost-barren field. Just a few straggly, dried-up cornstalks that somehow missed being cleared during the harvest.

"Not here," Vernon said. "Off in the woods. It's stuck, bawling in misery, and I can't rescue it on my own. It's kicking, getting itself more stuck, and risking injury. I'm looking for Seth or Jon."

"Can we help?" Zeke asked.

"*Jah*, but I think we might need more than just us. The cow's wedged pretty tight. Do you think your *daed* and brother are back from town yet?" Vernon glanced at Gracie.

She looked toward the driveway. "I don't know. Hop in. We're headed home anyway."

Vernon glanced down at his wet and muddy pants, then shrugged. "*Danki*." He climbed into the back of the buggy next to the empty picnic basket.

"Two baskets down, a buggy load yet to go," Gracie murmured.

Huh? Zeke glanced at her and out of the corner of his eye caught Vernon's frown.

"Sandwiches." Gracie must've noticed his expression, too.

Vernon still looked confused.

"From the wedding that wasn't," Zeke clarified.

Vernon nodded, as if it made perfect sense now. "My bride is preparing for our wedding in three weeks," he said quietly. "I can't imagine what you are going through."

Maybe he did understand.

A white van pulled out of the driveway as Zeke approached the beat-up mailbox. At least it was no longer dangling precariously from the post, even if it took pink tools to get the job done.

Two men stood in the yard, facing the direction of the vanished barn. A pile of lumber and other items were partially covered by a tarp.

Right. Barn raising tomorrow. And probably visitation starting for Toby. Zeke's presence wouldn't be required at the visitation—or funeral—unless they wanted him to accompany Gracie.

"They're home." Gracie stated the obvious as they turned into the driveway.

"Can we get to where the cow is by buggy?" Zeke looked at Vernon.

"Probably, but I don't know the way by road. We'll need a rope to secure the cow to the buggy, if we free her," Vernon said.

Zeke slowed the horse as they drove behind the *haus*.

"I'll look for a rope." Gracie stood in the still-moving buggy.

"Hold on, now," Zeke said, reaching for her, but she hitched her skirt and vaulted out. His breath caught and his heart stuttered when her feet narrowly missed the turning buggy wheels and she had to twist sideways to avoid slamming into a boulder, but she somehow managed to land on her feet and took off at a dash toward the *haus*.

Her *daed* yelled, "Halt!"

Charlie Horse stopped. But Gracie didn't.

Vernon made some odd sound. One that might've been a yelp.

Zeke agreed, once his breath caught up with him and his heart resumed beating. "*Jah*, the woman is dangerous."

"She kind of reminds me of some trick rider I saw at the county fair once. Do you think it's because her groom is missing and she has no reason to keep living?"

Zeke didn't really think that was the reason. He glanced at Vernon. "I don't know, but that's a good guess. My *daadi* always said, 'One should stay alive, if only out of curiosity.'"

Vernon chuckled.

Maybe Zeke should talk to her *daed*. His gaze shifted to Seth Lantz, approaching the buggy with a thunderous expression on his face.

Because…because Zeke *let* Gracie jump from a slow-moving vehicle? As if he had any control over the woman?

Or because Zeke had lost his straw hat and now violated the unspoken Amish dress code?

Or if Seth Lantz had issues with Zeke's driving, he needed to watch when Gracie took the reins. That might give him a few more silver hairs.

Vernon climbed out of the back and approached Seth. "I found your other cow, but she's stuck and scared and I can't get her out without help. Gracie went to get a rope."

"And she's probably in pain since she hasn't been milked." Seth focused on Vernon, the thunder fading.

"Find a log to use for a stool so we can ease some of her discomfort."

Vernon nodded and trotted off. Zeke frowned at the flimsy excuse. Just kneeling on the ground would work. Or they could find a log where the cow was.

Seth's attention returned to Zeke. His face hardened.

Zeke tightened his fists around the reins. Or maybe he should've released them and slunk from the buggy in shame.

No. No. He hadn't done anything wrong. He hadn't even kissed the girl when she made that, um, suggestion. He raised his chin. Firmed his shoulders. But a muscle ticked in his jaw.

"I trusted you with my daughter, Bontrager."

A white blur flew past Zeke, and Slush landed beside him on the seat, tongue lolling. He grinned at Zeke and leaned into his shoulder.

At least the dog still liked him. And was showing his support. Not that it was worth much.

Zeke managed a wordless nod. He tried to think of something to say other than, "Yes, sir," like the boys at the boys' ranch might say when pressured, but in the Amish world that might be considered a bit disrespectful.

But really, what had he done to violate Seth's trust?

"I know your type." A long silence while Seth stared at Zeke as if unearthing all his hidden secrets.

Zeke resisted the urge to squirm.

"Handsome, twinkling blue eyes, a smile that could cause a woman to look twice, a devil-may-care attitude, and the girls turn cartwheels to get your attention."

Not hardly, but oh, that *was* what this was about. Gracie's foolish stunt getting out of the buggy. Seth thought she was trying to impress him. Zeke opened his mouth.

"She's in a fragile place right now." Seth's words were almost a growl. Oblivious *Daed* thought she was mourning? Or did he recognize his daughter's attraction when she was supposed to be mourning and believe Zeke was encouraging her?

Worse, brother number twelve stood behind his *daed*, his muscular arms crossed. At least the other eleven brothers weren't there, armed with chain saws.

Except, Gracie wasn't as fragile as they thought. And…

Wait. Gracie jumping out of a moving buggy was meant to get *his* attention?

Or was it meant to impress Vernon?

Because other than her driving, she hadn't done anything else dangerous around him.

Except maybe to bare her soul. And mention the four-letter word that still seared his thoughts. *Kiss.*

So not happening.

Zeke forced himself to meet Seth's eyes. "I'll have a talk with her." Again. "I already told her and her friend I'm not here to date. But you should know, Hallie isn't sure, but she thinks she saw Timothy in town. Gracie didn't want to follow up on it."

The husky whined. Dipped his head, then shook it, as if he were shooing the thought away.

Zeke shared the sentiments.

Seth stilled, opened his mouth to say something, but then shut it as Gracie ran out of the *haus*, a coiled clothesline rope in her hand.

"Let's go free the cow." She tossed the rope into the buggy.

"You're staying home with your *mamm* and Patience. And when I get back, we'll have a chat about your stunt riding," Seth growled.

Gracie's eyes widened. She glanced from Seth to Zeke, then back. But to her credit, she didn't argue. She simply nodded and headed toward the laundry hanging on the clothesline in the side yard as Vernon came back carrying the stump of a tree. Perfect stool height. Zeke had to give him credit for that. Perfect, like everything else he did...except he wasn't smart enough to see through the blatant excuse to get him out of the way.

At Seth's pointed look, Zeke got out and carried the empty picnic basket to the porch. Slush jumped out and followed, close at his side. He turned as Seth took the reins. Vernon sat beside him, attempting to explain exactly where he found the cow. Jon climbed into the back.

Zeke hesitated, unsure if they even wanted him to go along. Or if they did, should he grab his bag so they could find someplace else for him to stay, somewhere far away from Gracie?

Seth peered down at him from the buggy seat. "Go get the pink toolbox and come along, boy."

Wow, he certainly was failing with the father figures in this area. Just like at home.

He retrieved the pink toolbox from the empty kitchen and climbed into the buggy next to Jon. Slush started to crouch to make his leap, but Seth pointed to the ground. "Slush, sit. Stay."

The dog whined but obeyed, giving Zeke a mournful look.

Zeke was tempted to give an equally mournful look to the dog and slouch in the seat, but that would make him look guilty for whatever sins the Lantz men accused him of. Like perhaps encouraging Gracie to be a daredevil. As if that was his fault.

Somehow, Seth was able to follow Vernon's rather bumbling directions, and they found the cow. Well, actually, they heard her before they found her. She was wedged in what remained of a shed. Two walls. The other two sides and the roof were missing. A shoelace connected to a man's work boot was driven into the wall next to her. The cow bawled pitifully from her awkward position of what appeared to be midbuck, her head and forelegs protruding through the wall.

Seth got the log stump out and set it near the thrashing cow. Vernon grabbed her tail to keep it from slapping their host in the face, and Jon and Zeke went around to the front to survey the situation.

Zeke rubbed the cow's nose and spoke softly. "Shhh. It's okay, Bessie. We're here to rescue you."

"Her name is Cowntess. With a *w* and not a *u*." Jon gave him a sideways glance.

Zeke grinned. "*Grossdaadi?*"

"How'd you guess?" Jon's eyebrows rose.

"Gracie told me the horses' names." Zeke kept his voice soft and continued rubbing the cow's head. "I'd love to meet him sometime."

"I hear tell that you have. He was working at the school this morning when you arrived."

Right. Zeke had forgotten. But that brief encounter hardly counted.

"The other cow is named Dairy Queen," Jon said.

"I guess you have royal cows," Zeke quipped.

"They think they are, anyway." Jon grinned.

"Whatever you're doing is calming her. Keep it up," Seth called from the other side of the wall.

Zeke continued crooning to the cow while petting her. He quietly sang a few hymns to her. The cow gazed at him with her big brown eyes. Jon took the pink hammer and carefully dismantled the damaged shed around the cow, working to get her free. As soon as Seth finished milking the cow, he murmured instructions to Vernon as they started working on the inside.

"Step aside," Seth said. "Go get the rope from the buggy. Too bad I didn't think to buy a pail when I was in town. Hate to waste the milk, but Cowntess's comfort is the main thing. I hope she's not injured."

Something crunched on the other side of the wall.

Jon carefully removed another section of wall as Vernon came around with the clothesline. He handed the rope to Zeke. "Here you go, cow whisperer."

Zeke set his lips and glowered at him but slipped the rope around the cow's neck anyway.

"Hey, I meant that as a good thing." Vernon clapped Zeke's shoulder, as if he were a father figure and not Zeke's peer.

Interesting. But at last Cowntess was freed. Jon dropped the hammer and took the rope from Zeke and led her off to the side, away from the pile of wooden rubble to solid footing, where he checked her over for injuries.

Vernon and Zeke gathered the pink tools Jon had left scattered on the ground and repacked them into the matching toolbox. Then Vernon carried the toolbox to the buggy.

Seth came through the cow-size hole as Zeke piled the

discarded scraps of damaged lumber next to the remains of the shed. The older man planted his dirty work shoes just in Zeke's peripheral vision.

Zeke looked up.

There was a measure of respect in Seth's eyes. "I misjudged you. I wouldn't have been able to free the cow without injury if you weren't there to calm her."

Zeke stood. Nodded. If only it were so easy to please his own *daed*.

"I was going to ask you to pack your bags—"

Zeke swallowed. He'd figured so. "I haven't unpacked yet. I'll grab my things when we get back." Maybe he'd be placed with Kiah after all.

"I changed my mind. As I said earlier, you are good with Patience. Slush likes you, and they say dogs are a good judge of character. You are gentle with animals, and you've done what I've asked without complaint. It's just Grace that concerns me. Today is her wedding day, and she's looking at you the way she never has her groom."

Zeke opened his mouth, then shut it. It wasn't his place to tell Seth Gracie's secrets. And he wasn't 100 percent sure of what to think of Timothy based on Gracie's comments and her own behavior. "I promised I wouldn't hurt her." At least he thought he had.

"I'm afraid she might hurt herself." Seth smiled, but it was weak, fleeting. "Let's get back. I need to have a talk with her."

Zeke nodded, but only because he didn't know what to say. Hopefully, Gracie would open up to her *daed*.

* * *

Grace folded the cool, clean laundry, but inside her temperature was rising. Why did *Daed* and Jon have to turn around in time to witness her foolish jump from a moving vehicle for a stupid, childish reason? She wanted Zeke to notice her. To think she was different from other girls. More fun. More...independent.

And *jah*, she might be, but Amish men didn't want different. They wanted a woman who could cook, clean, and bear children while maintaining a quiet, calm persona that would make her a submissive, perfect Amish wife who...

Ugh. In other words, they wanted what she was not, and worse, she had to go and prove it. Beyond a shadow of a doubt. Well, she could cook and clean as well as the next girl. It was the quiet, calm persona she had trouble with.

She'd better not mention the time she tried trick riding like she'd seen at the fair just to impress a boy. That hadn't turned out so well. The horse hadn't understood why she was attempting to stand on his back and had bucked her off. She'd broken her leg in three places and had to spend six weeks in an itchy cast. *Daed* had told her she was lucky she hadn't broken her neck.

She should be grateful that Timothy had noticed her. Wanted to marry her. And did his best to mold her into something she wasn't. He demanded; she obeyed. Buggy racing was a thing of the past. Sneaking out with *Englisch* friends and trying to learn how to drive a car...Well, that had ended badly anyway. She'd driven straight into the woods and hit a tree. And her *Englisch* friends wouldn't let her try to drive again.

Though, to be honest, she'd been too scared to try again. Once was enough. A slow-moving buggy pulled by a running horse was much safer than a fast-moving car. And horses had enough sense to avoid trees.

Giving that up hadn't been a problem.

She could pretend to be the perfect Amish girl...

But she'd joined the church. She'd vowed to give up the things of the world in preparation for marriage. To put away childish things.

She shouldn't have to pretend. She should *be*.

Maybe the "rules" were less about controlling her and more about love wanting to keep her safe. She thought of Toby's sockless foot, Hallie's scream, Timothy's *mamm*'s fears and worry... and truly didn't want to put her family through that. Especially after all the pain she witnessed today.

Tears stung her eyes. She needed to apologize to *Daed* and Zeke.

Maybe even to *Gott*.

Gott probably had to come first.

Grace folded the last sheet, laid the bag of clothespins on top of the folded laundry, and lifted the basket. Carrying it inside, she set it on the table and ran upstairs to her bedroom. She quietly shut the door. She wasn't sure where *Mamm* and Patience had disappeared to. Grace hadn't seen them since she returned home with Zeke and Vernon. But since the *haus* was silent, it was a good time to pray.

Grace dropped to her knees beside the bed and bowed her head. But words wouldn't come. She was so selfish. How could she ask *Gott* to make her into a perfect Amish woman when she was so far from perfect it was laughable? Not to mention Timothy was still missing, Toby's family was in mourning, and Peter's family was in limbo with him dangling somewhere between life and death.

"When I was a child, I spake as a child, I understood as a child, I thought as a child: but when I became a man, I put away childish things," she said, reciting a verse from 1 Corinthians 13. "Lord, help me to put away childish things. I'm so ashamed of myself and my behavior right now. Help me to think and act like an adult and not a child. Help me to have the words to apologize to *Daed* and to Zeke."

It would be hard to confess to *Daed* but beyond difficult to talk to Zeke, admitting that she'd developed this really quick crush on him because he treated her as if she had value and actually listened to her. Besides, she was smart enough to know nothing would ever come of it, not even if Timothy was gone. Zeke was from Indiana. It might as well be an ocean away.

A howl came from beneath her bedroom window. A long, low, mournful sound. Grace pushed herself up from the floor beside the bed and went downstairs. She sat on the back porch, and Slush pressed up against her.

She smoothed her hand over the dog's now clean, silky fur. Zeke had done a great job washing and brushing Slush. "Where is everyone?" The *haus* was too quiet, and *Mamm* never left except to visit family or friends, for church activities or work frolics, or...

Grace snorted. Okay. They could be anywhere. *Mamm* might've heard of a neighbor's need and taken off to serve however she could.

A note would've been nice, though.

A horse snorted and whinnied, followed by a cow's

answer. Charlie Horse pulled the buggy around the side of the *haus* as *Daed* parked by the stack of building supplies for the barn raising.

Maybe she should have held more sandwiches back…

No. People would bring food in. Besides, they still had plenty of sandwiches.

Jon untied the cow from the back of the buggy and led her off to pasture where she joined the other cow.

Grace stood and Slush bounded off to greet Zeke, as though he'd been gone for hours.

Daed approached Grace, his face grim. His hands gently closed over her shoulders, and he gave her the tiniest of shakes. "What was that all about, daughter?"

For a moment, Grace was tempted to play dumb and say something obvious, like, "There was a cow stuck in a shed, *Daed*." But he wouldn't believe that.

Grace's gaze went to where Zeke crouched beside the dog, roughly loving on the animal. Slush's mouth was open in what could be a grin, and his tail wagged while he made crying sounds as if Zeke had been gone *forever* and at long last was home.

Funny how she could sort of relate.

"Oh, Gracie." *Daed*'s voice was filled with… something that might be sorrow. "I was afraid it was something like that. He's not from here."

"I know," Grace whispered.

"What's wrong with Timothy that you don't love him as you should?"

Grace caught her breath, and her gaze shot from where Zeke and Slush frolicked to *Daed*. Had Zeke told *Daed* her secrets?

But no, because if he had, he'd look guilty. He didn't. Was he right and she should tell *Daed* her concerns and fears, even though the wedding was postponed if not cancelled? Would he wave them away as *Mamm* and her friends did, claiming it was just "cold feet" and "every bride got them"?

She probably should explain. Even if he didn't listen and told her the same thing everyone else did.

Grace inhaled and stepped out of *Daed*'s loose grasp. "Can we talk?"

* * *

Zeke straightened as Slush got his fill of loving and wandered off to greet Jon and the cows. Gracie and Seth walked toward the road, talking. They were long overdue for this conversation. He whispered a prayer that Seth would listen to Gracie and reassure her somehow. Or help her call off the engagement if Timothy was alive and that's what Gracie wanted to do.

"I picked up some shingling nails in town." Jon approached. "Want to help me check the roof?"

Zeke looked up at the roof of the two-story building. "Did you buy a ladder?" He glanced toward the building supplies stacked on the ground. No ladder waved its tiny rung at him.

"I figured we could crawl out Gracie's window onto the overhang. From there it's easy access to the roof."

Zeke eyed the overhang. "Her bedroom is the one over the back porch?" There was a measure of forbidden knowledge in that, even though he knew where her room was inside. He hadn't matched it up with the exterior layout yet. A twinge of excitement worked its way through him, but he tried to squash it down. He had no reason to care, no reason to use that knowledge. That right belonged to Timothy.

A twinge worked through Zeke at the thought.

"What about hammers?" Zeke glanced at Jon. "Though, I suppose, if you count the red-and-yellow plastic baby rattle one in the blue toolbox, we have two. I call dibs on the pink one."

Jon laughed. "We bought hammers, except we didn't grab them when going to rescue the cow. We'll need tools for a barn raising."

"And the pink ones aren't tools?" He raised an eyebrow to remind Jon he'd used the pink hammer. Oh, he shouldn't goad the man.

Jon laughed again. "Do you want a manly tool or not?"

"I'm man enough to handle pink."

"That you are. But still, do you want a regular hammer?"

"*Jah*, please."

Jon unearthed a plastic bag from the dark recesses under the tarp and led the way inside the house. "We didn't buy shingles yet. The roof will come after the barn if it needs to be replaced."

Obviously. Hallie's *daed* had said much the same thing. The funeral would come before roofs, too. And if this community was like his, visitation would start tomorrow and last two days. Then the funeral.

Although, if Zeke went, it would only be for Toby's family, because Zeke didn't know Toby. Other than that he went buggy racing during a tornado. And courted Hallie. No. If he had the option, he wouldn't go. Vernon probably wouldn't be there, either. They wouldn't be expected to attend.

So, why was he even thinking about it?

Zeke shouldered through the door that had started to swing shut and followed Jon upstairs.

Gracie and Patience's shared room was plain, with a high bed, a footstool to climb in, and a red-and-white patchwork quilt folded at the end. Clothes hung on pegs on the wall. A stuffed teddy bear rested on one side of the bed. Two packed and sealed boxes were on top of a hope chest, probably ready to be moved to Gracie's new home after the wedding. He wondered what was in there. But he'd probably never know.

A lavender nightgown was folded on top of a pillow.

Zeke's heart lurched. He looked away and followed Jon.

They walked around the bed to the narrow space between the mattress and the wall. Jon shoved open the window, removed the screen, set it outside, and climbed out. No hesitation. He must've done this before.

Zeke hesitated just inside the window. There just seemed something so wrong about sneaking out of a girl's bedroom window. What would Seth have to say about it if Zeke were caught? What would Gracie think?

What if, when he came back in, he caught her with her hair uncovered or down, and...

His face heated.

Zeke leaned out the window as far as he could but didn't see either Seth or Gracie approaching. Vernon was out in the pasture with the cows and Charlie Horse, looking at something on the ground.

Jon peeked over the ledge above him. "Coming, Bontrager?"

"Just contemplating how much trouble I'd be in if I was caught."

Jon smiled. An evil-looking smile. "I don't suggest finding out. But this time it's okay. Trust me."

"*Trust me*. Famous last words, those."

No reply came from Jon, other than a possible chuckle. But Zeke stepped out onto the porch roof, walked to the low overhang of the triangular portion of the roof on the second floor, and climbed up.

From the rooftop he could see Seth and Gracie walking slowly on the edge of the road. Gracie was talking, using her hands to emphasize whatever point she was trying to make. Zeke couldn't see Seth's expression, but Slush trailed them, tail low hanging and still.

In the distance, two women, maybe Gracie's *mamm* and Patience, walked, each carrying a cardboard box.

Jon handed Zeke a hammer. "If you can stop gawking at Gracie long enough, you can start over there." He pointed to the far side of the roof.

"I wasn't gawking at Gracie. Just curious what has Vernon so enthralled in the pasture and what your *mamm* and Patience are carrying in those boxes." And mostly wondering what Gracie was telling Seth and how he was taking it.

"No clue about Vernon, but I know what's in the boxes. Chickens. Ours were all lost in the tornado. Someone offered us some of their flock."

Well, that answered one question. Except, "With no barn, where will you put them to roost?"

Jon snickered. "Cute. I should've said baby chicks. They'll keep them in the kitchen, for now."

Oh. And that was enough looking like an idiot. Zeke accepted a handful of roofing nails from Jon and made his way to the opposite side of the roof. A chicken coop was probably in the short-term plans.

The Lantzes' roof was mostly in good repair. There were a few loose shingles, but a nail here and there fixed the few problems Zeke found.

They were just finishing up when an ear-piercing scream was followed by a wail. Zeke glanced at Jon; then both of them scrambled for the edge of the roof. Zeke dropped to the overhang, but the bedroom window was shut, the screen still sitting where Jon had placed it.

He peered in the window. Patience was dancing around the room, waving her hands over her head and shrieking. She turned toward the window and must've seen him because she screamed again.

Jon landed beside him, with the bag containing the hammers. "What's going on?"

"Indian rain dance?" Zeke guessed. "And then I scared her." He tried to lift the window. "She locked it." He tapped it. "Patience?"

Another scream. More arm flapping.

And then Zeke noticed movement near the ceiling. "A bird."

"Open up, Patience." Jon leaned against the window. "We can help."

Patience screamed again and dived toward the window. She fumbled with the lock but finally got it. Tears streamed down her face.

Zeke tugged the window open on the outside and crawled in, Jon on his heels. Dashing across the room, Zeke pulled the bedroom door closed to keep the bird confined to the one area.

Knocking the lavender nightgown on the floor, Jon

grabbed a pillow and tried to guide the bird toward the open window.

The bird didn't get the hint. It flapped around in the corners of the ceiling, looking for exits where there were none.

Patience shrieked again.

"Boys! Stop teasing Patience!" The shout came from downstairs.

Zeke grabbed the other pillow and handed it to Patience. "Go sit in the corner, cover your head, and don't move. We'll get the bird out."

With a whimper, Patience did as he said.

He turned to Jon. "Let's not chase it but let it quiet down instead. Maybe then we can catch it."

"Not likely." He swung in an unsuccessful attempt to guide the bird out the window and then tossed the pillow on the bed. "Now what, wise guy?"

Zeke tried to hide the shrug that wanted to escape. He didn't know. But chasing it was just aggravating the bird more.

It did quiet down some, flittering around the upper pane of the window. The part that didn't open, of course. It stilled long enough for Zeke to identify it as a wren, possibly. It fluttered to the top of the curtain rod and sat there, staring at the two men as if they were its mortal enemies and . . .

Too bad they couldn't communicate they were there to help.

The wren made harsh chirring sounds, seemed to decide Zeke was a likely candidate for attack, then flew at his face.

Zeke might've squawked, though he tried not to because of Patience.

Jon snickered, a sound that turned into a controlled roar as the bird targeted him.

The bedroom door was flung open. Gracie stood there, staring at them. "What on earth are you doing?"

The bird flew out the open window.

Of course.

Jon grabbed the screen, fumbling in his hurry to install it.

Patience wailed, launching herself up and into Gracie's arms.

Zeke picked up the nightgown and flopped on the bed, suddenly beyond weary.

Had he only arrived in Hidden Springs just that morning?

CHAPTER 13

Grace patted Patience's back and made shushing sounds as Jon finished installing the screen, gathered his scattered tools that must have fallen from the bag, and high-tailed it from the room with a glance at Zeke. "Come on, sleepyhead."

Zeke didn't move. One arm was flung over his eyes; his other clutched her nightgown against his chest. His breathing had evened out, and Grace was tempted to let him sleep despite his filth from working so hard sawing up innumerable trees, plus repairing or rescuing: two roofs, a dog, a cow, a mailbox, and who-knew-what-else after being up all night with a laboring horse.

Not to mention there was kind of a forbidden thrill in knowing that Zeke was asleep on her bed. Hugging her nightgown.

He didn't get much of a chance to rest, though.

Just as Patience's cries turned into sniffling gasps as if

she'd been deprived of oxygen, Jon stuck his head back through the door. "Do we need to wake Sleeping Beauty with a kiss?"

That shocked Patience into silence. Then, "Kiss Zeke?"

Jon's eyes widened, and he glanced at Grace with a what-now expression. "I could let Slush in to do it."

"*Mamm* not like." Patience frowned. "Animals not in *haus*. Except baby chicks."

"We could shake him awake." Jon frowned.

Patience shook her head. "I kiss Zeke."

Jon grimaced. Unless they wanted to hear Patience screaming again, a kiss would be required. He sighed and looked back at Patience. "Maybe kiss him on the cheek," he amended softly.

Grace nodded. If Patience kissed him, then on the cheek would be best. Because any lip kisses by any Lantz girls with Zeke would be . . . well, not good. They'd probably be great. But that would be a discovery for another day.

If ever.

Was it wrong to hope it would happen? Someday? Soon?

Patience wiped her tearstained cheeks with her sleeve and, with a happy smile, trotted over and gave Zeke a very loud smack on the cheek.

Jon cringed as Zeke bolted upright.

He stared at Patience, eyes wide.

"I kiss Sleeping Beauty." Patience patted his hand.

Zeke's gaze shifted from Patience to Jon to Grace, then back. His cheeks reddened. "Aw, Patience, *danki*, but I'm not Sleeping Beauty. That would be you."

But his gaze shifted to Grace and lingered as if he meant her. Her face warmed.

"Get off of my sisters' bed, lazy bones," Jon said, but his tone was teasing.

Zeke might not have recognized it, though, because the redness of his cheeks brightened. He stood, mumbled what might have been an apology as he avoided their gazes, and followed Jon from the room.

"Let's go find out what has Vernon so spellbound in the pasture. He's been gazing at the ground since before we went up on the roof," Jon said.

Zeke paused and glanced back at Grace but still didn't look her in the eyes. "Talk later?" he mouthed.

She nodded. She wanted to tell him about her conversation with *Daed* anyway. But Zeke appeared exhausted, and the conversation might not happen that evening. In fact, with the disrupted sleep of the previous night and the early hour for the barn raising tomorrow, they'd probably all be headed to bed as soon as they finished chores.

Patience sniffled beside her. "That bird scare me."

Grace put her arm around her sister's shoulders. "It was probably afraid of you, too. Come on—let's wash up and go help *Mamm* in the kitchen."

And maybe sneak out to the pasture with Jon and Zeke to find out what Vernon was looking at out there. She'd seen him earlier but hadn't thought twice about it until Jon mentioned it.

For a second, fear stabbed at her. Was it Timothy? Or one of their two still-missing horses? But no. It couldn't be a body or a live person or animal, because Vernon would've been quick to let them know.

After her earlier buggy jump and the following talk

with *Daed*, she wasn't willing to risk appearing unlady-like again by following the men out there. Sigh. She had to wait to satisfy her curiosity.

Grace helped her sister, followed her downstairs, and since *Mamm* was busy getting the baby chicks settled, gave Patience the laundry basket of folded clothes. "You can take care of the laundry." She turned to *Mamm*. "I'll be right back, *Mamm*. I have something I need to see."

Well, maybe not *need* to so much as *want* to. But she didn't want to be left out of the discovery in the pasture.

Without waiting for *Mamm* to reply, Grace dashed out the door and followed the men to the pasture. *Daed* had joined the other men, his attention trained on a trail of...

Grace stumbled to a stop. Had the contents of a woman's top dresser drawer exploded in their pasture?

Daed stooped to pick up a red, lacy garment with a tag that said something "Secret" that was so sheer anything under it would be very visible—and not secret. It dangled from his hand like a limp flag.

It was first in a line of colorful unmentionables strewn across the pasture.

"Run get a bag, Gracie, and pick these up. They don't need to be out here with all the men coming tomorrow."

They didn't need to be out there with the four men currently eyeing them.

Vernon's face was a mottled red, and he held a collection of colorful unmentionables as if he'd been picking them up. Jon kicked at a leopard-print underwire bra. Zeke handed something in a hot-pink case to *Daed*.

Grace edged nearer.

It was a cell phone. The top of the zippered case was clear plastic. And visible from the screen inside the case were words that someone with the initial P had written: Tim, leave me alone or these go public.

Grace's heart skipped a beat or two. Her stomach hurt.

When *Daed* scrolled down on the screen, photos of bruises in various shades of painful appeared.

Why would anyone take pictures of bruises? And who was P?

Daed's expression turned dangerous. But all he said was, "Gracie. The bag. Now."

Grace turned and ran. But since she'd told *Daed* about Timothy's controlling nature, she felt much better.

Still, her thoughts whirled. Tim was a popular name among the Amish and *Englisch*. It couldn't be her Timothy. Could it? And if so, who was P, and why did she have so many fancy undergarments?

* * *

The evidence was circumstantial at best, but assuming Zeke guessed the identity of the unknown Tim correctly, if he was alive, he'd soon be surrounded by Gracie's twelve brothers and wish he were dead. And Zeke, Vernon, and Seth might be part of the crowd surrounding him too. Well, a whole bunch of upset, protective Amish men. Maybe even the pun-loving *grossdaadi* who'd assigned Zeke to this family earlier this morning.

Zeke really wanted to meet the *grossdaadi*. Officially. And spend time in conversation with him. Maybe he'd be at the barn raising tomorrow. Or would he have to keep managing volunteers until the Red Cross arrived?

"I also found cushioned church pews broken in pieces over yonder," Vernon said, pointing.

"Hmm. An *Englisch* church's pews?"

"There was an *Englisch* church dismantled on the way into Arthur. All that was left was the sign: 'God can calm the storm.' Actually, it said 'He,' but 'God' was implied." Zeke glanced at Seth.

The older man was frowning again.

Did Seth somehow know that Zeke somewhat struggled with that? But then there were those unplanned words he'd said to Toby's father. *We can't choose whether or not storms come. But we can choose where we stare during a storm.* Or was that the bishop's response? Zeke tried to smother a yawn. His memory of the day's events and words was beginning to get very foggy. But other than the time he'd briefly passed out on Gracie's bed, he hadn't slept for almost forty-eight hours. It would be good to crawl into bed tonight.

Except, he wanted to talk to Gracie.

Maybe she'd understand if he postponed the conversation until tomorrow. Clarity of mind and sound judgment were essential for communication with her, and he was lacking in both at the moment.

Or maybe they were the same thing.

Okay, thinking was overrated. He'd confused himself. Talking definitely would be on hold until after he rested. If not, he'd find himself doing something incredibly stupid, like kissing Gracie.

And then those twelve brothers would be circling him.

Gracie ran back to the pasture with a plastic bag flapping beside her to collect some of the woman's lingerie. The wind gusted, pressing the blue material of her dress against her legs. Emphasizing her curves.

Did she wear something like the garments on the ground under her plain dress?

His face heated, and he forced his attention away from her. He needed busywork. Something he could do without thought or conversation. And not mess up.

Seth clamped his hand on Zeke's shoulder. "I'd engage you in a battle of wits, but I can see you're unarmed."

Zeke blinked. Opened his mouth...and shut it. The man was right.

"*Daed*, that's unkind. He was up all night with a laboring horse before coming here." Gracie came to his defense.

Seth frowned, his gaze sober. "Then I suggest as soon as you eat, go straight to bed. No sneaking out later with my daughter."

Oh, the man knew him so well. Zeke swallowed. Nodded. "Actually, I need rest more than I need food. If I may be excused?"

"See you bright and early in the morning." Seth walked farther into the field.

"I'll send Patience in to wake him with a kiss, and then we could sneak out later," Gracie quipped loud enough for her *daed* to overhear. And Jon. And Vernon. But maybe she was just being...impertinent. No, that wasn't the right word. Um...he shook his head. The word wasn't coming. Time to make himself scarce.

Zeke turned and headed toward the *haus*, leaving Seth to deal with his daughter if he so chose.

Because that idea held merit.

Especially because Zeke liked it way too much.

Except for the part where Patience would wake him with a kiss. It'd be ever so much better if it were Gracie.

* * *

The rest of the evening dragged by. It was amazing how much of a difference Zeke had made in such a short time. She missed him being around. His quiet listening. The wise comments. Their conversations. The glances and touches.

Grace finished her chores and headed up to bed. The morning would come early as the people in the community would arrive to start work on the barn. It would be finished before nightfall. Probably before the evening meal.

She crawled under the covers, which were still wrinkled from Zeke's brief nap, and bounced out of bed the next morning, excited about spending the day with him.

Funny how on the night of her wedding she'd gone to bed filled with dread, and the very next night was filled with joyful anticipation that fueled her dreams. The way she always assumed the night before her wedding would be.

Joyful anticipation.

Not dread.

Not relief to wake up and discover the wedding was...postponed.

What did that tell her about her planned wedding? Future husband? Both?

"It's just cold feet. All brides have them." She whispered the words she'd been told too many times to count in just the last month alone. Words spoken yesterday by

Mamm. Plus pressure from Elsie…And *Daed*'s silence during their talk hadn't exactly said this, but it hadn't refuted it, either.

She shuddered. But even that didn't dim the anticipation of seeing Zeke.

She put on a clean dress, maroon this time, and pinned it shut, then fixed her hair, securing the *kapp* over it.

Even though it was not yet dawn, men's conversations already rose outside. She peered through the window. Maybe ten men had arrived so far, and they unloaded their big, heavy toolboxes from their buggies or wagons. An older woman, Erma, carried a large tray into the *haus*. Cinnamon rolls. Oh, Erma. Her cinnamon rolls were the best. Sticky, gooey, melt-in-your-mouth goodness. Grace had to have one before they were all gone. And they'd go quick. Erma only made twenty-four when she brought them to events. Always. And the men she heard talking through the window would be lining up, more would be arriving…Oh, she must hurry.

With a smile on her face, Patience mumbled something in her sleep. Probably about cinnamon rolls.

Grace hurried out of the room and ran right into a solid, bare chest, still warm and damp from the shower. Sparks shot through her. She stumbled back, blinking. The man was little more than a blur in the dim early morning light, but from her physical reaction, it wasn't Jon. Or Vernon.

It was Zeke. The man who filled her dreams and every waking thought.

Her heart thudded. Her stomach tumbled. Her mouth went dry. She swayed.

"Easy there, Gracie." Zeke's voice was husky from

sleep. His hands gently closed around her upper arms, steadying her.

She wanted to lean into him, step into his embrace, and...

No. No. No.

She couldn't. She wouldn't.

Her breath lodged, seized, and then came back in an embarrassing gasp.

"Are you okay?"

Worse, he'd noticed.

He stepped nearer, his fingers tightening almost imperceptibly. "Gracie?"

She jerked away and ran, losing her balance on the first step of the stairs and nearly falling.

"Easy there." His hands reached down and closed around her waist, fingers splayed, and hauled her back against his firm, and still very bare, chest. Except, he lost his balance and sat down hard on a step, and she landed—still in his arms—on the step below.

Oh, her heart. It tried to pound its way out of her chest. Her bottom stung along with her pride.

And her brain ceased functioning, because she sat there, in his arms, letting the unfamiliar feelings wash over her like a tidal wave.

He sighed, maybe with relief that he'd caught her before she fell, or it might have been dismay at their tangled legs and inappropriate appearance to anyone who wandered by. Not that anyone would. They'd be lining up for those scrumptious cinnamon rolls.

She was in no hurry to move. This—not cinnamon rolls, but *this*—would fuel her dreams for the next week.

"Gracie?" This time, concern filled Zeke's voice. His

hands moved. Adjusted themselves so they weren't so accidentally close to anywhere they weren't supposed to be. Sweet of him to be looking out for her, respecting her, that way.

Her whole body warmed. Tingled.

"I must be dreaming," she whispered. In real life, stuff like this didn't happen. Her dreams were fueled by her active imagination, and...

He chuckled. "A nightmare, I'm sure. I didn't mean to run into you or knock you down the stairs."

Except, *she* ran into him, and she almost fell down the stairs in an attempt to do the right thing.

And well, she *wanted* to kiss him. A peck. On the cheek.

Or maybe she might accidentally on purpose miss his cheek.

She shouldn't.

But...oh, she would. This might be the only chance she got.

And since she most certainly was dreaming this...

She twisted in his arms and kneeled on the step.

His eyes widened. "Gracie," he whispered.

She leaned in...

A blur, and Patience appeared behind Zeke. She was still in her white nightgown, her hair in disarray. A flashlight spotlighted the floor in front of her. "Gracie? Why you in Zeke's lap? Where Zeke's shirt?"

Except, her sister had never appeared in her dreams before...which meant this wasn't a dream and she was really about to...oh my goodness...

With a gasp, Grace planted her hands against his bare chest and shoved away. She lost her balance and this time tumbled the rest of the way down the stairs, backward, on her rump.

Oh, the shame. The cinnamon roll line had just observed her entrance, Patience would tattle, and Zeke couldn't come down to check on her without the entire community seeing him shirtless and destroying his reputation...

And hers.

CHAPTER 14

Zeke's breath caught. Had Gracie intended to kiss him? Intended, because with what could only be bad timing, Patience had interrupted.

Longing had flashed across her face, followed by horror, and then embarrassment. With a gasp, Gracie had planted her cold hands against his bare chest, still warm from his shower—his heart had pounded—and shoved away. Before he could react, she'd lost her balance and tumbled the rest of the way down the stairs.

Zeke was pretty sure he was still sleeping, and what might have been a very pleasant dream had just turned into a nightmare with every thump, thump, thump as she fell down the stairs.

Backward.

On her rump. Mostly.

She made a quiet "eek" sound, but Patience made up

for it in volume by screaming and bursting into tears. Make those ear-piercing wails.

Okay, this was real life. There was no way he'd imagine that noise.

He caught his breath, lurched to his feet, and started down the stairs, when a whole crowd—well, a small gathering—of Amish women all rushed to Gracie's side where she was sprawled at the bottom of the stairs.

He turned tail and attempted to run for his room before the women saw him shirtless, in his pajama pants. But then his bedroom door opened, and Vernon stumbled out, in much the same condition.

"What happened?" Vernon blinked owlishly.

"Gracie fell down the stairs," Zeke said simply. No need for embellishment.

"Gracie was in Zeke's lap," Patience declared loudly enough for the women gathered below to hear. "And he shirtless." She held up her flashlight, shining it full on Zeke's face and blinding him.

Danki, Patience. Zeke shut his eyes and sighed. Seth would be sure to send him away now. Maybe even all the way back to Indiana. And wouldn't *Daed* love that? Zeke hadn't even lasted twenty-four hours. He imagined his father berating him.

You're reckless and have a complete disregard for the rules. And worse, you're a goof-off. You'll always be a goof-off.

He turned back toward the stairs to rebut the situation somehow. He tried to think what to say that wouldn't get Gracie into trouble. Or him.

The women gathered below gasped, staring up at him.

And Vernon. And Patience. All still in their nightclothes. And they gasped again.

Vernon had enough common sense to back away. Quietly. But at least he wasn't spotlighted. A door shut.

"Patience, go get dressed." Jon was still upstairs and now standing somewhere behind Zeke.

The flashlight slid away from Zeke.

With *Daed*'s harsh words still ringing in his ears, Zeke turned to face brother number twelve. Jon was at least partially dressed.

"It's my fault. I tripped and started to fall down the stairs, and he caught me," Gracie said, her voice strained.

Truth, but not the whole truth.

"Looks to me like he missed," an unknown woman replied, and the whole group twittered.

And with that the tension was over.

Jon grinned and clapped his hand on Zeke's bare shoulder. "*Danki* for trying."

Zeke didn't want them to believe a lie, but if he told the whole truth, it'd get ugly fast. And did everyone really need to know that Gracie apparently had intended to kiss him and Patience had not so conveniently interrupted?

He didn't think so.

"Good thing he missed. Timothy wouldn't have liked another man's hands on his bride," another woman said from the foot of the stairs.

Jah, *danki* for the reminder. Zeke's heart folded in on itself.

It might've been his imagination, but it seemed a heaviness descended upon the household—a thick, dark silence. But before Zeke could figure out why that might be, someone giggled nervously.

And with that, the women's conversation shifted to talk of Gracie—"Are you hurt, dearie?"—to the mystery of Timothy's disappearance and when the wedding might be rescheduled when he was found.

Zeke aimed a probably sick-looking smile at Jon and headed back to his bedroom to get dressed. And take on the day.

After a good night's sleep, at least he could assist with a barn raising with his wits in place, so long as he stayed far from Gracie.

And so long as Jon or Seth didn't single him out to get his story of what exactly happened between him and Gracie. Because if asked, he would tell the truth and not lie, even though they might never believe his side of the story. What Amish girl would be bold enough to attempt to kiss a near stranger on the stairs in a *haus* full of Amish there for a barn raising?

The answer hit him with enough force to knock the air from his lungs.

A woman desperate for escape. Was she so desperate to not marry Timothy that anyone would do? Even a stranger from Indiana?

Oh, that hurt.

Gracie wasn't really attracted to him. Any single, un-attached male would do. He really was the loser *Daed* called him for falling for it.

Because it meant he was nothing more than a means to an end.

He'd still be her friend, but he'd guard his heart.

He didn't want it trampled.

* * *

Grace's body ached from head to toe, but since she could move, albeit slowly and painfully, she figured nothing was broken. Just bruised.

Kind of like her emotions.

She slowly got to her feet, every muscle and joint in her body protesting at the movement. Her cheeks burned, but not as hot as the shame filling her to overflowing, spilling out from her pores. She'd meant to apologize to Zeke for her behavior, and instead she'd made it ten times worse. A hundred times worse. Maybe even a thousand times worse.

Zeke would be ever so glad to return to Indiana and get away from the too-forward Illinois hussy.

But oh, why couldn't a man like him have noticed her first? Asked her if she wanted to go on a buggy ride? Treated her like she mattered? And instead she got Timothy.

At least *Mamm* was happy. His parents were happy.

It was just that she suffered from... She sighed heavily. Cold feet.

Icy, cold feet.

Make that frozen feet.

"Does it hurt terribly, dearie?" Erma grasped Grace's arm and held on as she shuffled her way into the kitchen, slower than the slowest snail would go. But bless her heart—she was doing it for Grace's benefit, because even on her pokiest day, Erma walked fast. "Maybe it'll help to put some ice on it."

She'd pretty much have to pack her body in ice or take a handful of pain pills, but she deserved nothing less after her forward, foolish behavior.

But oh joy, there was still one cinnamon roll, waiting on the metal baking sheet on the table. Grace eyed it and inched closer, reaching out the arm that wasn't gripped by Erma...

A bearded man grabbed the baked delight and turned away, adding insult to injury as Grace watched the very last melt-in-your-mouth piece of deliciousness get carried out the door. The whole reason why she had been hurrying in the first place.

She could've cried.

And that settled it. This whole thing was Erma's fault. Because if she hadn't brought cinnamon rolls, Grace wouldn't have been hurrying; she wouldn't have run into Zeke and almost fallen down the stairs and then gotten sidetracked enough to try to kiss him. *Jah*, it was all Erma's fault.

Erma pulled out a chair and held on to Grace's arm as Grace lowered herself into it; then Erma bustled to the freezer and pulled out a bag of mixed vegetables. "Where does it hurt most, dearie?"

Um, everywhere? But mostly her pride. And her conscience. But she couldn't put ice on those. Nor on her bottom, which would likely be black and blue.

Grace waved it away. "I'll be okay."

Erma returned the vegetables to the freezer and then poured herself and Grace mugs of coffee and carried them to the table. She added cream and sugar. Sweet, but Grace didn't like coffee. "*Danki*," she murmured and tried not to grimace as she tasted the bitter brew.

The women, who'd arrived early, bustled around, carrying breakfast foods and drinks outside to a table that'd been set up from sawhorses and lumber. No more cinnamon rolls, but there were breakfast burritos, toast, hard-boiled eggs, cereal bars, fruit, bacon, and some fruit-filled pastries, as well as assorted juices and coffee to drink.

Jon, Vernon, and Zeke filed past to join the gathering crowd outside. Grace tried to catch Zeke's attention to mouth her apology, but he wouldn't look at her.

She couldn't blame him.

Her eyes burned, and she swallowed at a stubborn lump in her throat. The coffee she'd forced herself to swallow didn't stay put and she gagged. She slapped her hand across her mouth and raced from the room.

Every step ached. Her back, her neck, her rump, her...everything.

The first-floor bathroom was occupied, so she dashed upstairs. And barely made it. She didn't even get the door shut, though she swatted at it.

Patience stumbled in and rubbed Grace's back as she knelt on the floor, heaving and crying.

"Jesus, calm Gracie's storm," Patience prayed.

And the innocent words made Grace cry harder.

Lord, please forgive me for all my sins already this morning. Help me to make things right with everyone I wronged. Especially Zeke.

Oh, her behavior.

A fresh round of shame washed over her.

Patience dropped to the floor next to Grace and wrapped her arms around her.

So much for being strong for Patience. Maybe her sister was stronger than Grace thought.

Gracie twisted enough to wrap her arms around Patience. "*Danki. Ich liebe dich.*"

She rose to her feet, washed her face, and rebrushed her teeth; then she and Patience went downstairs together, hand in hand.

Some of the women were whispering together, hands over their lips, eyes focused on Grace as she appeared.

Patience released Grace's hand and went to feed the peeping baby chicks in the boxes on the floor.

Erma wrapped Grace in a hug. "I wish I would've known, dearie. I never could drink coffee when I was in the family way. But Timothy's *mamm* will be ever so glad to hear. Especially if he's . . . gone."

Grace stared at her. "Family way?" What? Why would they think that? Timothy and she had barely even kissed. Maybe only three times. And that wasn't enough for . . . Oh. Oh no, no, no, no, no. Erma didn't sound judgmental, but others would, even if it wasn't true. Grace's stomach roiled again. She swallowed the bile and made a second dash from the room.

* * *

Zeke helped the men as they used a pulley system to raise the prebuilt sides of the barn into the air. Then, as several men held the ropes in place, he and a few others shimmied up and started attaching the sides. Around him conversation hummed, and jokes were shared as well as good-natured gibes.

Zeke listened to the ebb and flow of conversation, present but not a part of the group. He missed joking around with his friends and coworkers.

Vernon seemed to be working in the same solitude but on the opposite side of the building, so Zeke couldn't even talk with him. Not that he had any idea what they'd talk about. What could a known goof-off say to someone as perfect as Vernon? Except, maybe, ask him to share his secrets so Zeke could learn from them.

Zeke should've stayed home. Then he wouldn't be used by a pretty girl desperate to escape. He wouldn't be the laughingstock of the Lantz men. He and his younger brother and Kiah could be hanging out, having fun after work, and…

Kiah. Zeke lowered himself to sit on a beam and looked around the crowd of men. Surely, Kiah had to be there somewhere. But he didn't see him. Very few men from Shipshewana were there. Just him, Vernon, and a couple of Mennonite men that Zeke didn't know very well.

An Amish man down below started mocking a street preacher he'd heard in town. Something about how the tornado was *Gott*'s wrath. "The funny thing was he is a pastor at that there church the tornado destroyed. Made me think maybe *Gott* was judging him."

Several of the Amish men concurred, but unease slithered up Zeke's spine and he shuddered. The *Englisch* man who oversaw the boys' ranch where Zeke volunteered preached about everyone needing to be saved. That it wasn't based on works, or on who one's family was, or on what religion you were, or on anything except the blood of Jesus. *I am the way, the truth, and the life: no man comes to the Father, but by me.* The verse was engraved on the front of the chapel at the ranch. It always made Zeke a bit curious. He and his coworkers always sat in on the sermons, but he never was brave enough to ask about what he heard. Especially since Amish generally believe salvation is based on church membership and works.

The Mennonite missionaries stilled. One stood on the beam up near the top of the barn and loudly cleared his throat. "Amish or *Englisch*, we all need to be saved. If anyone has any questions, come see me."

"Or me," the other Mennonite said.

The two missionaries exchanged glances and returned to work.

Zeke fought the urge to go over there. It'd be a bad move when surrounded by Amish men who'd agreed with the storyteller.

Below him someone muttered, "I'm Amish. I don't need to worry about salvation."

More murmurs of assent.

Zeke's stomach twisted.

"I agree with the missionaries," a quiet voice said behind Zeke. "Salvation is not so widely preached among the Amish, but it's a fact. We need *Gott*, and He is calling for us to come to Him. There's this *Gott*-sized hole in each one of us that no one can deny, if they are honest."

Zeke's *Gott*-sized hole responded with a tug and a rush of longing. But Zeke wasn't sure who the man was talking to. No one answered. But maybe the loud-mouthed ones below didn't hear him. Zeke carefully swung a leg over the beam he was sitting on and swiveled around to face the thin, wiry guy he'd first seen at the public school yesterday morning. Gracie's *gross-daadi*. And he was on the beam next to him, his pale-blue gaze focused on Zeke.

"Cliff Lantz. And you're Zeke Bontrager."

"Good memory." Now that he was face-to-face with the pun-loving *daadi*, Zeke didn't know what to say.

"I make it a point to remember people I like."

People he liked?

"I remember you arriving. You were kind to the dog. Stood up to the man who kicked the dog. And returned him to his family."

"And you named the horses and cows here."

Cliff grimaced. "And the hog." He glanced toward a tree, but other than a rope, nothing was there now. "Named her Crispy Bacon. She's gone to the butcher. Guess she's going to live up to her name. Tornado killed her."

"I'm sorry. Loved the names you came up with, though."

"How's your stay so far? Any unmarried daughters?" There was a twinkle in Cliff's eyes.

Zeke shook his head. "With twelve brothers, ain't it a wonder?"

Cliff roared with laughter. "I knew I liked you."

They both fell silent, working on the barn, for fifteen, maybe twenty minutes. Below them, the joking and gibing continued. Zeke eyed the missionaries. Could *Gott* really love someone like him? Someone his own *daed* couldn't love? He longed for that unconditional love and acceptance. Something inside him urged him to seek the missionaries out. Would he have a chance to talk to them privately sometime? Maybe on the way home.

Then Cliff shifted. "I think I'm going to talk to one of those missionaries."

Zeke puffed out a breath of relief. "I'll go with you. If you don't mind."

"It's easier with two, ain't so?"

"Much." Zeke swung down to the ground and headed in the direction of the missionaries. Vernon was already there. *Huh.*

Patience approached with two glasses filled with what appeared to be water. Probably had apple cider vinegar added to it like they did at home. Her eyes shimmered with tears. She handed a glass to Cliff, then turned to Zeke.

Zeke took a cup. "*Danki*, Patience. What's wrong?"

"They say Gracie in family way. She *not* in way."

She was pregnant? Zeke's stomach twisted and cramped. Had Timothy forced her to...? His heart skipped a beat. She wasn't with child. It wasn't true. When she'd appeared to try to kiss him, she'd said, "I must be dreaming." When Patience caught them, she'd pushed him away. He could hear the pain in her voice when she talked about Timothy's behavior and her doubts. He thought of the curve of her assets in the windblown dress, and Patience's obvious tears and denial.

A verse in Proverbs came to mind. He paraphrased it in his mind: A person with wisdom has patience. It's in one's glory to overlook an offense.

Distance was good for his sanity's sake, but Gracie needed a friend and a listening ear. He'd just keep making it clear that he wasn't here to date. And if it turned out she'd been trying to play a game with him, well, then *Daed* would be right if he called him a fool for falling for it.

Cliff stilled. He stared at Patience. "What did you say?" His voice was dangerously calm.

Zeke's stomach roiled. A throbbing began in his temples.

Patience tearfully repeated it.

"That boy," Cliff muttered. "That boy."

Jah. Twelve brothers would be circling the missing groom.

If he was still alive.

CHAPTER 15

Grace brushed her teeth again, then headed downstairs to somehow set the gossips straight without coming out and saying she was *not* pregnant. That just wasn't spoken of except in whispers to trusted family members. The loose dresses hid—for the most part—the shape of a woman's body.

Mamm was on her way up, and they met in the middle. "What is going on? I'm hearing whispers that you—"

"Let's go to my room." Grace grabbed *Mamm*'s hand and tugged her upstairs. Once there, Grace shut the door. Her back twinged as she twisted it.

Mamm's forehead was wrinkled, her lips curved down. "Gracie, I simply cannot believe you would do such a thing. Timothy—"

"I didn't. I'm not in the family way. Timothy and I, we never . . ." Grace's face heated. "It's Zeke. He, I mean—"

"What!" *Mamm*'s eyebrows shot up.

Okay, never mind heated. Grace's face burned. "No. I mean I might have developed a crush on Zckc. I know nothing will come of it, so no reason to send him away. I'll marry Timothy..." She gulped. "If he's alive. If he shows up."

Mamm smiled. "I'm glad to hear that."

Jah. But the thought made Grace's blood pressure rise. And not in a good way. "But I might have flirted with Zeke and then I felt guilty, and between falling down the stairs and the coffee Erma gave me, everything mixed wrong, and well, I got sick."

Mamm's expression cleared. "Sarah Jane made the coffee. She gets way too many grounds in it. But don't tell her I said that. I'm surprised more don't get sick from it. Don't worry. I'll set the gossips straight." She glanced around the room. "You need to take a moment and straighten your room; then make sure the boys' beds are made. I'll have the misunderstanding cleared up by the time you finish."

Grace hoped so. It would be beyond terrible if that gossip spread further than the kitchen. She couldn't imagine what Zeke might think. Maybe that she was more than a flirt—that she was also very loose. Easy. She shuddered.

Mamm gave Grace a gentle hug and bustled from the room. Moving slowly, due to her aches and pains, Grace made the bed that she and Patience shared and picked up Patience's discarded nightgown, folded it, and placed it under the pillow. Patience normally took care of things, but she must've been excited to get downstairs, too.

The room straightened, she went down the hall to her brother's room. It was clean, nothing out of place.

Then she peeked into the room Zeke and Vernon were staying in. They'd been in a rush. Both twin beds were jumbled, tangled messes, and the contents of both men's bags lay strewn across the room, divided by a swath of bare floor in the middle.

Grace made the beds but hesitated to touch their personal belongings. It'd be wiser to let them pick up their dirty socks and other garments themselves.

She went down the hall to the room across from hers—the bathroom. She took a couple of pain pills, then looked around. That was clean. The towels Zeke and the others had used were dropped in the hamper, and there was a kind of manly piney scent lingering in the room.

She hadn't noticed when she was in there earlier. But then she'd only been focused on herself. And when she was in his arms, she'd thought it was part of her dream.

Maybe she could find a candle with that scent. To remind her of him.

It was time to stop hiding. Hopefully, *Mamm* had quieted the rumors.

Grace firmed her shoulders and, careful not to move any unnecessary muscles, returned downstairs. She entered the bustling kitchen. Uninterrupted chatter continued, but at least no one whispered behind cupped hands. Someone had discarded Grace's barely touched cup of coffee, and everyone did chores that were assigned by one person—typically bossy, take-charge Deborah Fisher.

Deborah wasn't there. She was related to Toby, though, so she'd be at visitation.

Hallie would be there, too.

Grace gulped. Should she go to support her friend? Or stay home for the barn raising?

Mamm came in from outside carrying an empty tray in one hand and a plastic dishpan full of dirty glasses against her hip. Patience stood at the sink, washing dishes. And sniffling.

She glanced over her shoulder at Grace and lifted her hands from the suds. Dripping, she rushed to Grace and wrapped her warm, wet arms around her. "You not in way, Gracie."

Grace returned her hug. "I…" What was Patience talking about?

Erma caught her gaze and, with a sheepish smile, mouthed, "I'm sorry."

Oh. Patience had heard the rumors. And misunderstood.

Grace tightened her grip on her sister. "*Danki*, Patience."

Patience smiled brightly and returned to the sink.

The door opened and Gracie's other best friend, Elsie, poked her head in. "Gracie, my family is here for the barn raising. *Daed* said I could go to the visitation if you go with me. I think we need to be there for Hallie."

Grace sighed. "I'll ask." Hopefully, *Mamm* would agree.

Mamm had returned outside sometime while Grace and Patience were hugging, so Grace hurried to join her friend in the yard. *Mamm* was arranging more breakfast burritos on a tray. A man snatched one as she worked.

"May I go with Elsie to the visitation?" Grace stopped beside her.

Mamm waved her hand in a shooing motion. "Go on. We have plenty of help here for now. Try to be back in time to help with the noon meal."

"*Danki, Mamm.*" Grace hurried after Elsie to the buggy her family had brought. She scanned the skeleton of the future barn, looking for Zeke, but she didn't see him anywhere. Of course, men clung from every beam already in place, and some men were perched on the eventual roof. Zeke could've been any one of them working at dangerous heights.

Daed crouched beside one of his four-year-old grandsons, showing him how to use a hammer.

And oh, wait. Zeke stood next to *Daadi* Cliff and Vernon, talking to two men Grace didn't know. Zeke's eyes locked on hers for a brief moment; then he deliberately looked away.

Oh, her heart. What had she done?

* * *

Zeke tried not to watch Gracie walk with her friend to a closed buggy. *Tried* being the key word. His gaze kept drifting to her as he listened to the Mennonite missionaries explaining the ABCs of salvation: Admit you have sinned, believe on the Lord Jesus Christ, and confess with your mouth. All things from scripture he had thought about or that he and Cliff had discussed.

All things they had done at one time or another, though Zeke had never thought to pray and ask *Gott* to save him.

"The truth is once you believe the promises of God, you not only have hope—your life is forever changed," one of the missionaries said.

"I think I'd like to pray." Cliff bowed his head.

Jah. Zeke wanted to, also.

"Repeat after me," the same missionary said, closing his eyes.

Zeke bowed his head with the others and silently repeated the prayer the missionary uttered.

Peace, or something, fluttered to life inside Zeke. Filled him. He couldn't keep from smiling.

Not even Gracie and her issues could dampen his thoughts...

He took in a deep breath. Okay, maybe they could affect his smile but not this new, amazing peace that settled deep within him despite the outside turmoil.

Lord, danki *for saving me. Help me to minister to Gracie as I should. And help Timothy to be found alive.*

A rock settled in the pit of his stomach. But Timothy should be the one to raise his own child, if she was in the family way. But wow, it hurt. He might be a fool for believing she was as attracted to him as he was to her and that her stories about Timothy were true... He exhaled. Then he would be a fool. He needed to be her friend.

Help Gracie to find happiness and peace with her situation. He sighed. *Help me to find peace with it, too.*

Zeke thanked the missionaries and returned to work. Most of the Amish hadn't paid any attention to them being gone. But of course, except for Cliff, they were strangers. Zeke reached for a beam to swing himself back up, but Cliff grasped Zeke's arm. There was peace in his eyes, too. "Want to go visiting with me tomorrow? I need to look for that boy."

So Cliff felt the same burden with Patience's not-so-welcome news.

"I heard that someone who resembles Timothy was

seen in town," Zeke said quietly. "They weren't sure if it was him or not."

A strange light flashed in Cliff's eyes. "Oh, it's him. I'm sure of it."

* * *

The field near Toby's *haus* had about a dozen buggies parked in it. But people would be coming and going the rest of the day and the next for visitation. A church bench wagon was parked in the driveway. The family must've borrowed benches from another district.

Grace trailed Elsie into the *haus* and filed past Toby's body, looking at him one last time. She and Elsie murmured condolences to his parents; then they went to sit down beside Hallie, one on each side of her. Hallie's icy fingers closed around Grace's, and a strange sort of gasping sob escaped.

Grace shifted closer to her friend as Timothy's parents came in, their eyes red rimmed. His *mamm* openly wailed as she viewed Toby's body, then embraced Toby's *mamm*. She was still crying when she sat on the other side of Grace and murmured, "Horrible, horrible, horrible."

Grace gulped and grasped Lavina's hand with her free one. "No word yet?"

"Nothing. It's like Timothy vanished into thin air," Lavina sniffled.

Which was kind of what he did, getting sucked up in a tornado.

"And Peter is hovering between death and life. He hasn't woken up from his coma yet. Maybe never will."

Grace had nothing to say to that. She squeezed Lavina's hand. And Hallie's.

They fell into silence, except for sniffles and an occasional sob.

Grace glanced at Toby's body in the casket, then closed her eyes to pray for Toby's soul. Then her prayers wandered from him to Peter and his family, to Hallie and her comfort, to closure for Timothy's family, to Zeke.

Oh, Zeke.

Danki, Lord, for bringing him into my life. Please heal our relationship that I messed up by being impulsive, and if it's Your will—she pulled in a breath—*please open the doors for us to be together.*

Though that was an impossible dream.

As impossible as Timothy walking in the backdoor.

And then he did.

Maybe.

CHAPTER 16

Zeke faced Cliff. "Are you sure of it?"

Cliff shrugged. "I'm as sure as sure can be. There's just a smidgen of room for doubt. The boy looks just like him, but he sure as shooting doesn't act like him. Not that I ever liked the boy that much anyway." He lowered his voice a little and Zeke leaned closer to hear him. "He seemed a bit two-faced to me. Acting and talking one way around the adults and Gracie but a totally different fellow when he thought he was alone or that no one who'd report back to the bishop or preachers was around. He used drugs, alcohol, and sometimes chewing tobacco or cigarettes . . ." Cliff shook his head and swung back up to the beam where he'd been working.

Zeke followed suit. "Lots of Amish *youngies* do."

Cliff frowned. "Not just the *youngies*. It's who you are when you think no one is looking that matters." He shook his head. "That said, Alvin—he's Timothy's *daed*—said he told Timothy that if he wanted to live at home and inherit the family business, then he needed to straighten up, join the church, and marry some sweet Amish girl like our Gracie."

So that was why Timothy ordered Gracie to let him take her home? Told her they were getting married?

Zeke's stomach hurt.

Cliff pounded in a nail. Picked up another.

Zeke didn't like Timothy very much at the moment. Gracie did have valid concerns. He glanced down at Seth, who was crouched beside a young child, helping him hold a hammer correctly. What had Gracie told Seth, and was he at all concerned?

"Never dreamed the boy would actually— Well, *jah*, I know some kids get pregnant outside of marriage, but..." Cliff puffed out a breath. "Figured with Alvin's warning, Timothy would respect our Gracie."

Zeke made a noncommittal grunt. Based on Cliff's summary, Timothy didn't sound like the sort of man Zeke would want courting or marrying his sister.

"I prayed hard that *Gott* would stop the wedding if Timothy shouldn't marry Gracie. He did, in a big way. I prayed *Gott* would send a nice young man for our girl to marry instead." Cliff raised his head and looked into Zeke's eyes. "He sent you."

Gracie had prayed the same thing. Had *Gott* gone to extreme lengths to bring Zeke here? He was so out of his league at the mercy of such a powerful *Gott*. A chill worked through Zeke's bones. He shivered. His thoughts stalled.

The wind suddenly gusted. Cold, cold air. Straw hats

went flying. Someone at the top of the barn yelled something.

Zeke looked up from his perch. And a man came tumbling down.

*   *   *

Grace sucked in a breath and her heart skipped several beats as she stared at the man who entered. Hallie's hand squeezed hers painfully.

Lavina gasped loudly as the man who might be Timothy walked up to the casket and silently stared down at Toby. The man sort of resembled Timothy, except for a bad cut on one side of his face surrounded by bruising, and an eye that was swollen shut. His head had a large white bandage covering part of his brown curly hair. Blood seeped through part of the bandage. He wore *Englisch* clothes: ragged blue jeans and a bright-green T-shirt.

It seemed as if everyone filling the benches stilled. Breathing was suspended. No one moved.

"Timmy," Lavina breathed, but the man standing beside the casket showed no reaction.

Was he deaf? Or did he have amnesia? She should feel concern for the man's obvious injuries that apparently kept him away from his family...But she felt more concern for his mother and Toby's *mamm* than for her missing groom. Which was an uncomfortable awareness that her feelings weren't cold feet but a true lack of love...And how would she explain that to her parents and Lavina? Hopefully, this wasn't Timothy, because she didn't want to have to deal with those lingering questions yet.

Toby's *mamm*, Tabitha, stepped up to him with a watery smile. "Timmy. So glad you stopped by." She reached to pull him into a hug, but he held up a hand and moved away.

"Don't. Touch. Me," he growled. He sounded like Timothy did when he was sick. Kind of husky.

Tabitha looked away, a tear running down her cheek. Her shoulders shook. "Why are you acting like this, Timmy?" Her voice broke.

"Do I know you? And who's Timmy?" He scowled, pushed past her, and limped toward the front door without so much as a glance at Grace.

"If he's not Timmy, who is he and how'd he know to come?" someone asked in sort of a confused yet judgmental way. Grace didn't turn to see who.

Lavina trembled beside her, then lurched to her feet, still holding Grace's hand, and stumbled toward the man.

Grace let go of Hallie's hand and allowed Lavina to tug her along. Grace's legs quivered and threatened to fail her, but whether that was due to her painful fall down the stairs or because of fear, she didn't know. Her heart pounded, and her lungs struggled to find enough air.

"Timothy. Stop! Please." Lavina released Grace's hand and grasped the man's arm. "Gracie and I have been so worried."

Well, she'd been more relieved, but *jah*, *worried* worked. She also felt confused, hurt, mad, numb, and guilty for having feelings for Zeke.

The man stopped and jerked out of Lavina's grip as he glared at them. "Who are you? What's with you people?"

No spark of recognition flashed in his eyes when they slid over Grace. None. There was just...a dark nothingness. Like her feelings for the man right now.

She couldn't marry a man who didn't know who she was. More relief washed through her.

"Timothy!" his *daed*, Alvin, roared. "Stop your foolishness!"

"Whatever." The man rolled his eyes skyward and turned his back on them and walked out.

Lavina collapsed on the floor, wailing, and Alvin gathered her into his arms.

"It's an ill wind that blows no good," someone said in a tone low and dark.

Grace shuddered as she stood there, paralyzed with fear and doubt. Was he Timothy? Or not? Was he just pretending to not know anyone? But why would he do that? He had to know his *mamm* was worried if he was truly Timothy. Grace swallowed the fear that threatened to take hold of her, firmed her shoulders, and followed him outside.

A chill wind had picked up. She wrapped her arms around herself in a hug. The strong breeze tossed her *kapp* strings and ruffled the short hairs at the back of her head. She went down the stairs. "Wait."

The wind blew the stench of cigarette smoke toward her as well as something else she couldn't identify.

The man straddled a rusty green bicycle, one foot already on a pedal, but glanced at her. He cocked his head in a way that was so familiar. It reminded her of the fun Timothy. The one she sometimes liked to spend time with.

"What?"

But there was no friendliness in his voice. Just barely controlled rage. Also familiar.

He was Timothy. He had to be.

"Look, I don't know you people. I don't want any more of your drama."

She sucked in air. Let it out in a whoosh. "Then why'd you come if you aren't Timothy? Toby was his best friend."

The Timothy look-alike stared at her. "I just felt I should. But I don't know you, and I don't know who Timothy is." He hesitated. "I'm James."

Timothy's middle name was James.

Grace narrowed her eyes, stared at him. He was familiar but not. She tried to imagine him without the bruises, without the eye swollen shut, without the bandage. He looked like a man who'd survived a tornado.

"Look, nice to meet you, but my head is throbbing." James's brown eyes—make that eye, since the other was swollen shut—widened. He winced, his face pale. Then he turned and pushed off, mumbling. It sounded like he said something about "finding Paige" under his breath. *Who is Paige?*

Grace watched him go.

Was he or wasn't he Timothy?

When he turned onto the road headed toward town, Grace spun around and went back inside.

Lavina was still huddled on the floor in Alvin's arms. Tabitha stood at the window, arms crossed, back ramrod straight, and muttered under her breath. Toby's female relatives whispered behind cupped hands. Hallie and Elsie stared at Grace, eyes wide, unspoken questions in their eyes. *Was he Timmy?*

What had just happened? What did it mean for the future?

All Grace had was a *Who knows?* that she couldn't verbalize, so she shrugged a nonanswer to their questions and returned to her seat. She bowed her head but stared at her folded hands on her lap.

She couldn't help but compare the maybe-Timothy who just left to the Zeke who'd arrived yesterday about this time.

Well, tried to compare.

Because there was no comparison.

Grace just couldn't see Zeke being rude and inconsiderate to a roomful of strangers at a visitation.

But then the Timothy she knew wouldn't have acted that way, either. He was always kind and well behaved in gatherings. It was when they were alone that he seemed to barely hang on to his anger.

But why would an *Englisch* man show up at an Amish viewing and be disrespectful to the bereaved? It made no sense.

None whatsoever.

* * *

Zeke watched in horror as the man hit the ground with a thump, bounced a few times, then lay still. Too still.

He quickly pulled out his cell phone, dialed 911, and told the operator what happened, then gave the phone to Cliff to recite the address.

A woman wailed, screamed a name that Zeke didn't catch, then fell on her knees beside the fallen man.

Hammering ceased. Joking and gibes stopped. Some

men climbed down to help; others stayed put. They'd be in the way anyway. Work stopped.

Cliff handed Zeke the phone.

Zeke slid it into his pocket and watched, feeling helpless. He knew CPR, but someone was already doing that. He wondered if he'd met the man—he couldn't tell who he was from this far away.

Zeke was about to climb down, but then in his peripheral he caught movement. He turned his head and...oh no. No, no, no. Patience approached with a tray full of water glasses.

If she saw this, her reaction would be deafening. Maybe enough to wake the dead. Of course, that might be a good thing. But just in case, he'd better not risk it.

Zeke glanced at the fallen man. "Got to go," he said to Cliff, hooked his hammer on the tool belt someone had loaned him, and swung down.

He caught up with Patience three or four feet into the barn, before she noticed the man. He took the tray from her, handed it to another man, then steered Patience out of the way. "Do you want to go for a walk?"

She beamed at him. "You walk with me?"

Zeke forced a smile, though it probably flopped. "*Jah*, if you would."

"I love to."

They left the barn, and he walked beside her to the road.

He tried to remember which way to town and picked the opposite direction. He wasn't sure if an ambulance would frighten the girl or not. Maybe if the lights were flashing and siren screaming.

Slush came running, jumped a swollen drainage ditch, and fell in step beside them, tail wagging.

Zeke would miss the dog. Patience. This family. He gulped. Gracie.

It was weird, like he'd come home and found where he belonged.

Which, of course, was plain foolishness. His home, his family, his friends, his job, his life were in Indiana.

"I tell Gracie she not in way." Patience bounced on her heels.

Zeke looked at her. "What?"

Patience huffed. "She not in family way. I tell her. She stay."

That clarified that she must've thought Gracie was literally in the way. Unfortunately, that didn't change anything, but a smile formed and spread. "You're sweet, Patience."

"I like you, Zeke."

"And I like you."

Patience pointed. "Look. There Gracie."

A horse clip-clopped down the pavement pulling a closed buggy toward them. Zeke didn't know how Patience knew it was Gracie, or even where Gracie had gone. But two women were in the buggy. It neared and one of the women said, "Halt."

It was one of the women Zeke had tried to rescue from the tornado shelter. The one with the matchmaking *mammi*. He cringed a bit.

Gracie climbed out, and the buggy rolled on. Her brow was furrowed, her mouth set. "*Mamm* said I had to be back before noon." She stopped beside them.

Zeke glanced toward the sky. Not noon yet. Maybe half an hour. "Where'd you go?"

The wind gusted again. Hopefully, no one else fell. Oh, he'd forgotten to pray for the man who had fallen in his haste to get Patience away from the scene. Zeke dipped his head. *Lord, if it's Your will, let that man who fell be okay. If he's not, please comfort his family and friends.* There'd been so much loss as a result of this storm.

"Visitation for Toby. Where are you going?" Gracie shifted.

"Zeke ask me on walk." Patience beamed.

Zeke gazed in Gracie's eyes and attempted a meaningful look.

Gracie hesitated, opened and shut her mouth, then nodded.

"I tell him you not in way," Patience said.

Gracie's face reddened. "*Danki*, Patience. No. I'm not in the family way. Not even a remote chance of it."

Zeke's face heated. But oh, joy flooded him along with immense relief. This news was so good to hear. He wouldn't need to worry about that issue now. He grinned, reached for Gracie's hand, and squeezed. "I am so glad. Would you like to join us for a walk?"

"Sure. We need to talk sometime."

Jah, they did. "Tonight."

Her return smile seemed strained. "I can't wait." She tightened her grip on his hand.

He didn't want to release it. He wanted to hold on tight. But with a sigh, he let go. "*Jah*. Looking forward to it." Sort of. Unless she admitted she was using him. And then he'd keep his distance from her.

But if she genuinely liked him... maybe they could clear some things up.

And finish that unspoken conversation they'd started on the steps before she fell.

Oh *jah*. Please.

CHAPTER 17

Grace fell into step beside Zeke, remembering the sparks of his hand holding hers. Well, technically, she was beside Slush, since he was between them. She limped along, but the pain was getting better with the movement of walking. Patience rambled on about her morning, working in the kitchen washing glasses, then filling the clean glasses with vinegar water and delivering them to the men working. "*Mamm* say it important job."

"It is a very important job." Zeke glanced at her sister, then looked to Grace. "How was the visitation?"

"I not like to go." Patience shuddered.

"Well, *jah*, I don't like to go, either. But they are necessary to show a sense of community and joining together in mourning the dearly departed." Zeke kicked at a broken shingle lying in the road, then bent to pick it up. "Although, in some cases, they are not so dear until they are departed."

Patience frowned. "I not understand."

Grace agreed with Zeke. When her great-*aentie*'s husband died, he stopped being the ogre that *Aentie* Linda complained about and turned into a saint who could do no wrong.

"Anyway. Visitation. As per usual?" Zeke asked.

How could she answer that? She considered her answer and glanced at Patience to see how closely she was listening. Then she stared at Zeke, willing him to understand what she wasn't saying. "Um, *jah*. It started that way. But then some man walked in and, um, sort of upset the norm."

Zeke gave her a sharp look. "Timothy?"

Grace nodded, then shrugged. "I think so, but I'm not sure."

"You marry Zeke. Not Timothy," Patience insisted.

Grace's face warmed.

Zeke grimaced, a bit of red tinge to his cheeks. "Let's not talk about that right now, Patience."

Jah, because while Grace had a massive crush on Zeke, twenty-four hours was hardly enough time to fall in love. They barely knew each other. She didn't even know his favorite flavor of ice cream. Or when his birthday was. Or a thousand other things that were shared during the courting season. But oh, she wanted to learn all she could about this man.

"I no like Timothy. He mean to me." Patience's eyes widened, and she slapped a hand over her mouth.

"How was Timothy mean to you?" Grace stopped and stared at her sister. Patience always made herself scarce when Timothy came over.

Patience shook her head. "No."

"Come on, Patience. I need to know."

"Can no tell."

"We can't fix it unless you tell us," Zeke said.

Moisture glistened in her eyes. "He make fun of me. Call me mean name, like 'ugly retard.'"

Zeke made a low growling sound deep in his throat.

Slush tucked his tail.

Grace's eyes burned. "Oh, Patience. Why didn't you say so?"

Tears dropped off Patience's chin. "He tell me bad thing happen if I do." A loud sob escaped. "Now bad thing happen." She sniffled, and tears flowed heavier.

If *Daed* and their brothers knew what Patience had just said, Timothy—if he was Timothy—would wish the tornado had finished the job.

Zeke made another low rumbly noise.

Slush dropped to the muddy ground and rolled.

Grace wrinkled her nose at the dog, then gathered Patience into her arms. "You should have told me. You are not ugly. And—"

"And you are the sweetest, most lovable girl I know, and as long as I'm here, I'll take care of you. I promise," Zeke broke in. His eyes narrowed as he looked at Grace. "When you spoke to your *daed*, did you tell him any of this, Gracie?"

"I didn't know!" Okay, maybe she shouldn't have raised her voice.

Patience wailed louder, lurched into Zeke's arms, and buried her runny nose against his chest.

He rubbed her back. "There, there."

Slush stopped rolling and got up, leaning his muddy body against Patience's formerly clean dress and giving Grace a look that clearly communicated, *What did you do?*

An ambulance approached from the direction they'd been walking. It turned into the driveway.

Thankfully, Patience didn't notice. Grace fought the urge to run. Who got hurt? *Daed*? One of her brothers? *Daadi*? Why hadn't she thought to ask?

Though Zeke didn't know many in the community. He wouldn't have been able to tell her.

A police car followed the ambulance.

Oh no, no, no.

Grace looked at Patience snuggled in Zeke's arms, the dog leaning against her. Her sister was well taken care of.

"I've got to go." She looked at the action and tilted her head that way to signal. Now she understood why Zeke asked Patience to go on a walk. He took even better care of her sister than she did.

Zeke nodded, kindness and understanding in his eyes. A glint promised they'd have that talk later. "Then go."

She turned and ran.

* * *

Zeke wanted to cry along with Patience. She was such a sweet girl, and to be verbally abused by Gracie's missing groom... He sighed. It was just unfathomable that anyone would treat another person that way. Especially one who couldn't defend herself.

But if what Cliff said about Timothy was true, then Gracie's postponed wedding had been a gift of *Gott*. Nothing less. Especially if she found the courage to tell him no, if he was still alive. Zeke tried to dissect his memory of her expression for hurt or grief, but all he remembered was irritation.

It was nothing short of amazing that Cliff and Gracie had prayed the same thing and that *Gott* had answered. Maybe *Gott* also answered Cliff's other prayer to bring a new man for Gracie.

Zeke's heart pounded as he tried to soothe Patience and ran a hand over Slush's muddy fur.

The same *Gott* who forgave him his past mistakes. If *Gott* truly answered prayers, then maybe Zeke should add his own prayer that the full truth about Timothy would come out and Gracie would be set free. Even if she wasn't for Zeke, she deserved better than Timothy.

But Cliff's prayers made it baffling why *he* hadn't spoken to Gracie's *daed*—his son—about what he'd observed. It didn't make sense that Seth wouldn't care enough to approach his daughter about it if he knew, because he seemed like a loving, caring father.

Or maybe Cliff didn't want to talk to Seth because Gracie's *mamm* was friends with Timothy's *mamm* and, according to Gracie, very much in favor of the marriage. But if they were truly friends, wouldn't they be honest with each other about why Timothy was courting Gracie?

Oh, this was getting beyond confusing, not to mention Zeke was fairly certain this kind of restoration wasn't in his job description. People were ever so much more complicated than buildings.

Then again, people were more important than anything made out of wood or stone. Relationships mattered.

That was why Zeke wanted to help with special-needs individuals as well as troubled boys at the ranch.

Zeke recalled his own reckless and *youngie* days where he might have gotten involved in the things Cliff said Timothy was doing. If his boss hadn't made him spend time with special-needs or troubled boys, he might have judged harshly what he didn't understand. Perhaps *Gott*'s grace kept him from truly becoming what *Daed* once accused him of being. "Hmm," he murmured.

"What?" Patience sniffled.

"Just thinking." He shifted and the dampening material of his shirt touched his skin. He would have a wet patch, compliments of Patience's tears, but it was a badge he'd wear with honor.

"Why he mean, Zeke? Why he not nice like you?" Patience sniffed.

"I don't know, Patience. I don't. All I know is that suffering is part of life. I've never met a strong person who hasn't suffered. And you're a strong person." He'd learned to stand on his own feet in construction in part because of *Daed*'s harsh and unfair judgment.

"I pray Jesus to calm the storm. Why He not listen?"

Oh, she asked tough questions. "I think maybe He is working behind the scenes. That He still has more parts of the storm to calm." Like Timothy. Maybe like Zeke's relationship with *Daed*. Though how that'd be soothed with Zeke miles and miles away was beyond him. "All I know is the fiercest storm, the highest wall, the harshest word have no power against our *Gott*. He will prevail." An inner peace guarded his heart like the ultimate storm shelter.

"He just speak and storm obey." Patience attempted to snap her fingers.

"Weather storms obey Him. But now He's dealing with people. He could make us obey Him, but He's given us free will so we have to want to listen. It's like if your *daed* tells us to do something, we have to choose to obey."

How many times had Zeke disobeyed *Daed*? Maybe that had something to do with his miserable opinion of Zeke. He probably owed *Daed* a huge apology.

He'd call home tonight and apologize to *Daed*.

Patience sniffled again and wiped her nose on her dress. "I hungry."

Zeke glanced at the sky again. It was near noon, but neither the ambulance nor the police car had left yet. Would she be upset to see them working on someone?

But of course, Patience didn't know about the man falling. She turned and trotted toward home.

Slush whined and looked at Zeke.

Zeke fought his own whimper. If Patience witnessed anything, she might not handle it well. But on the other hand, he couldn't tell her no, that she couldn't go home. He shrugged at the dog and followed behind Patience closely.

The ambulance drove up to the end of the driveway.

Quietly. No lights.

Maybe because of all the horses or maybe because there was no need for the drivers to rush to the hospital.

Zeke's eyes stung. So much loss.

Seth met him when he rounded the end of the *haus*. Patience darted ahead of him inside.

"It's Jon."

Jon. Brother number twelve. The one Zeke had the beginnings of a friendship with. His vision blurred.

"A driver is on the way to take my wife and me to the hospital."

A measure of hope filled him. "He's still alive, then."

In the distance, sirens started to wail.

"He was when they loaded him in the ambulance. Gracie is a mess." Seth inhaled deeply. "I trust you. But just in case, her *grossdaadi* and eleven brothers are still here. For now."

Which translated into *I don't trust you*. Zeke nodded. "Got it."

"By the way, Gracie told me you told her to talk to me. I appreciate it. I had no idea she felt that way." Seth had a grim expression.

"You need to talk to Cliff and to Patience. There's more you don't know."

Seth grimaced. "I was afraid of that." A heavy sigh. "Gracie ran to her room. I trust you," he repeated.

And with that bit of not-so-helpful information mixed with the implied warning, Seth walked away.

Zeke stayed put. If only life came with instruction manuals for fathers. Or maybe one for young men attempting to understand fathers.

What was he supposed to do?

* * *

Grace bypassed her room and ran into Jon's room, locked the door, and threw herself on his twin bed. He was still alive but unconscious, and his fiancée, Aubrey, was sticking to his side, even riding in the ambulance with him to the hospital.

Not fair, not fair, not fair. It was her brother, for pity's sake. Her favorite brother. The one only two years older than her, the one who taught her to drive a buggy, the one who taught her how to swim, the one who went looking for her and Patience when they got lost in a record-breaking Illinois blizzard and couldn't find their way home from school.

Grace wanted to argue, but it seemed fiancées trumped sisters and even parents. Which she kind of understood. If it were Zeke, she'd want to be with him.

Her breath lodged in her throat. Zeke. Not Timothy.

And Timothy was her fiancé.

Oh, that said so much.

One day, slightly more than twenty-four hours, and she'd fallen in love with a man who wasn't her groom.

A man who'd never be her groom.

A man who'd leave her and return to his life in Indiana.

A man who her favorite brother actually liked...unlike Timothy.

She remembered their antics with the bird in her room just yesterday and then "Sleeping Beauty" and Patience's kiss.

Tears flowed as she clutched Jon's pillow to her heart. Oh, Jon...

CHAPTER 18

The joking and gibes had stopped. Except for the hammer-and-nails melody of a barn under assembly, conversation had ceased, replaced by a heavy blanket of silence.

Zeke strode in, hoping to regain his perch, just for the nearness of a friend. Men had their gazes cast down, their eyes red rimmed, mouths set. Maybe some prayed. Maybe not.

Zeke added a whispered prayer of his own.

Vernon had taken Zeke's place on the beam next to Cliff. Figured. Now Zeke had to find someplace else where he probably wouldn't have a friend to talk to. Not that they'd talk. Not with the oppressive absence of sound. Still, having a friend nearby would've been comforting.

Jon Lantz. It was nothing short of a miracle he hadn't died on impact considering the great distance he'd fallen.

If allowed, Zeke would visit him in the hospital. He liked Gracie's brother number twelve.

Cliff caught Zeke's attention and nodded toward the *haus*. Zeke glanced that way. Women, including Patience, carried out food for the slightly delayed noon meal. With the church benches gone and other districts' benches in use for funerals, the men would be eating dinner on the grounds, literally. Unless they sat in the back of wagons.

But Zeke's appetite was gone.

He shook his head and murmured, "Not hungry." Hopefully, Cliff could read lips.

Cliff sighed so heavily his whole body sagged. "Gracie."

Right. Except Seth didn't trust Zeke.

"Go to her."

Cliff was kidding. He had to be.

Zeke might be stupid compared to straight-A Vernon, but he didn't have a death wish.

Exaggerated motions from above caught Zeke's attention.

Cliff was again pointing toward the *haus* as if Zeke were daft.

And maybe he was. Because this time, he obeyed.

But if the biggest gossip in this district caught him in Gracie's bedroom, then it wouldn't be his fault.

He trudged toward the *haus*, past the ladies setting out the noon meal—which included platters full of wedding sandwiches—through the kitchen, and into the front room where the stairs were located. Up the stairs where he and Gracie almost kissed. Her bedroom was right across from the bathroom. The door was open, but the room was empty. Gracie wasn't there.

Disappointment warred with relief. He wanted to be her hero, but at the same time, he didn't deal well with tears.

But then her muffled sobs reached him. He wouldn't know what to say, but maybe he could hold her. Pray for her. As he had for Patience on the road. He followed the sounds to Jon's room. The door was shut and locked.

He pulled in a deep breath and knocked. "Gracie?"

Silence.

Except a sniffle.

"It's Zeke."

A squeak or something came from the other side of the door, followed by creaks.

"Your, uh, I mean, both your *daed* and *Daadi* Cliff sent me to find you. Sort of," he explained to the closed door.

The door opened with another creak—the hinges needed oiling or adjusting—and then she stood there, head dipped, tears dripping off her chin.

She swiped at the tears and looked up, her gaze still watery, mouth quivering. "I feel like such a big baby. But really, Jon..."

She hiccupped, made sort of a gasping sound, then wonder of wonders, she was in his arms.

Or at least he thought she was.

But before he had a chance to decide for sure, she was gone, retreating to one of the twin beds in the room.

His body burned from the brief touch.

"Sorry. I didn't mean to bump into you. I was checking to see if anyone witnessed you coming in. Since the coast is clear, you can shut the door."

"I'd rather keep it open to protect our reputations."

And to keep from misbehaving, because wow, he liked her. He wanted to be close, closer than he had any right to be.

"My reputation is pretty much in shambles, thanks to my intolerance of coffee."

He chuckled but then thought better of it. Though it was absurd to get a bad reputation over a beverage. "I'm sorry. I didn't mean to laugh."

"I understand. *Mamm* was going to try to set the gossips straight, but since the rumor reached the barn, it might have to be misproven by the test of time."

Oh! Now her comment made sense. But Zeke's brow furrowed. "Misproven? Do you mean disproven?"

"I meant misproven. As in it's a misunderstanding to be proven false."

He couldn't keep from laughing outright.

"I am sorry, though, for what I did on the steps. Trying to kiss you, I mean. I thought maybe I was dreaming, and since kissing you will never happen in real life, then . . ." Her face warmed. "I never would've tried if I thought it might be real."

His heart warmed. She'd wanted to kiss him, too . . . but only felt that brave in her dreams.

"Patience has never appeared in my dreams, though. Not like that. And, well, I didn't want you to think I was desperate." A nervous giggle escaped. "I might be desperate, but I really wanted to thank you for listening to me." She picked up a pillow and clutched it to her chest.

Relief filled him. She wasn't trying to trap him, after all. She wasn't using him. He wasn't a fool for falling for her.

"You can sit down, if you want, but if you stay, you might be subjected to more dramatics." Her voice broke.

Zeke nodded. "That's why I'm here. Your *daed* and *grossdaadi* both sent me. I didn't realize it was Jon until after I got back, or else I would've warned you." He sat on the other twin bed on the opposite side of the room. In case the gossips peeked in. Because if he had his choice, he'd sit beside her, arms around her, holding her near while she cried on his shoulders.

He plucked at the wet spot Patience had left.

If he and Gracie went for a walk, someplace out of sight of casual observers, he might be able to hold her, too.

He shouldn't think like that, especially since she was weeping into the pillow she'd pressed to her face.

He sighed, feeling helpless. After a moment, he bowed his head. *Lord... please comfort her...*

Was it pointless to pray for comfort and then sit on the other side of the room and not offer it when he had the arms and shoulders needed?

Or should he stand up, cross the room, and pull the one woman he'd been attracted to in, well, ever into his arms and hug her?

Like he did with Patience. Purely platonic.

Right.

Well, she could think it was platonic on his part. He alone would know the truth that the hug was paid for with his heart.

Okay, now who was being dramatic?

He sighed again. He was being dramatic when he should be that comfort that both Seth and Cliff seemed to think he could be.

Zeke planted his hands on either side of himself and pushed up, then crossed the room. He hesitated in front of her. Should he sit beside her and offer a one-armed hug? Or kneel on the braided bedside rug and wrap both of his arms around her?

Oh, the temptation. And since this was likely the only opportunity he'd have to hold her...

He pulled in a deep breath, gently removed the pillow from her grasp, and knelt before her. "We can't have you smothering yourself." He opened his arms wide, giving her plenty of time to decide she didn't want to hug him.

Then, joy of joys, she was in his arms, crying on his shoulder, while his arms were around her, his hands rubbing her back in little circles, kind of like how *Mamm* comforted Zeke's eighteen-month-old nephew when he cried.

She buried herself nearer, wrapped her arms around him, and cried, saying something about learning to drive and the worst blizzard in Illinois history that made little to no sense because the words were garbled against his neck.

Or maybe because his senses were tuned into the fact that she was in his arms, her mouth moving against his neck as she talked, and not focused on the words she was saying.

He tried to pray, disjointed sentences like *Comfort her* and *Please let Jon live and be okay* that probably made as much sense to *Gott* as Gracie's words did to him.

His knees were beginning to hurt, and he began to seriously consider moving beside her on the bed and giving her a one-armed hug instead when Gracie pulled back a little, then surged forward, knocking him on his rear.

"*Danki*. For being a friend."

Then, Lord have mercy, her lips were on his.

He handed his heart over in its entirety, tugged her more fully into his arms, and settled into her tentative... not tentative... kiss.

His heart pounded, and he closed his eyes.

Her hands cupped his face, her fingers just reaching to tangle in his hair.

A kaleidoscope of colors burst, forming flares, rainbows, and stars.

He might not survive this assault on his senses.

He wasn't sure he wanted to try.

He surrendered to the madness.

* * *

Grace was right. Kissing Zeke wasn't good. It was great. Beyond great. Amazing.

His hands trembled against her back, pressing against her in what might be desperation, until she lost her balance and tumbled more fully into his arms.

Somehow, he scooted around until he leaned his back against Jon's bed...

Oh, Jon...

She gasped, sucking in air, and then, in desperation, plunged her fingers into Zeke's soft, silky hair. She needed to forget. And what better way...

Zeke made some sort of sound deep in his throat and settled her against him, taking control of the kisses, taking them from whatever temperature they were to something beyond comprehension.

She made an answering moan, wrapped her arms around him, and held on for dear life.

This—this was better than anything she could ever imagine.

She was melting…melting…melting…

Then, horror of horrors, it was over.

She was no longer in his lap. Instead, her lips felt bereft. She trembled beside him.

He gasped for air, his eyes wide with dismay as he scooted away.

Dismay. Confusion. Regret. Anger. A whole arsenal of emotions—none of them good—crossed his face.

He took another gasped breath, then stumbled to his feet. "I…I'm sorry. I never meant…I mean, it shouldn't have happened. Oh, Gracie. It…I…I only meant to try to comfort you. I feel—felt—so sorry for you and all you're going through. I never meant to take advantage of you. Gracie, it'll never happen again." He made a terrible groaning sound and left the room at a lurching run.

She covered her bruised, well-kissed lips with her shaking hand.

She'd wanted to say thank you.

He was sorry? It wouldn't happen again? He felt sorry for her?

So when he took over…What was this—some sort of pity kiss?

She managed to pull herself to her feet, only to have her unexpectedly weak knees give out. She collapsed on Jon's bed again, fell back against the pillow, and rolled to face the wall.

A huge sense of loss washed over her, covering her in grief.

It'd never happen again?

She wouldn't be able to live without it.

* * *

Zeke stumbled down the hall, somehow made it to his temporary room that he shared with Vernon, and fell on his knees beside the bed. *Oh, dear Lord. What did I do? Seth trusted me! He trusted me, and I…oh, merciful Lord. Please forgive me.*

Would he need to confess to Seth that he'd violated his trust and taken advantage of his vulnerable daughter?

Or Cliff? Would he need to know?

Would Zeke end up surrounded by eleven of the twelve brothers, all armed with pitchforks or chain saws?

Not rational thinking perhaps, but he gulped.

Someone, somewhere, began beating something. And in his mind, it turned into a drumbeat, summoning the natives to war.

It'd probably be wise for him to pack his bags and find another host family. Preferably one without a daughter. Or at least one without twelve brothers.

He got up and started shoving his things into his bag.

"Ezekiel."

He looked up and stared into Seth's eyes.

"What are you doing?"

Zeke put the socks into the bag just to avoid answering. Besides, wasn't it obvious?

"I thought I'd see if Gracie wanted to go to the hospital with us. We'll leave Patience here because the women will look out for her, but since you have a special bond with her, I figured you'd keep an eye on her, too. However, it appears as if you are planning to leave." Seth's eyebrows rose. "Is something not to your liking here?"

"I kissed her. I mean, she kissed me." Zeke groaned.

"Actually, I mean, we kissed each other." His face burned.

Seth's mouth quirked.

Zeke looked down and picked up his pajama pants.

"Who kissed who first?"

"Does it matter? The deed was done. I violated your lack of trust."

"It wasn't a lack of trust. And *jah*, it does matter." There was a touch of humor in Seth's voice.

Odd. Not exactly the response Zeke expected.

"She kissed me first. But I was a very willing participant—at least until my brain caught up with me," he mumbled to the floorboards, lacking the courage to look Seth in the face. He braced for the firing squad of angry family members.

Seth laughed. He actually laughed. Very strange, considering his youngest son was on the way to the hospital and Zeke had just confessed to kissing his daughter. Anger would be more appropriate.

Zeke looked up, frowning. Had the man gone daft?

"You're welcome to stay, if you think you can adjust to the family dynamics...and drama. My daughter is...impulsive. And in light of some of the things I was told, I completely understand. Keep in mind, though, that understanding is not the same as condoning. Especially considering we still need to find Timothy."

"I understand." Zeke folded his pajama pants, stood, and placed them on his pillow. "*Danki*." There was a foreign twinge of hope that he got to stay awhile longer, though it'd be harder on his heart to be so close to Gracie—especially now.

And this—this level of parental guidance was amazing. He felt the discipline without the shame. And the grace of a second chance...

"And I thank you. I learned some very troubling things from both of my daughters and from my *daed*. I appreciate you convincing them to talk to me. I don't understand why they wouldn't have in the first place." He frowned. Shrugged. "*Danki* for making yourself available to listen."

Zeke didn't know what to say. *You're welcome* would imply he'd done it on purpose, and it was purely accidental. He swallowed. "I'm praying for Jon."

"Appreciate it." Seth walked across the hall. He knocked on Jon's door, then entered, crossing to wherever Gracie was.

Zeke headed for the stairs. In light of what just happened, if he and Gracie ever talked about what she told her *daed* regarding Timothy, they'd need to be well chaperoned.

Because Zeke wasn't totally sure he would be able to keep his promise not to kiss her again.

Especially since he was already going through withdrawal.

CHAPTER 19

Grace huddled on Jon's bed, her face pressed into his pillow. Creaks sounded behind her, but she ignored them. If Zeke dared approach her after giving her a pity kiss, she'd...she'd...she didn't know what she'd do. But it wouldn't be pretty.

She gulped air and tried to focus on the words *Daed* had said yesterday when they'd gone on their walk and talked about her concerns about marrying Timothy. He'd offered advice on what she should do if he resurfaced for real, and on her new feelings for Zeke. A man so totally out of her reach it wasn't funny.

"Look for what *Gott* might be teaching you, grow, and make choices based on what you've learned." *Daed*'s words had confused her then, but he had added, "I'm not *Gott*. He's the one you need to ask."

She would, whenever she'd stopped crying long enough to pray.

The bed sagged behind her, and a hand rested on her shoulder.

She gasped and rolled over, prepared to give Zeke a piece of her mind. And maybe bop him with a pillow.

Daed. His gaze was sober, his eyes filled with shadows she didn't recognize. They scared her.

"Jon...?" His name came out on a wail.

"Oh, honey. I don't know. I came to ask if you want to come with us to the hospital. The driver will be here in a few minutes."

"*Jah*, I would. *Danki*."

Daed pulled in a deep breath. "I, uh, caught Zeke packing."

Grace caught her breath. "What? Why?"

Daed grimaced. "Something about he kissed you, you kissed him, you kissed each other."

He'd told *Daed*? How could he? She sniffled. "Fine. He can go. He's a jerk. It was a pity kiss."

"So you're over your earlier feelings for him? You pity him?" *Daed* frowned and shook his head.

"What? No! Why would you ask such a thing?" Grace ignored the first question. Her feelings for Zeke were a confusing jumble.

"Zeke said you kissed him first."

Grace's face heated. And she had nothing to say. Nothing.

"He's not here to date, Gracie."

"I know," she whispered. "He's made that clear." And she'd told *Daed* that very thing when they talked yesterday.

Gravel crunched in the driveway and *Daed* stood. "If you're coming, come quickly now." He left the room.

Grace scrambled to her feet and ran after him.

As she followed *Daed* to the waiting van, men were going through the food line, piling their plates full of more of the leftover wedding food. Hopefully this would be the end of it. She was heartily sick of fried chicken and mashed potatoes, and that was more than she'd ever thought possible.

Zeke wasn't anywhere in the line. Not that she was looking for him. Okay, she was. She found him standing beside *Daadi* Cliff and her brother Reuben in the unfinished barn. The three men stood in a circle. Heads bowed.

Her heart hurt. Zeke truly was a good man, and she was so needy. Desperate. High-maintenance. He probably didn't have the foggiest of ideas what he was getting into when he climbed into the van in Shipshewana to come to Hidden Springs. Certainly he wouldn't have expected a girl to be completely swept off her feet, fall madly into a crush with him, and then behave inappropriately.

He probably still didn't know what he was getting into when he got out of the vehicle in front of the tree blocking the road and offered to help her.

And just twenty-five or twenty-six hours later, she'd fallen in love with him and proceeded to push him away. Lying about it being a crush. After kissing him. And after he made it clear he wasn't here to date.

No wonder she'd gotten a pity kiss. And yet oh, what a kiss. If that was a pity kiss, what would a true kiss be like?

"Gracie."

She forced her attention away from Zeke long enough to glance over her shoulder.

Daed stood by the open van door. "Are you coming?"

Oh. Right. They needed to go. She turned her back on the men and got into the van next to *Mamm*.

Daed slid the door shut and climbed into the front passenger seat.

When she came home, she owed Zeke another apology and...

Wait.

Daed said he was packing his bags.

She tried to contain a sob, but it escaped.

Zeke might not even be there when she returned.

She'd ruined her chances, and now when she came home, he'd be gone.

Probably for good.

*   *   *

Zeke bowed his head with Cliff and Reuben as they all prayed for Jon. And Zeke did pray for Jon, but his heart was troubled. He should have taken the time to pray about this mission trip before they'd left Shipshewana and for what *Gott* had planned for him to do instead of going into it blind. He should've made a decision about how he would act, planned as best as he could, prepped his mind for the possibilities he might face, and trusted *Gott* for the outcome. Maybe, if he'd taken the time to do that, he would've been better prepared emotionally and mentally and not so overwhelmed by the severity of the aftermath of the physical storm in addition to the effects of the ongoing emotional storm.

Of course, no amount of preparation and planning would've prepared him for Gracie.

Patience's words came to mind. "Jesus, please calm the storm." *Jah, Lord. Please. Calm the Gracie storm, the Timothy storm, the Jon storm, and the other emotional storms I'm not remembering. Oh, and the storm waiting at home with* Daed. *And my impossible feelings for Gracie.*

He blew out a breath of frustration. She deserved a good, solid man. Someone like dependable, perfect Vernon.

A hand landed firmly on his lower arm.

Zeke raised his head and opened his eyes.

Cliff stared back at him. "I'm sensing some negativity here. Positive thoughts, boy. Give it all to *Gott.*"

Right. And Zeke had gotten sidetracked from his tasked assignment—given by Reuben—to pray for Jon.

"Sorry. I'm having some trouble focusing."

"That is obvious." Cliff studied him, and Zeke stiffened his spine to avoid squirming. "Maybe it'd help you focus if you prayed out loud."

Zeke shook his head to rid himself of troubling thoughts. "I'm fine." He quickly dipped his head again and this time, prayed. *Lord, touch Jon, help him to live, and heal him. Guide the doctor's hands. Comfort his family and friends.* Zeke included, *Yet not my will but Thine be done. Amen.*

He raised his head, as did the others.

"I'm going to get a bite to eat." Cliff was already heading toward the end of the food line.

"I'm not hungry," Reuben said, stating Zeke's feelings.

Cliff stopped, turned. "Both of you need to eat something to keep your strength up. Come along, now."

Reuben grimaced. "*Daadi* Cliff has spoken. We must obey." There was a bit of sass in his voice.

Cliff put his hands on his hips. "I'll have none of your lip, boy. You may be bigger than me, but I am still your elder."

Reuben glanced at Zeke. "He talks tough, but as the oldest of the twelve brothers, my oldest child is as old as Patience—fourteen."

"*Jah*, but that changes nothing. You're still my grandson." Cliff shifted his stance. "Come along, Zeke; we've got to get you away from this bad influence, teaching you that it's okay to disrespect your elders."

The mild arguing was probably meant to distract from the worry over Jon, because no one laughed or even cracked a smile. Their eyes were grim.

Zeke obediently got in line behind Cliff and Reuben. He'd force something down because Cliff was right. He needed to keep up his strength.

As he waited at the end of the line, he scanned the women serving them. Patience was there. He didn't see Gracie, though.

He raised his gaze to her bedroom window. She'd probably gone to the hospital with her parents.

Lord, please let Jon live. And help me to solve the puzzle of Gracie.

* * *

Grace paced the floor in the huge emergency waiting room. Even though some *Englisch* people sat at the far end of the room near the television, she felt totally and completely alone. *Mamm* had stopped to use the restroom, and *Daed* had gone to talk to someone at the front counter.

Was Aubrey still with Jon? Or had she been rerouted to yet another waiting room?

Was Jon alive?

Grace pressed her fingers to the corners of her eyes, willing the tears to stay at bay. It was surprising that no one had called her on being such a big baby, crying at every little thing ever since the tornado.

If only *Gott* would calm the storm. It'd be nice to sit in some peaceful spot, not worrying about the winds and the rain destroying her.

Emotionally, she was bruised and battered.

She dropped down into the nearest chair as *Mamm* bustled into the room. *Mamm* dropped her never-leave-home-without-it bag on the seat next to Grace and crossed the room to where *Daed* still stood at the counter.

Grace opened *Mamm*'s bag enough to peek in. Knitting. As upset as Grace was, she'd be dropping stitches constantly. Knitting wasn't near as relaxing as *Mamm* claimed.

She picked up the *Englisch* magazine next to her and scanned the cover. Some man she'd never heard of was getting married to the mother of his love child. Whatever that was. Why did anyone even care? She returned that and picked up the next one. Someone else shared fool-proof tricks on how to snare the man of your dreams.

Tricks and snare?

She could imagine *Daed* shaking his head in dismay and muttering something about what the world was coming to.

Still, she opened the cover, found the page number,

and then glanced up to make sure *Mamm* and *Daed* weren't coming.

The article talked about use of makeup, deep V-neck shirts, and high slits on the sides of dresses. Peekaboo shoulders. Whatever. Make him think of sex.

There was more to love and marriage than sex.

But then again, it hadn't mentioned love or marriage. Just snaring and sex.

She turned the page. Tricks to perform better in bed.

Grace's face burned as she closed the magazine and put it back. Nothing useful there. Instead, her mind felt soiled.

Underneath that was some kind of geographic magazine.

She opened that to a photo of a big-busted woman with no clothes on her top half. She carried a basket full of some sort of fruit on top of her head.

Grace shuddered. Maybe *Daed*'s opinion was right. What was the world coming to?

She dropped that magazine on top of the other discards and folded her hands on her lap. A sober-faced woman in purple scrubs admitted *Mamm* and *Daed* through a door off to the side.

The door shut behind them.

Nothing to read...except maybe a Gideon Bible. The TV in the corner was off. She was left alone with nothing to do except the one thing she desperately needed time alone to do. So no time like the present...

Grace bowed her head and started to pray.

Gott, please spare Jon's life.

And help me sort out my own.

She didn't know how long she prayed that same

prayer over and over before another woman in yellow scrubs appeared. "Grace Lantz?"

She attempted to speak, but her voice cracked. Broke.

The woman's gaze held compassion. "Follow me. I'll take you to your family."

Grace's nose ran. She reached for a tissue, then realized her face was wet, so she grabbed another tissue.

"My brother. Is he ... ?" Her words were raw.

"I don't know. The doctor was going to meet with your parents and your brother's wife."

Wife? Jon and Aubrey weren't married yet. But she might've lied so she'd be allowed to stay by his side. Grace couldn't blame her.

Grace grabbed *Mamm*'s abandoned knitting bag and followed the woman down a confusing maze to another waiting room. This one was much smaller, and she was all alone.

"Your family must be with the doctor. They'll be back soon. Help yourself to coffee." She pointed to a coffee maker on a small stand. Disposable cups were stacked beside it, and a basket full of stirrers, sugar, and powered creamer was next to that.

The woman was gone before Grace turned to thank her. But Grace didn't want coffee. Even on her best days she detested the foul-tasting stuff, as she was reminded this morning.

And today was painfully obvious that it wasn't anywhere close to being her best day.

She settled down next to another stack of magazines and picked up the top one. A cooking magazine. That one she could read.

By the time she'd finished the entire magazine and

come up with a few new ideas, daylight had faded outside the windows. And still she waited...

Her brothers, *Daadi* Cliff, and Zeke filed in. They hadn't bothered to clean up.

Zeke! He hadn't left yet. She might've beamed. She lifted her hand in a tiny wave.

"Any word?" *Daadi* Cliff asked.

"Nothing. I haven't even seen *Mamm* or *Daed* since we arrived."

Daadi Cliff frowned and left the room.

Zeke crossed the room and sat beside her. "Are you okay?"

She reached for his hand and clung, unable to answer. Pity kiss or not, she craved his strength.

CHAPTER 20

Zeke eyed the eleven brothers, but none of them seemed too concerned about him sitting next to Gracie or even that they were holding hands. It seemed odd. But they probably all realized he and Gracie had an immediate connection. The brothers had all plopped into other chairs or made a beeline for the coffee station.

Gracie grimaced. "I'm worried sick. But Jon must still be alive, and *Mamm* and *Daed* are somewhere. They surely would've remembered I came with them if they started to leave. And I still have *Mamm*'s knitting that she never leaves behind. I'm surprised she made it this long without returning for it."

"Hmm." Zeke made the noise to communicate he was listening, because he didn't know what to say. That seemed the story of his life. A brainless idiot around Gracie. No. He gave a slight shake of his head. He was finished with negativity, as Cliff encouraged him a few hours ago. *Think positive.* Zeke may not be a former straight-A student like Vernon, but he seemed to fit in better with the Lantz family and the community. Vernon didn't appear to possess many skills that equipped him to interact with strangers. He was more of a loner. And Seth apparently recognized that, sending Vernon off alone, while keeping Zeke around people. Around the family.

Nobody had said as much, though.

Vernon had been left to see to the cows and the horse and put away the tools while Zeke had been willingly dragged along with the family to the hospital, even though he'd dreaded Grace's reaction to seeing him again. Dreaded the temptation...and yet, seeing her sitting there alone in the room had erased all of his promises to himself to keep his distance. And her grip on his hand...

He eased his hand out of Gracie's grasp long enough to entwine their fingers. "Tell me about Jon."

Her wide-eyed glance and raised brows clearly communicated confusion.

"I know he's the youngest brother of twelve, that he's engaged to be married, and that he seems as pun loving as your *daadi* Cliff. I know I like him. But what does he do?"

Gracie's brow furrowed. "Well, up until yesterday he worked as a blacksmith and a farrier out of our barn. It originally had this one side that was open on both ends like a walkway. Handy for customers and plenty of ventilation for the forge."

So Jon lost his business in the storm. Zeke would've been struggling if he'd lost as much as Jon, and yet the man had a positive attitude. Or was it faith that *Gott* would somehow see things through? Zeke could learn a lot from the man.

"He's only a couple of years older than me. He's the one who looked out for me, the one who taught me how to drive—"

"And that's scary. Have you seen how she drives?" One of the other brothers—Zeke didn't know his name or which number he was—winked at Gracie.

"You hush. You've wrecked more buggies than I have." Gracie narrowed her eyes at him.

Another brother chortled. "She told you, Joseph."

Joseph appeared to be close in age to Jon. His beard looked short and bristly and new, as if he was recently married.

Seth must've had a busy fall with at least two sons getting married, plus Gracie's wedding-that-didn't-happen. Yet.

And here he was, holding hands with the bride-to-be-that-wasn't-his.

And never would be.

Comfort. She needed his comfort. And his shoulders were wide enough to carry her burdens. Just as he was going to have to trust *Gott* to carry his.

While the others talked and teased around him, Zeke shifted on the uncomfortable chair. It was padded, but the padding was in the wrong spot to conform to his build. The room stank of burnt coffee and lemon-scented bleach. A bad combination.

He glanced down at her not exactly small, but smaller-than-his, hand. Her skin was rough and calloused, the sign of a hard worker. Would *Mamm* like her? Would his sister, Elizabeth? If Timothy was permanently out of the picture, would Gracie consider coming to Indiana to meet his family?

Moving to Indiana to merge into his life? Would he consider moving here?

"Is the barn finished?" Gracie asked. "Because when Jon and Aubrey marry..." She choked to a stop.

Joseph nodded. "All except for Jon's shop and the finishing work on the inside. But that's all stuff that can be done whenever."

A deep, dark silence followed Joseph's words. Would Jon even have need of his shop? It seemed as if Zeke wasn't the only one who wondered.

Cliff bustled back into the room. He stopped just inside the doorway where he would have a good view of everyone. "Okay. They took Jon back to an operating room to do immediate surgery on a bad break on his right shoulder. He has some broken ribs but miraculously hadn't broken anything else. He hasn't woken up yet, but they say he has brain activity. They're obviously admitting him to the hospital and say that rest is the best thing for him, and the coma is 'nature's' way of protecting him." Cliff huffed. "I say it's *Gott*'s, and it's a plumb miracle the boy survived the fall."

Zeke agreed.

Gracie sniffled.

About a half an hour later, Reuben stood. "I'm going to head home. I'll take care of *Daed*'s livestock if Vernon didn't. My wife took Patience home with her and our fourteen-year-old daughter, Becky." He glanced at Zeke as he said this.

As if Reuben was accepting Zeke and willing to let him in on the family dynamics.

"Patience can spend as much time as needed with us. Do you want to come home with those of us leaving now?" Reuben's gaze slid to Gracie.

She caught her breath in a sob and shook her head. "I'll go home later."

"Home." Reuben's eyes bored into Zeke's with a clear warning. Maybe brother number one wasn't as accepting as he'd thought. But the man had good reason, especially if Seth had told them that Gracie had kissed Zeke and he'd given into temptation and kissed her back.

He wanted to assure the eleven brothers that he could be trusted. He'd promised it wouldn't happen again, after all.

Although, when would Seth have had the time to tell them that?

But the brother simply shifted his gaze down to their still-interlocked fingers and let that stand as enough incriminating evidence.

"It was a pity kiss. I don't need his pity or those kinds of kisses. So you have nothing to worry about." Gracie glared at her brothers. The brothers all looked around. Confused. Because how would they have known about the kiss?

"What are you talking about, Gracie?" a brother asked.

Her faced flamed red. "Never mind."

It was nice that she was thinking about their kiss, too. But what did she call it? A pity kiss? Zeke shook his head. "A what?" The question burst from him. "A pity kiss?"

Someone chuckled. Zeke didn't notice who. He was too busy staring at Grace with his mouth hanging open in shock.

Cliff sighed. "Your *grossmammi* and I will spend the *nacht* to chaperone Zeke, Vernon, and Gracie, especially since Seth and Barbie will be staying here with Jon and Aubrey."

All well and good, but . . . "What is a pity kiss?"

* * *

Grace's face warmed. She released her hand from Zeke's and popped out of the chair, needing to distance herself from her brothers' knowing stares. From Zeke's confusion. Why was he confused anyway? He was the one who said he felt sorry for her. "I need to use the facilities." Her stomach chose that moment to remind her she hadn't eaten since supper the *nacht* before and rumbled loudly. "And find food. I'll return if I don't get hopelessly lost in this maze of a hospital."

"I'll go with you." Zeke stood. "To make sure you don't get lost."

"And to learn the definition of a pity kiss," her brother Dan said, with an elbow jab at Aaron.

Zeke quirked his eyebrows. "That, too."

There was a short-lived chorus of chuckles.

Grace dipped her head to try to hide her embarrassment. "I'm sure someone will give me directions. I don't need a babysitter." She headed toward the door.

"I'm coming." Zeke followed her. "Because obviously we need to talk."

Grace sighed and stopped at the door. "Someone keep an eye on *Mamm*'s knitting bag." Oh, she'd forgotten to grab her purse when she left home. She didn't want to beg from her brothers, so her stomach would have to go without. "I won't be gone long."

She headed down the hallway toward the bathrooms, which, thankfully, were well marked. "See? I'll be fine." She pointed to the signs. "I won't get lost."

"What about food?" Zeke stubbornly insisted on following.

"I changed my mind." Her stomach rumbled a very vocal complaint, and she hurried into the bathroom.

She emerged a few minutes later to find Zeke leaning against the wall outside the door. He straightened. "I'll buy your meal."

"Because you pity me?"

He frowned. "No. Because you forgot your purse. Because I'm hungry, too. Because we need to talk."

She didn't want to hear what he had to say. But she needed to apologize to him again, so she sighed and then followed him to the elevator.

He pushed the button and the door opened. A couple emerged, then Zeke got on. She followed and stood on the opposite side of him.

Zeke stood there a moment surveying the buttons, then glanced at her. He hesitated a long minute, his gaze holding hers; then he inhaled, looked at the panel again, and pushed a button.

His mouth worked a minute; then he shook his head, pressed his lips together, and leaned against the wall.

"You said you felt sorry for me." She stared at her shoes.

Silence for a beat. Two. Three. "I do."

And she lost her appetite. Or rather, her stomach churned again like earlier after the coffee. Her already broken heart stabbed again with fresh pain.

The elevator rumbled to a stop, and the doors slid open.

She walked out.

He followed.

"See? It was a pity kiss. You kissed me because you thought I was pathetic." Why couldn't she let this go? Why did she insist on humiliating herself?

His brow furrowed. "No. It means I feel awful about all the bad things that happened in your life recently. Not that I think you're pathetic." He glanced at her. "And that certainly is not why I kissed you."

"But—"

"Besides, you kissed me first. Should I believe that you think *I'm* pathetic?"

"No! I wanted to kiss you but didn't actually intend to. I wanted to say *danki* for all the nice things you've done. For listening to me."

His mouth quirked, but he didn't answer. Instead, he opened the door to the cafeteria and motioned her in.

She looked at the hot case full of fried chicken and mashed potatoes and groaned in frustration. She reached for a blueberry muffin and a slice of pie and set them on the tray he placed in front of her.

Zeke glanced at her choices, added three sandwiches and another slice of pie to the tray, and then carried it to the drink dispenser. "What do you want to drink?"

She took the cup he handed her, added ice and cola. "*Danki* for buying my meal."

"You're welcome." His look was gentle. He paid, then led the way to a table for two in the corner.

"So why did you kiss me? And apologize?" Ugh. She *was* pathetic.

He set the tray on the table and pulled out a chair for her. "Why do we need to rehash it?"

She lowered herself into the chair and shrugged. "Just curious."

He pushed it in, took his seat, and divided the food, giving her one of the sandwiches. He opened one and took a bite.

"Tell me about your girlfriend back home." *Jah*, she was fishing.

He swallowed. Frowned. "I don't have a girlfriend. The girl I used to court will marry Vernon in a couple of weeks."

"Oh, how awful. That must be so hard for you." But she was ever so glad he was available.

"I shouldn't have said that. It's okay. I'm over her." He shrugged. "Besides, I never felt for her what..." He shook his head.

Her heart sagged. "You met someone new, then?"

He sucked in a breath. "*Jah*. You."

"Me?!" She wanted to bounce out of the chair, around the table, and into his arms.

He held up a hand. "But the missionaries and others warned that I'm not allowed to date or court while I'm here. You are engaged, and you have twelve brothers who would have my hide if I hurt you. Not to mention I live in Indiana and you live here. And despite evidence to the contrary, two days really aren't enough time to fall in love."

Yet she had. And apparently, he had. And this last part made her heart giddy.

But what he mentioned seemed to be insurmountable obstacles. Besides, she promised *Mamm* she'd marry Timothy when he was found. Her heart ached.

"And that is why I shouldn't have kissed you. It's also

why it won't happen again." Despite his words, his gaze drifted to her lips.

They tingled in response.

There had to be some way around this.

*   *   *

There wasn't any way around it.

Facts were facts.

Zeke hadn't planned to say anything to her about it, because what was the point of her knowing? But he wouldn't lie to her, or let her believe a lie. That would only hurt her. Something he'd done anyway with admitting the truth. He saw the hope, the joy, then the despair in her eyes, followed by something he didn't recognize. Determination, probably. Gracie was stubborn and determined.

"Where there's a will, there's a way," she said.

He didn't see a way, but okay. If she said so. He nodded and took another bite of one of his sandwiches.

"*Danki* for getting me a sandwich." She unwrapped it and peeked inside. "Tuna salad. One of my favorites." She took a bite. It was good. The second bite was just as good.

"You're welcome. I figured you were hungrier than a blueberry muffin."

"Mm-hmm." She quickly finished her sandwich and unwrapped the blueberry muffin. "Maybe, but I got chocolate cream pie, and that would make up for a major lack of food."

"If you say so." He didn't see how. He finished his first sandwich and opened his other sandwich.

"Chocolate can solve the world's problems." She sliced the blueberry muffin in half. "Want half?"

"*Danki*." Zeke accepted half of the muffin. "So chocolate would solve our relationship problems?"

She winced. "No. We're going to figure it out, though, right? With the help of chocolate."

"Okay." He'd dump everything they needed to talk about out on the table before they were interrupted. He wanted answers. "What are you going to do about Timothy when he's found? And speaking of which, you never did tell me about the conversation with your *daed* or about the Timothy who showed up at the visitation." He stiffened.

She frowned. "He looked like Timothy. Or at least what he might look like after being sucked into a tornado and banged around. He had a scraped cheek, a black eye, and a bloody bandage on his head. But he was rude, acted like he didn't know me or his parents, and said his name is James."

"So he might not be Timothy. Unless he suffered a brain trauma and forgot who he was, people, and things," Zeke said, alternating between hope that Timothy was truly gone and guilt that he should feel bad for the man if he was so injured he'd forgotten who he was.

"I believe he is Timothy. His parents do, too. And he knew enough to come to Toby's house for the visitation."

"If he's the same one your *daadi* Cliff met, he thinks he's Timothy, too. Just a smidgen of room for doubt, he said." Zeke took a sip of his soft drink.

Gracie sighed. "*Jah*."

"What did your *daed* say?" Zeke reached across the table and touched her hand.

"Not a whole lot. He mostly listened, but he frowned a lot. He looked sad and upset, but then he said, 'Look for what *Gott* might be teaching you, grow, and make choices based on what you've learned.'"

"So, he's giving you permission to dump Timothy?" Zeke hoped.

"I don't know. He also said, 'I'm not *Gott*. He's the one you need to ask.' But it may not do any good to ask, because I promised *Mamm* I'll marry him if he shows up. And a promise has to be kept."

Zeke swallowed. He ran his finger over the back of her hand. "Gracie…that was a bad promise. Think about it. You heard Patience. And…and maybe you should talk to your *daadi* Cliff about Timothy, too. It's your call, but I think your *daed* is right. Pray about it, but I think you already know you should move on."

No sense asking her to move on to him—because even without Timothy in the picture, Zeke couldn't see how they'd work, having a long-distance relationship. And if they decided to marry, would he give up his job and move to Illinois? Or would she leave her family and move to Indiana?

His gaze drifted south to her sweet lips as she flipped her hand over, palm up, and grasped his.

His pulse rate soared.

And he wanted to spirit her away to a private place and kiss her again.

CHAPTER 21

Grace stirred the straw around in her icy soft drink. She wanted to question Zeke about his ex-girlfriend but kept biting the questions back. Now wasn't the time. But she might not get another private moment to ask. She took a sip, then decided to go for it. "I don't want to upset you, but tell me about your ex-girlfriend. Why did she choose Vernon over you?"

Zeke's eyes darkened, and he pulled his hand away from hers. He shrugged. "Vernon is perfect. What can I say?" His voice held a twinge of pain.

Grace shook her head. After supper last *nacht*, she'd overheard her brother and *Daed* discussing which man to give what jobs to. And both of them agreed that Zeke was the harder worker, the most pleasant to have around, and—a big plus—Patience and Slush liked him.

All things she couldn't say about Timothy. Except the hard worker part. At work frolics Timothy always used to try to show off by doing the most of whatever they were supposed to be doing. Like when they had a corn-shucking frolic. He always did more than the next guy. And strutted around when he won the prize. He had to be the big shot.

Whereas Zeke did kind things for others and never mentioned them, like helping Hallie's *daed* repair the roof, or moving a tree off a shelter to free Elsie and her family. And Zeke's pain when comparing himself to Vernon hurt her to the core.

She slapped the table. "Vernon is *not* perfect. What really happened?"

"He got promoted to shift manager at the RV factory my *daed* works at, and Naomi—that's my ex-girlfriend—overheard *Daed* berating me for being such a lazy bum and how I should be more like Vernon." His voice was tinged with bitterness. "So she dumped me and pursued Vernon."

"Why would your *daed* think you're a lazy bum?" Because he was so not. She finished her half of the muffin.

"I hated my job and spent more time goofing off than working. To be truthful, his opinion was justified." He shook his head. "Your *daadi* Cliff told me to lose the negativity and think positive. So, on the positive side, I now have a job I love and a boss who respects me, but I told you all that. I just have no way to prove my worth to *Daed*. I don't know how to even begin, other than try to get hired back at the factory and drive myself crazy with the boredom. And because I embarrassed the family name by getting fired from a job I hated, he doesn't hesitate to let everyone know I'm a worthless, rebellious loser."

She winced at the harsh words. If his own father had been spreading those lies, no wonder Zeke doubted himself. Too bad he couldn't see his true worth the way her family had.

"You are *not* a loser. My *daed* and brothers seem to think you passed some Lantz family initiation test. *Daadi* Cliff loves you, you use pink tools without self-consciousness, you are willing to give a dog a bath and spend time with needy me and Patience, you listen, and"—she pointed her chocolate cream pie–covered fork at him and his growing smile—"you're honest."

He leaned forward, grabbed her hand, and with an impish look in his eyes, aimed the pie-filled fork toward his mouth. "Mmmm," he mumbled as his lips closed around the fork.

Her mouth gaped. "Pie thief!"

"Almost as good as your kiss. Wait. Maybe it's better." His eyes gleamed, lighting a fire deep inside her.

"I guess you'll have to rely on memory because you said it'd never happen again." She wrinkled her nose at him and stuck out her tongue.

Then retaliated by stealing a bite of his pie. She thought it might be cream cheese based.

"Ugh. It's peanut butter." She reached for her soft drink and gulped to wash the taste out.

"So I guess it's safe to say my kiss is better than my pie." He winked.

She was trying to think of a sassy comeback while fighting the very strong urge to march around the table, plop herself down in his lap, and proceed to kiss him senseless despite their very public setting and the others eating in the cafeteria, when a chair twirled toward them from somewhere and landed beside their table. A figure appeared behind it.

Gracie looked up into Timothy's—or James's—one unswollen eye.

His dark gaze latched on to her, some kind of challenge in its depths. "Mind if I join you?"

* * *

Zeke frowned as he looked at the *Englisch* janitor he'd seen yesterday morning at the school. He didn't appreciate their playful teasing being interrupted by this stranger's rude behavior, but as he opened his mouth to tell the man so, he caught the horror in Gracie's eyes.

And he knew.

This was Timothy. Or James, the one who Cliff thought was Timothy.

The man was a jerk. A man who had kicked the dog and threatened Patience.

The intruder sat without waiting for an answer.

But Gracie was busy shoveling the rest of her chocolate cream pie into her mouth as if it really could solve problems and she needed an immediate fix.

Zeke shut his mouth as the man turned to stare at him with the look men used when they were sizing up the competition.

So Zeke did the same.

The man turned his attention back to Gracie with a smirk. "I heard that you're engaged, in the family way, and running all over town with another man. Is he the one you're cheating on or the one you're cheating with?"

Gracie sucked in a noisy gasp, dropped her fork,

stood, picked up her icy soft drink, and proceeded to dump it over the man's head. "What about you? You and Paige? You have no room to talk."

Then she took her empty cup and stalked toward the exit.

Paige? The *P* on the cell phone they found? It took another second for Zeke's brain to kick in enough for him to follow.

He followed Gracie to the drink dispenser, where she calmly refilled her cup, and left.

When Zeke glanced back, the man had risen and was mopping himself off with their discarded napkins.

Zeke caught up with her at the elevators. She speed walked when she was angry. "Wow. Remind me not to get on your bad side."

She glowered.

"Okay. Is he Timothy?"

"He's a *jerk*."

Jah, that was a given.

Zeke didn't know whether to make sure she made it safely to the surgical waiting room or return to the cafeteria and question the man.

He pushed the elevator button that would take them to the floor the waiting room was on. She fumed during the ride, not speaking, and when she got off, she speed walked toward the waiting room, her body stiff and definitely communicating *Don't talk to me*.

He'd keep silent. She'd talk when she was ready. But for now she was back with family who would protect and defend her. He glanced in at the brothers. *Jah*, she was safe. And his curiosity was getting the best of him...

He stopped. "I left my peanut butter pie on the table. I'll be back—just want to get it if it's still there."

She didn't answer.

He backtracked quickly, hoping none of the remaining brothers in the room wanted to blame Gracie's mood swing on him.

Timothy, or James, was still in the cafeteria, now sitting in Zeke's former seat and eating Zeke's abandoned peanut butter pie. Actually, he shoveled the pie into his mouth like a starving man.

Zeke paused long enough to buy another sandwich and slice of pie, then returned to the table. He put the sandwich in front of the other man and sat in Gracie's abandoned seat. "The sandwich is for you."

The man glowered at him, anger deep in the depths of his eyes. But after a moment, he nodded. "Thanks. I'm starved."

Obviously, or he wouldn't have eaten another man's pie—especially one with a bite taken out. Zeke took a bite of his new slice, then looked at Timothy—James. "Are you visiting a friend here?"

The man's dark eye filled with shadows. "Yeah. Peter may not survive. It's not looking good."

Peter. Wasn't that the name of Timothy's other best friend? The one the bishop mentioned?

"I'm sorry to hear that. What happened?" Would this man tell the truth?

Timothy—James—shrugged. "I don't know exactly. One minute we were guys having fun, and the next I woke up out by the highway. I hurt all over, and the people who picked me up said I would have a shiner." He touched the bruise around his swollen eye.

"I couldn't remember who I was, so I called myself James, and when I did finally remember my identity, it seemed easier to disappear as James rather than return to being Timothy." He sighed. "The people who picked me up helped me find some clothes since I lost mine somewhere, then took me to the shelter set up at the school. I think I saw you getting off the van there." His face colored. "I didn't think I was so crazy drunk to lose my clothes."

Zeke had heard the term before at the boys' ranch. It meant stoned and drunk at the same time. Some of the boys called it "crunk."

He fought to keep his expression neutral. Not judgmental. But this was Timothy. There was no doubt.

Timothy devoured the sandwich. "Thanks again, man."

"Can I get you something else?" Zeke asked.

Timothy looked at the food in the serving line longingly but shook his head.

The man had been humbled by the storm and seemed a bit broken, as if he was trying to figure out who he truly was at the core. But there were still the harsh words he said to Gracie right before being doused in soda. Zeke frowned. Considered him. "It's okay. I'm willing."

Timothy looked down, his hair and bandage saturated from his soda bath. "Another sandwich would be great. They're only feeding us one meal a day at the shelter until the Red Cross arrives."

"I'll be right back." Zeke stood and went to buy two more sandwiches, a bag of chips, and a drink. He set them in front of Timothy, then reclaimed his seat. "No offense, but if the shelter isn't feeding you well, why don't you go home?" He was certain the man wasn't suffering from amnesia since he just admitted the truth, but there was something about the man's expression that made him seem somehow vulnerable. Or lost. Or hurting.

Timothy's face reddened. "I lost my direction."

For some reason, Zeke didn't think he meant that he forgot his way home. He raised a brow and waited.

Timothy ate a couple of chips and half of one of the sandwiches. "My parents are forcing me into their idea of a perfect man."

Jah, Zeke got that.

"Chicken farmer. I hate the foul things."

Ah, *jah*. Zeke remembered that place. And the odor. To quote Timothy's mother, it was "horrible, horrible, horrible."

"Marry the perfect woman. Okay, she's not so bad, but I love another. Though she gets on my last nerve sometimes. A mutual friend told me where to find her, since her old trailer was blown away, but she won't let me in where she's staying. Told me I'm a mean drunk."

The mysterious *P* on the cell phone? Paige. Gracie called her.

And Timothy loved another—and not Gracie? Joy washed over Zeke. Maybe Timothy would be willing to break up with her and then Grace wouldn't have to keep her promise to her *mamm* after all.

"I just can't fit into the life my parents have mapped out for me, and this is my chance to break free. If I can find the direction I want to go."

Trust in the Lord with all your heart; and lean not unto your own understanding. In all your ways acknowledge him, and he shall direct your paths.

The verse popped unbidden into Zeke's mind. And even though he could relate to Timothy's issues, he didn't know what to say.

Except, "My *daed*'s the same way. Not chicken farming, but factory work. And because I chose my own way, I can do nothing right."

"What did you do?" Timothy asked.

Zeke chuckled but without humor. "I'm still dealing with the fallout."

He hated that he had no wise advice, but everything he thought of to say seemed too judgmental or too preachy. And according to the director at the boys' ranch, neither should be said out loud...and yet the words were screaming in his own mind for him to pay attention.

I'm trying to trust You, Lord. Are You directing my path?

Timothy finished the other half of the sandwich and the rest of the chips during the silence. Then he gathered the trash and stood. "Look. Thanks for the food. I appreciate it. And please don't tell anyone anything I said." He inhaled. "Except Gracie. Tell her I'm sorry. I was out of line."

Especially since he'd been cheating on Gracie long before Zeke came on the scene.

"I think you need to tell her that yourself." Zeke stood. Hopefully, Gracie had calmed down by now.

Timothy sighed, a wild look appearing in his eye. Nodded. "Tell her I'll be in touch. I need a fix." He walked off, carrying the sandwich he hadn't eaten.

Zeke watched him go as Timothy's words about his chance to break free replayed. Funny how Zeke felt the same, as if coming here might be his chance, too. As much as he wanted Timothy to be punished for past mistakes, he had Zeke's sympathy for the current situation.

And then he remembered words the boys' ranch director had said many times.

Rock bottom will teach lessons that mountaintops never will.

* * *

After backtracking to use the facilities, then walking the halls for a while in a futile attempt to calm down, Grace stalked into the waiting room, found an empty seat, and plopped down in it, hard enough that the drink in her cup slopped out the top, onto her hand and dress. Her fault for not grabbing the plastic lid and for not controlling her temper.

Her eyes burned. Her lips quivered.

Six brothers had gone home. The five brothers remaining in the room stared. Whispered. Jaws hardened.

And with a grunt, *Daadi* Cliff rose to his feet. He strode, fists clenched, toward the door. "That boy. Oh, that boy."

Five brothers followed.

As much as she hated her brothers fighting her battles for her...

Good.

Her brothers and *Daadi* Cliff would put that cafeteria jerk in his place.

She basked in that knowledge for a bit; then the truth hit with blunt force.

They didn't know she was with the man who most likely was her errant groom.

They thought she was with Zeke. Which, she was, but...

Oh no. No. No. No.

She set her drink down on the end table, bolted to her feet, and rushed toward the door...

And plowed headlong into *Daed*.

Her overprotective family was long gone, pursuing the wrong man.

Daed caught her by her upper arms. He had a terrible expression on his face.

"*Jon!*" she wailed, and crumpled against him.

CHAPTER 22

Zeke cleaned up the mess the three of them had left at the table, returned Timothy's still-sticky chair to the other table, and looked around, hoping to apologize to the janitor for the dumped soft drink. The only people in the room were eating, though. He didn't see any of the cafeteria crew—the cashier had even disappeared. Messes happened, but maybe not often on purpose.

Satisfied that he'd done his best, Zeke left the cafeteria, only to be met at the elevator by a barricade of Lantz men. Five brothers and a *grossdaadi*. They crossed their arms in unison. A bit of déjà vu from his worst nightmare, even if there were only six family members—and none had chain saws.

Zeke stopped. Frowned. "What's wrong?" He'd delivered Gracie safely to the waiting room, albeit upset, and...Wait. Were they blaming him?

And she hadn't defended him?

At least he'd gotten exactly half of the twelve that were threatened if he hurt her.

"Care to explain what happened?" Cliff broke formation.

"Um, I bought her a meal, and we were eating." No need to mention the flirting part. "And talking. When a certain somebody decided to join us." He attempted to give Cliff a meaningful look.

Cliff frowned. "Somebody you know?"

Apparently the meaningful look failed.

"Actually, no. First time I met him. Sort of. I mean, I saw him at the school yesterday morning, pushing a broom."

Cliff's eyes widened. "Gracie's missing groom."

Grunts and grumbles came from the five brothers. They stepped closer. One looked around.

"*Jah*. He basically accused her of cheating on him, and she retaliated with a large glass of ice and soft drink dumped on his head."

The five brothers relaxed.

Cliff shook his head. "That girl. Oh, that girl."

Oops. Zeke hadn't intended to get her into trouble. That wasn't the typical turn-the-other-cheek Amish response. He'd meant to show them that she could take care of herself.

"I talked to Timothy after Gracie left." Fed him, too, but they didn't need to know that or exactly what else he'd said since the man had told him to tell Gracie but not anyone else. He skimmed over the details. "He needs a lot of prayer as he figures things out." And probably a good rehab center, but that would be Timothy's choice.

"Is he still intending to marry our sister?" The words

were heavy with warning. Zeke didn't know which brother asked. And he didn't know what the warning meant.

"I don't know." He hoped not. Gracie deserved better than a drug-addicted drunk who loved another. But that would be Timothy's and Gracie's choice. Not Zeke's. And since he wasn't here to date or court but to work, there was nothing he could do about it.

Except pray.

And pray he would.

"Sorry for accusing you." One of the brothers lightly punched Zeke's arm. "You're a good man."

"*Jah.* Too bad Gracie hadn't discovered him first," another brother agreed.

Oh, that warmed Zeke's heart.

"Never did see what Gracie saw in Timothy," a third brother said.

It was taking forever to learn names at this rate, but it was entirely too awkward to point to them individually and ask, "Who are you? And you? And you...?"

"Maybe you should ask Gracie what she saw in him," Cliff suggested, as if he knew the truth about the abusive behavior and wanted her to tell her brothers.

"And encourage her to chase Zeke here?" a brother teased.

A chorus of agreements.

"Don't let them drive you away," Cliff said, grasping Zeke's arm. "They're only teasing."

The brothers fell silent. He really needed to learn their names. He'd find some way of asking on the elevator. Jon was the beardless one, and then there was Joseph—the one with scruff who'd recently married. And he knew Reuben, who was the oldest. Three down, nine to go.

"I'm not here to date," Zeke reminded them. "And the linc is drawn in quicksand. Crossing it means immediate punishment, I was told."

And that was the cold, hard truth.

"Hmm." *Daadi* Cliff eyed him. "So skip the dating and cut straight to marrying?"

* * *

Tears flowed down Grace's face, and she fought to stay upright. Here she was, filling her empty stomach and flirting with Zeke while her brother breathed his last breath. Dumping her soft drink on Timothy's head while the doctor notified her parents. Her selfishness shamed her.

She moaned, covering her face with her hands. "Jon. Oh, Jon." How would she ever live without her favorite brother? They shared everything, including the same wedding season and apparently both not getting married... Another wail burst out of her.

"Gracie! Get a hold of yourself. Hush, now." *Daed*'s hands tightened on Grace's upper arms, and he gave her the tiniest of shakes. Then he pulled her into his hug. "No, Gracie. Listen. Jon is alive. He's still in surgery for his shoulder blade, actually. It's Timothy's friend, Peter. I know you have valid reasons for your concerns about marrying Timothy if he's alive, but you probably should prepare for the possibility that he's gone, since both of his friends he was with—"

"He's alive." Gracie found her strength to stop wailing.

Daed jerked and clutched her tighter. "You sure?"

She nodded. "He was in the cafeteria." Tears still dripped, as sympathy for Peter's family and friends filled her. And so quickly on the heels of Toby's death. And all because of Timothy's foolishness, wanting to go out for one more wild night as a free man before he was bound by the chains of matrimony.

But maybe he wanted to marry her as much as she wanted to marry him—not at all. Maybe he'd felt pressured to do it because of their *mamm*s being best friends and imagining their children marrying ever since they were newborns sleeping in the same crib while their parents visited.

Gracie shook her head and swiped at her wet face. "Jon will be okay, right?"

Daed sighed. "He's in the hands of the Lord."

Which was a nonanswer. And clearly stating that *Daed* didn't know, and...and...Well, the rest was too terrible to consider.

Down the hall, the elevator door dinged as it opened. And one by one, her five brothers, *Daadi* Cliff, and Zeke emerged.

Daadi Cliff had his arm around Zeke's shoulder. "Just remember the twelve sons of Jacob. With a few exceptions, those are the names of Seth's twelve boys. Reuben, Simeon, Levi, Judah, Dan, Joseph, and Benjamin. The exceptions are Nathan, David, Aaron, Isaac, and Jon. Don't worry. You'll get to know everyone in time."

Time was one thing Gracie knew they didn't have. How long would Zeke be allowed to stay?

Daed walked toward the men. "Zeke. Do you think you'd be able to build furniture? Luke, Toby's *daed*, needs help with the furniture side of the business—he also builds caskets—and the bishop said Luke had requested you by name. Furniture orders are backing up, and he's not yet buried his son. I thought I'd send you and Vernon to help out tomorrow. There'll be a few others from your area that are being asked to help out there as well."

Zeke nodded, his expression sobering. "*Jah*, I'm sure I can do it. I'm so sorry for all the loss."

Daed nodded. "It's a terrible time, to be sure."

Grace winced a bit and said a quick prayer for Luke and his wife in their grief…and for Peter's parents.

"It's a blessing to have the men from your area come to help us," *Daed* said, clapping Zeke on the shoulder. "There's a group of Amish and Mennonites coming from Missouri, too. They're due to arrive late tonight or tomorrow." He turned. "Gracie, with your mother and I at the hospital with Jon, you're needed at home. Since you went to Toby's visitation today, there's no need to go tomorrow for the second day of it."

Grace sniffled. "I'm glad to help." But it'd be lonely at home without Patience or anyone there to visit with or to share the workload. And she didn't want to whine about it. She needed to do her part during this time of great need.

Even if it meant that Zeke would be a couple of miles away. At least it was closer than being in different states.

She hated visitations anyway.

And funerals were even worse, with three hours of preaching plus the trip to the cemetery. Though with multiple deaths from the tornado, they might have combined services.

Zeke cleared his throat. "If it makes it easier, I could

move into Luke's hayloft while I work for him. I'm not sure how to get there, and—"

"No!" The word burst from Grace unbidden.

Zeke and the male members of her family jerked to look at her.

Her face burned. But how were she and Zeke supposed to talk if he wasn't even there? How were they supposed to court without courting? How were they supposed to flirt? What about stealing kisses? How…

Zeke's face reddened. Dan laughed. *Daadi* Cliff dipped his head, but his shoulders shook.

Daed stared at her. "Grace Lynn."

Horror filled her.

"Did I say all that out loud?"

Nobody answered. They didn't need to. She knew.

She wished for a hole to open up for her to drop into. None did. Of course, that would've been too easy.

A long silence fell.

Grace swallowed and stared down at her shoes. "I'm sorry. I know he's not here to court. And I was just kidding." Except that was a lie, and everyone knew it. *Ugh.* "I mean, *jah*, having Zeke stay at Luke's would solve a lot of problems." And create more. She sighed heavily.

There was a round of awkward chuckles.

"Zeke?" *Daed* asked.

"Your decision," Zeke said quietly.

Oh, she hated that she put him in this position. Shame filled her.

"We'll discuss it after the funerals," *Daed* decided. "I came to get your *mamm*'s knitting. Jon will be in surgery for hours. I want the rest of you to go home. And Gracie…"

Silence fell. One beat. Two. Three.

Grace looked up.

Daed stared into her eyes. "I trust you."

* * *

Zeke firmed his shoulders, determined to do everything in his power to help Gracie earn and keep Seth's trust. Even if it meant they weren't alone at all. They could talk just as well in the living room with Cliff nearby as they could on the floor in Jon's bedroom, in each other's arms…His face heated. They probably could talk better around chaperones. Especially since they weren't courting. Besides, if perfect Vernon thought they were spending time together as a dating couple, he might decide to notify the missionaries in charge who'd remove Zeke from temptation's way. No romantic entanglements. Zeke almost snorted. He and Gracie had already been tangled romantically. At least two times. And how sweet it was! He looked forward to future entanglements…

Jah, the interest was there, on both sides. But they needed to develop a friendship, too. Though even the beginnings of one was well established. But Gracie needed to talk to Timothy before she and Zeke made any future plans. He would seriously miss Gracie when he returned home to Indiana, even if he made plans to come back here. He had a heart connection with her that he'd never had with anyone. Ever.

Despite the mental fog he was lost in, he managed to trail the Lantz family into the waiting room.

Seth grabbed his wife's knitting bag and gave Zeke a fatherly slap on the back. "Good night." He left the room.

Zeke whispered another prayer for Jon as one of the Lantz brothers—Dan, he thought—pulled out his cell phone. "I'll call the driver."

It'd be good to get back to his host family's *haus*, though Zeke intended to take a shower to get all the construction dust off and tumble straight into bed.

Calling *Daed* would wait another day. Zeke didn't know exactly what he'd say to him anyway. *I'm sorry for being such a huge disappointment to you* didn't seem to fit. It also seemed rather poor-pitiful-me-ish. *Daed* would pick up on that. It'd be better to pray about what *Gott* would have him say and that *Gott* would guide their conversation.

"Zeke." Gracie touched his sleeve, drawing him out of his mental wanderings. "We're leaving to meet the driver."

"*Danki*," he said.

She picked up her soft drink and moved to join the others as they headed toward the elevator.

Zeke watched the sway of her skirt for a few moments before he shook his head to hopefully remove the fog from his brain and followed her.

He needed to pray about more than one thing.

What to say to *Daed* and...

What to do about his relationship with Gracie.

CHAPTER 23

The next morning, the scent of strong coffee and fried eggs woke Grace. *Mammi*. Grace should've been up to help. She rolled over and stretched wearily. She'd had a restless night's sleep due to worrying about several things: Jon, what to do about Timothy, finding a new job since she quit her waitressing position to get married, and Zeke. Not to mention the bed seemed so empty without Patience sleeping beside her.

It was the first time that Grace could remember sleeping alone, though surely she had before Patience was born and until her sister was old enough to sleep in a real bed. The strangeness had contributed to her difficulty in falling asleep.

Her back twinged as she got out of bed, remnants from her fall down the stairs yesterday morning. She hoped it would loosen up again once she started moving. She moved a little slower than usual as she showered, dressed, and prepared to take on the day. Since no one would bring cinnamon rolls, she wouldn't be in a huge rush and wind up repeating the previous morning's drama. Though she wouldn't mind a repeat of the time spent in Zeke's arms.

Or the kiss.

Oh, the kiss.

Her heart pounded just thinking of it.

She'd absolutely love a repeat of that.

Except, with a different ending than him saying he was sorry and running from the room.

The smell of burnt bacon and smoke filled the kitchen. *Grossmammi* stood in front of the open refrigerator muttering to herself as she shuffled items around.

Grace crossed to the stove. Smoke poured from the oven and the bacon was crispier than crispy. The crispiest she'd ever seen. *Mamm* didn't make hers so well-done. She grabbed a pot holder, turned the burner off, and moved the skillet to a cool spot, then checked the eggs. They were crispy, too. The oatmeal was scalded and sticking to the bottom of the pan.

Stove-top foods saved—sort of—Grace turned her attention to the oven. She whipped open the door and waved away the black billows of smoke that poured out. It smelled toxic. She turned the oven off and stared at the blackened toast.

Mammi was usually a great cook, so this was weird. Was *Mammi* suffering a bit from dementia? Or was it caused by one of the new meds she'd gotten when she went to the doctor last week? Maybe this was why *Daed* wanted her at home to help—so *Mammi* wouldn't burn down their *haus*.

"Doesn't your mother ever clean her refrigerator? This is a disorganized mess," *Mammi* complained.

The refrigerator had been organized but probably was messed up with all the women working in the kitchen yesterday for the barn raising. But Gracie didn't argue. That would be disrespectful. Instead she pulled the burnt toast out of the oven. She turned to set it on the counter.

The kitchen door opened, and *Daadi* Cliff, Vernon, and Zeke came inside. Without a word, *Daadi* Cliff removed his work boots, then opened the kitchen window. Was this his new normal?

Vernon wrinkled his nose. "It smells...done." He bent to take off his footwear.

Well, that was tactful.

"Oh, Gracie, you baked." Zeke winked. His boots thumped into the plastic tray next to the others.

That would earn him a thump from a well-aimed pillow. Which actually sounded fun.

And promising...She peeked at his oh-so-kissable lips.

They twitched as if he had an idea of what she was thinking.

If only Grace could pass the blame for the overdone breakfast. Zeke hadn't had anything she'd cooked yet, and if the way to a man's heart is truly through the stomach, she'd just had an epic fail by proxy.

Mammi emerged from the depths of the refrigerator with a jar of strawberry preserves Gracie had helped *Mamm* make from their strawberry patch excess. *Mammi* plopped the jar on the table hard enough to make Grace wince. "Grace Lynn, when breakfast is finished, I need you to help me straighten that mess of a refrigerator.

Your *mamm* ought to be ashamed, letting it get into that condition. In the meantime, find the ketchup."

Grace swallowed the retort hovering on the edge of her tongue, nodded, and moved to obey.

Mammi was right. Food was shoved in everywhere. Bottles and jars were tipped over. The dill pickle jar had lost its lid. The cheese had been put in unwrapped and left to harden. *Mamm* would insist on cleaning this atrocious mess, too.

At least that would give her something to do today while alone at home. Perhaps some laundry and some baking of the good, nonburnt kind.

She found the ketchup bottle sideways in the vegetable drawer, buried underneath leftover fried chicken.

At least there wasn't much of that left. If *Mammi* let her, she'd figure out something to do with it for the noon meal.

Except, Zeke and Vernon weren't going to be there. They'd be building chairs. And however many orders Luke had pending. He supplied the local furniture store in addition to the Amish community.

She'd need to pack a lunch for the two Shipshewana men.

Cold fried chicken, cut-up raw carrots and celery, dill pickles, the last of the cherry tomatoes from the late garden, and an apple...She turned to check the bowl someone had moved to the counter. Exactly two apples left. Perfect.

She carried the ketchup to the table, set it beside *Mammi*, and then sat in one of the empty seats. The one across from Zeke. Not that she planned to play footsie under the table.

Although the idea held merit.

But no. *Daed* trusted her.

After the silent prayer, Grace got up to help *Mammi* carry the burnt offering over to the table. *Mammi* must've really been thrown off-kilter by the sad state of the refrigerator, because normally she was a really good cook.

The men filled their plates and ate without a word of complaint. Although they washed it down with generous amounts of coffee. Grace gulped juice.

Zeke bowed his head for his end-of-meal prayer and glanced at *Mammi* and then Grace. "*Danki* for breakfast. I really appreciate it."

"Hopefully, supper will be better. I got slightly distracted," *Mammi* said.

That was an understatement.

"Good thing Grace Lynn came in when she did. It might've been charred instead of burnt," *Mammi* added.

The men chuckled.

Grace felt good to be vindicated in their eyes. In Zeke's eyes. And amazingly, by waiting instead of leaping in impulsively, she'd ended up with a good result anyway.

"I'll pack lunches for you to take to Luke's." Grace stood.

"Thanks. We'll need directions, too," Vernon said.

"I'll give you boys a ride, go in and pay my respects to the deceased, and come back here after I do my chores at home. I'll be by Luke's at fiveish to pick you up." *Daadi* Cliff drained his coffee. He bowed his head for a moment, then stood. At the door, he paused to put his boots on, then stood stock-still. "Well, I'll be."

Grace peeked out the window, then did a double take.

One of their two missing horses—Ben Gay—limped up to the closed barn door.

"I'll check him over for injuries before we go and make sure he's fed and watered," *Daadi* Cliff said. "You boys go on upstairs and make sure your beds are made and the room picked up."

They needed to, based on the appearance of the room yesterday.

"Wow. One of your horses returned." Vernon moved to stand beside Grace.

"Which one is he?" Zeke glanced outside. "Author Itis or Ben Gay?"

"Ben Gay. You, straighten your room. Go on, now." *Daadi* Cliff headed outside.

Zeke and Vernon headed upstairs, and Grace got out the lunch pails. Two of them. One was pink with PATIENCE stenciled on it, and the other was blue with JON stenciled on it. Grace's yellow pail had long since gone missing somewhere. She'd used Jon's the last two years she was in school.

Grace traced her fingers over her brother's name. *Lord, please heal Jon. Let him live.*

If their old barn hadn't gone missing in the tornado, she'd run out and check the phone for messages. But there wasn't a phone in the new barn yet.

Mammi washed breakfast dishes while Grace packed two lunches and filled two thermoses with black coffee. It'd be easy enough for them to add milk and sugar at Luke's if they desired.

Vernon and Zeke both came downstairs, and Grace held out the two lunch pails. "Pick one."

After a moment's hesitation, Vernon glanced at Zeke,

who motioned for him to go first. Vernon chose Jon's. "I'll pray for Jon."

Zeke quirked a brow and reached for Patience's, letting his fingers graze against Grace's. He held up the pail. "This will be a reminder for me to pray for Patience. Pun intended. Of course, I'll pray for Jon, too."

Grace managed a fleeting smile. Patience was probably enjoying being with her nieces and nephews at Reuben's *haus*.

After Vernon took a thermos and went out the door, Zeke glanced toward *Mammi*, then leaned close to Grace. "I'll pray for you, too. Pun intended there, too." And with a gentle smile, he followed Vernon outside.

Grace watched him go. *Pun intended there, too*? What did he mean by that?

And then it hit. When you pray for rain, you pray that you'd get rain. Did he also mean that he would pray that he'd get her?

As in, she would be his girl?

She couldn't keep her smile contained.

Lord, I pray for Zeke. Please, Lord, let it be so.

* * *

Zeke followed Luke around his neatly organized workshop as he explained where everything was kept and showed him the list of orders. There were a couple of almost-finished chairs waiting that Zeke would take the time to study, just as a visual aid.

"I asked for you specifically since someone mentioned to me that you're experienced in construction. That know-how will come in handy here," Luke said.

"I'm also having you do the more simple chairs, not the fancier, pricy furniture. I'm not sure how familiar you are with some of the fancier equipment."

"I'll do my best." Zeke glanced around for Vernon. He stood still, arms crossed over his chest, as if he planned to step into the shift manager position here and oversee Zeke's work. Like he was when Zeke worked at the factory. In fact, Vernon had been the one who fired him.

He shook off the bad memories. The bad vibes. This was a different kind of work, and he was asked for by name. Here, Zeke would be the one to issue orders and delegate.

Zeke knew how to delegate. He taught construction at the boys' ranch when he was there. How well would straight-A Vernon do taking orders from Zeke?

"The bishop said there'd be a couple more boys coming to help out. They should be here soon, and you can get them started on what to do." Luke backed toward the door. "If you need me, I'll be at the visitation." His voice broke.

Zeke's vision blurred. He aimed a hopefully sympathetic smile toward Luke. "I'm praying."

Luke pulled in a deep breath and leveled his gaze on Zeke. "I'm keeping my eyes on Jesus to keep from being washed under the waves."

Huh. Zeke's words had somehow reached the heart of this hurting man. Only *Gott* could have orchestrated such a thing. Could it be that despite Zeke's lack of prayers, planning, and prep, *Gott* was somehow involved in the details of this whole trip?

But then Zeke had told Patience yesterday on their walk that *Gott* was working behind the scenes.

A chill worked through him.

Was *Gott* somehow using Zeke to work His will in this hurting community?

That was so humbling.

Zeke walked over to one of the almost-finished chairs to study it. The padding part wasn't done yet, but that was out of his level of expertise. He supposed Luke's wife did the upholstery or it was outsourced.

Vernon still stood like a statue, watching Zeke.

And this standing and watching was what Vernon got paid the big bucks for? This was what *Daed* wanted for Zeke? Unbelievable. He'd go stark raving mad.

Zeke nodded toward the other worktable. "You can start measuring wood to match the sample. Measure twice, cut once." He turned his back to Vernon and went to work sanding the cut boards on another table.

Another moment of silence. And then a board thumped onto the table considerably harder than necessary.

Zeke suppressed a grin. Perfect Vernon had a temper.

Fifteen minutes later, the door to the shop opened. Zeke glanced up as two men entered the room. One was Kiah; the other was a Mennonite named Henry that he knew from back home. Zeke put the sander down and went to welcome his best friend and Henry.

He couldn't wait to talk to Kiah at lunch and get caught up on his news—and maybe, if Vernon and Henry weren't near, tell Kiah about Gracie.

And about how *Gott* was working behind the scenes in this whole storm.

* * *

Grace cleaned and reorganized the refrigerator while *Mammi* went downstairs to the basement to sort laundry and start a load in their gas washing machine. They had it ever so much easier than some of their cousins who had to use wringer washers. Judging by thumps and bumps, *Mammi* did other cleaning, too.

She'd just finished sweeping and scrubbing the kitchen floor when *Mammi* came upstairs, removing her apron.

"When this laundry load is finished, I thought we'd go to the visitation for a little bit. Why don't you get cleaned up?"

Grace frowned. "*Daed* told me not to go since I went yesterday."

Mammi shook her head. "Pishposh. I need you to drive me since your *daadi* hasn't returned yet. Hurry now and get ready to go."

Grace grinned and ran upstairs. She removed her soiled apron and checked her dress to make sure it was still clean. Then she repinned her hair, replaced her *kapp*, and returned downstairs.

Maybe she'd have a chance to see Zeke.

Though unless he poked his head out of the shop, she didn't see how.

Daadi Cliff would say, "Where there's a will, there's a way."

She definitely had the will.

She'd find a way.

CHAPTER 24

Zeke showed Kiah and Henry around Luke's workshop, and after learning Henry had construction experience, he assigned him to work with Vernon. Not that Vernon had done much working. Mostly he'd slammed things around and watched Zeke sand and join seams, as if he didn't know how to do anything except supervise and make noise.

Kiah's job in Shipshewana was raising and training buggy horses, but he did have some barn-raising experience. With him helping Zeke, it was a good chance for them to catch up with each other while getting some serious work done.

"Where are you staying? Do you like it there?" Zeke asked as he measured the board on the workbench a second time, then sawed a needed angle.

Kiah took the cut board and handed Zeke another. "They placed Henry and me with the semiretired buggy repairman and his wife. They're older, and no children, I guess. They live in town in a tiny one-bedroom *haus*, and so we're sleeping in sleeping bags tossed on the living room floor. The kitchen is overrun by tiny, little ants. And we're fed bean soup and corn bread for every meal except breakfast. So far, breakfast is exactly two poached eggs and a bowl of oatmeal. I'm going to be skin and bones by the time we leave here." On cue, his stomach rumbled.

Zeke chuckled. "You exaggerate."

"Not by much," Henry said from nearby. "He didn't mention the innumerable cats, either. They're everywhere."

Kiah rolled his eyes. "For sure and certain."

"We've had fried chicken or sandwiches every meal so far. Except breakfast," Vernon grumbled. "And our noon meal today is more of the same. I peeked."

"I'll trade you cold bean soup and dry corn bread for your fried chicken." There was a note of teasing in Henry's voice.

"I accept," Vernon said.

Henry's eyes widened.

A strained silence fell.

"They're serving us leftover wedding food that is being used up before it goes to waste," Zeke clarified. He struggled to process Vernon's attitude. Zeke was raised to eat what was set in front of him without complaint. And the food at the Lantzes' *haus* was good, though the reason behind it had to be painful. Especially for Gracie.

Or maybe not, if it meant she didn't have to marry Timothy.

"How about you? Any unmarried daughters?" Kiah finally broke the silence.

"With twelve brothers, ain't it a wonder?" Zeke said, quoting Cliff.

"Eleven," Vernon corrected.

Zeke caught his breath, turned, and glared.

Vernon spread his arms wide. "What? He fell from the roof of the barn. There's only one possible outcome."

"As of last night, he was in surgery and still alive. Besides, with *Gott* all things are possible," Zeke said quietly.

"In the perfect world." Vernon turned away. "One daughter is as good as married, and the other is special-needs."

Zeke clenched his fist and then released it with a prayer for patience.

"So no romance for you, either." Kiah smirked.

"Not supposed to date while we're here, anyway." Zeke shrugged. But he struggled to keep a straight face and block out the memories of the kisses and flirting he'd shared with Gracie.

Thankfully, Vernon had nothing to say to that. Vernon might not have realized what nearly happened on the steps right before Gracie's fall. But if he missed their frequent glances at each other, the man was blind.

"Zeke's been taking the special-needs girl on walks." Vernon's voice was filled with thinly veiled contempt. "Guess there's someone for everyone."

Kiah gave him an irritated look.

"She's fourteen, Vernon," Zeke snapped. What had gotten into calm, easygoing, perfect Vernon?

And then he knew.

Zeke had been put in charge, making him feel less like a loser, and Vernon didn't know how to handle it. And

Zeke's prior feelings toward Vernon, the perfect supervisor at the RV factory, were like Vernon's now toward him. Resentment and maybe jealousy.

Zeke really did need to pray for patience and grace in order to work with Vernon.

Because out of the two men, Zeke handled the upheaval from the storm better.

* * *

Grace went out to the barn to hitch Charlie Horse to their one remaining buggy, but both the horse and the buggy were gone. Of course. *Daadi* Cliff needed transportation for his errands today since he'd sent his wagon home with Reuben to return his tool chest. And with no phone, they had no way of calling for a driver.

Despite her will, there was no way to get there. Guess she had to stay home and obey *Daed*, after all.

She didn't want to go inside and tell *Mammi* she'd have to walk to the visitation. To postpone the inevitable, she stopped by the stall to check on Ben Gay. She fed the gelding the piece of carrot she'd carried to give to Charlie Horse. She gave Ben Gay a final pat on his nose and was turning to leave the stall when gravel crunched in the driveway. A vehicle door slammed. And a few seconds later, the vet walked into the barn.

"Hi, Miss Gracie. Your grandfather wanted me to come out and check the horse's leg."

Daadi Cliff must have called from his own barn. And therefore might be back somewhat soon after his chores and could drive *Mammi* to the visitation, after all.

Maybe? Or no. He'd be a while because he would've called the vet first thing.

"He was walking with a limp when he returned home this morning." Grace led the way back to the horse's new stall. "If you aren't too busy when you finish, could you drive my grandma and me to a visitation?"

She wasn't exactly disobeying *Daed* if *Mammi* asked her to go, right? Well, actually, *Mammi* asked her to drive her there. So maybe she would be. She needed to do the right thing and obey *Daed*.

She sighed. "Or just Grandma."

The vet chuckled. "I'll be glad to take both of you, Miss Gracie. Just give me a moment to check over the horse."

"I'll go tell Grandma." Grace hurried toward the *haus*. She found *Mammi* fixing a cup of coffee. "*Mammi*, *Daadi* Cliff took the buggy, but the vet is here, and he'll be glad to take you to the visitation."

Mammi raised a brow. "And you?"

"That's up to you. *Daed* told me to stay home," Grace reminded her. And as tempted as she was to peek at Zeke, she would do the right thing. And somehow just saying what *Daed* wanted out loud made her feel more courageous.

"You're a good girl, Grace Lynn. However, I'd prefer you go, especially with all the rumors floating around about you."

"Rumors? Plural?"

Mammi nodded. "You need to be seen and let them know it's pure foolishness."

Grace knew about the pregnancy rumor, which *Mamm* said she'd end, but… "What are they saying, *Mammi*?" Her stomach churned.

"That your groom took an opportunity to jilt you. That and you were cheating on him. No idea who you were cheating with. I think the person who started that rumor has knots for brains."

Grace wrinkled her nose. The only person she'd been seen with was Zeke... And that hadn't started until after her groom jilted her.

"How would my showing up disprove rumors? They'll just whisper behind their cupped hands and stare at me."

Mammi frowned at her. "No matter. You and I both know the rumors are untrue. In fact, the bishop told me yesterday evening right before your *daadi* brought me over here that Timothy went to Toby's visitation, and his parents said the families want the wedding to happen next Thursday, and the bishop agreed! Isn't that wonderful? We could share that news!"

Grace just stared. Wonderful wasn't how she'd describe it. Instead, it felt like a noose tightening around her neck. But... that was a plural *families* and her parents had said nothing of the kind to her and, as far as she knew, hadn't had a chance to talk to the bishop.

But... she'd promised *Mamm*.

And no one said no to the bishop.

Her inner resolve crumpled in the face of the ultimate authority she was supposed to obey.

* * *

Furniture making was not something Zeke wanted to do for a living. Not at all. In fact, it was slow, painstaking work, mainly because he didn't know what he was doing and had to keep going over to study the chairs so he could decide what the next step would be, making notes of measurements and talking it over with Henry for his opinion.

And joking with his best friend seemed inappropriate with the visitation happening at the *haus*, so they'd all fallen into silence. A dark, brooding silence.

One made darker by Vernon's increasingly bad temper. He didn't take instructions from Henry well, either. Probably because Henry was asking Zeke for advice. Talk about the blind leading the blind. Hopefully they wouldn't put Luke out of business.

Henry murmured something about wrong measurements to Vernon—who'd written down the length and width needed.

Vernon said something that sounded like a curse.

Zeke's head whipped up.

Vernon glared, grabbed the board from the worktable so fast he almost smacked Henry in the face. He swung it around and stomped across the room. He threw the board down, then froze, staring at an almost-finished casket waiting at the side of the room. "There . . . there's something in there."

"I shut the lid to keep sawdust off the not-quite-finished upholstery." Zeke might not know what he was doing, but he didn't want to sabotage Luke's business. Zeke frowned at Vernon, but in the following quiet, there were definite scratching sounds coming from the casket.

He wouldn't put it past Kiah to play a practical joke, but a glance at his friend revealed wide eyes and mouth gaped.

"Probably a mouse." Henry turned his back and returned to work, remeasuring what Vernon should've measured twice. "Open the lid and let it out."

Vernon reached out a shaking hand and flung the lid open.

With an angry "yeow" and a hiss, a black cat flew from the casket.

Vernon screamed.

A moment later the shop door was flung open, and two women stared in.

Zeke knew that one face. *Gracie.* The other looked familiar, but before he could figure out why Vernon barreled toward them. "I'm done! This is pure stupidity, making us do a job none of us know anything about."

Gracie and the other woman stepped out of his way.

"I'd rather look for stupid lost cows," Vernon shouted as he went past.

"The door to the *haus* is open," the second woman said quietly.

"What just happened?" Gracie asked, drawing Zeke's attention away from Vernon.

Kiah gawked.

"Everyone at the visitation heard that," the other woman said. Zeke studied her. Either Hallie or Elsie. He wasn't sure which.

Gracie came into the room. "Well?"

"Oh, um…" Zeke blinked. "There was a cat in a casket. I didn't realize it was there and shut the lid to keep it clean inside. It wasn't too happy when Vernon let it out. I didn't mean for it to interrupt the visitation." Yet another thing he'd done wrong. If anyone reported to his *daed*, he'd have a whole slew of mistakes to throw in Zeke's face.

And so much for positive thinking. He sighed.

"These are a couple other guys from Shipshewana. Kiah and Henry." Zeke motioned to the men with him. He glanced from Gracie to her friend. "The one who left is Vernon. Kiah and Henry, this is Gracie and her friend…"

"Hallie," Gracie supplied. "Nice to meet you both."

"Hi," Henry said.

Hallie gave a half wave.

"So you must be a Christmas baby," Kiah said with a flirty smile, "with a name like Holly." He walked nearer and stuck his hand out.

"Hallie, not Holly, and no. Easter." Her eyes were still red rimmed. And oh, it was her boyfriend's body inside the *haus.*

Gracie shook Kiah's hand. Hallie ignored it.

Kiah raised a brow and glanced at Zeke. He'd try to explain her relationship to the deceased later.

"We were outside talking when we heard the scream." Gracie's voice was tight. She looked at him. "The bishop said Timothy and I are getting married Thursday."

Zeke frowned. But neither Timothy nor Gracie wanted it.

Of course, neither one knew the other felt the same. Well, not exactly. They needed to talk without Timothy insulting her and Grace losing her temper.

"My brother is in a coma and may not live, and both of Timothy's sidesitters are dead, and…and…"

Someone needed to speak up before it was too late.

Zeke swallowed. "Gracie, it's time for you to talk to

people. Has it occurred to you that *Gott* has given you a chance to have something more, something better, if you have the guts to take it?"

"Something?" Her gaze latched on his. "Or some-one?"

CHAPTER 25

Grace didn't know if she'd have the courage to talk to anyone—especially if it involved talking to the bishop. But still... *Please, Lord, let that someone else You might have for me be Zeke.*

Zeke's gaze softened. "Maybe. But first, talk to your *daadi* Cliff. He knows stuff. Talk to Timothy. It's his story to tell, but if you can't find him, talk to me because he told me. And then talk to the bishop."

When did Zeke have time to talk to Timothy? And what had Timothy said? Still, Zeke's words gave her a twinge of hope that she tried to hold on to like an anchor or maybe hide in, like a storm shelter. Earlier it was just a rumor that the bishop had approved her rescheduled wedding, but now it was confirmed, and she was sick to her stomach. She couldn't do it. The internal storm was really picking up force now. "They'll say it's all cold feet. They'll say it's all because of my crush on you." Her voice cracked and ended with a sob.

Hallie caught her breath. Grace didn't dare to glance at her. Zeke's friends jerked to stare at her. Then looked at Zeke.

A figure—two of them—appeared in Grace's peripheral vision.

"*Gott*'s given you those cold feet for a reason. And maybe the crush, too." Zeke winked.

Kiah's wide eyes looked between the two of them. Zeke's friend was cute, with blondish hair and green eyes. He was a little shorter than Zeke but looked friendly. But then his brow furrowed. "A crush? Zeke, you know we aren't allowed to date. And the line is drawn in quicksand."

Brown-haired Henry nodded. "Careful there, Zeke."

Grace ignored them because, *jah*, she knew that. Except the quicksand part, but that made no sense. "Maybe it's more than a crush." If she trusted her emotions, she'd believe it was. She studied Zeke's expression to see if he agreed. His gaze softened. Caressed. *Jah*. She loved Zeke Bontrager, even though she just met him forty-eight hours ago. And that felt new and exciting, and she'd never been more sure of anything in her life. It was a total contrast to Timothy and a true blessing to have discovered what love was supposed to be like.

"We haven't dated." Zeke glanced at Kiah, then Henry, before he looked back at Grace. He smiled and winked but said nothing.

And she felt foolish again, pouring her feelings out like that. In front of their friends. But she'd never felt this way before, and it seemed so unfair he would only be here for a little while and then gone. Forever. She wanted to grab hold tight and hang on.

She'd marry him next Thursday without hesitation. She wrung her hands. Instead, she'd be marrying Timothy. *Is this it, Lord? Did you want me to come to a complete and total end of myself? Well, I have. Now what?* She'd prayed that same prayer the night of the tornado. Maybe she should edit it so they wouldn't have more damages.

"What's going on here?" Luke moved to stand beside Grace in the doorway. His arms were crossed, and there was a stern expression on his face as he stared at the three Indiana men in the shop. "Vernon says you're playing practical jokes instead of working and that he quits unless he's the supervisor."

"Nothing will get done otherwise," Vernon stated.

Grace glanced over her shoulder and met Vernon's glare. She supposed the cat would've scared anyone into screaming, but what did he mean nothing would get done? She glanced at the progress on the workbench beside Zeke.

"And now I know why you've been getting all cozy with the Lantz family," Vernon spat, staring at Zeke. "It's a good thing I came along to report back on your behavior."

What? He only came along to spy on Zeke? Not to help?

"This is an in-demand furniture business." Luke's voice was filled with confusion and disappointment. He pushed past Grace and Hallie as he stepped farther into the room. "I requested you, Zeke, because I heard nothing but good things about you. And this is what I get?

Deliberately measuring wrong, wasting my supplies. I can't believe this."

Henry and Kiah moved to flank Zeke.

Zeke stood there. Silent. Fists clenched. Acute pain filled his expression. Was he replaying the memory of getting fired from the factory where Vernon was a supervisor and causing others including his *daed* to think he was a loser?

Grace's heart hurt. She looked down at her shoes, long enough to find her courage. Then she raised her chin and glanced at him. "Zeke. What you said: 'It's time for you to talk to people. Has it occurred to you that *Gott* has given you a chance to have something more, something better, if you have the guts to take it?'"

"Sir," Henry said, "Vernon here is the one who doesn't know what he's doing. Zeke told us all multiple times, 'Measure twice, cut once.' I trusted Vernon to do that, and I didn't double-check." He waved a hand at the workstation behind them as if claiming it. Zeke's station was much further along, and the furniture was done correctly. "The waste is my fault. Not Zeke's."

Vernon spluttered.

"What about deliberately hiding a cat in a closed casket?" Luke sighed and nodded. He glared over his shoulder at Vernon first as if sorry he believed him and now just wanted the "case closed" so he could get back to his son's visitation.

"Not deliberate." Zeke squared his shoulders. "I didn't want sawdust getting into it and closed the lid. I didn't know the cat was sleeping in it. I would've shooed it out, if I'd known."

"Zeke is super kind to animals," Kiah said. "And people. There are no ulterior motives. I always want him around when a horse is giving birth. He somehow calms them."

Grace remembered *Daed* and Jon talking about how Zeke calmed the stuck cow. And how Vernon had called him a "cow whisperer." He had the same effect on her…and on Patience. Slush liked him, too. He definitely wouldn't have trapped a cat on purpose.

"My *daed* says Vernon's a great supervisor. The best he's ever had." Zeke dipped his chin, maybe conceding to Vernon's self-proclaimed right to be the manager. It seemed unjust that Zeke wouldn't even get a fair chance, especially when it was obvious Vernon had lied about him.

"That's because it's all he knows how to do," Henry snorted. "Boss people around. He's lazy. We all know it."

Kiah nodded.

Grace's brothers and *Daed* had commented on that.

She glanced at Vernon as he spluttered again, his face turning a frightening shade of red.

Luke nodded. "I've heard enough. Vernon, you're fired."

"You can't fire a volunteer. I quit. And Zeke, that line was drawn in quicksand, and you crossed it." Vernon turned and stomped off.

Grace watched him go.

He didn't make any more comments or threats, but something filled Grace with unease. Vernon had heard her confess her crush on Zeke. He'd heard Kiah's reminder that they couldn't date…But then he'd also heard Zeke say they hadn't dated. But would he conveniently forget that part?

What did it mean that the line was drawn in quick-sand?

Hallie gripped her arm. "That one's trouble."

Jah, he surely was.

* * *

Zeke was doomed. Especially since he could see Vernon through the dusty shop window chatting on his cell phone. It didn't take a genius to know he called the head missionary in charge. He'd seen Vernon's expression at being proven a liar and being fired instead of promoted. He was out for revenge.

Zeke would be punished—somehow—for violating the no-dating rule. Even though he technically hadn't dated Gracie, he had broken the rules. He kissed her.

And he'd willingly do it again.

And Vernon, while he might not *know*, had heard enough to condemn Zeke. Or at least would make up enough to condemn him. And once again, Vernon would be the cause of Zeke's dismissal.

It hurt, though it was nice that both Henry and Kiah stood up for him. Even when Vernon was caught in a lie—though that was a confusing mix of feeling good and yet not at the same time.

And somehow, the thought of his reputation being shredded here hurt worse than it had at home. Because of her. Gracie. He wanted to be her hero.

He'd wanted to be the hero for the community, too.

Ha. He should've known better. Especially when he was paired with Vernon.

Vernon, who destroyed Zeke's relationship with his

father. Vernon, who stole Zeke's girlfriend. Vernon, who...

Zeke shook his head. *Enough of the negative.*

But Zeke couldn't see the silver lining on these dark clouds.

Luke came into the shop and studied Henry's work, then Zeke's. He ran a hand over the smoothly sanded wood and checked the joints. He made not a sound, but when he finished, he smiled, nodded, and patted Zeke on the back.

Zeke didn't know exactly what he meant by it, but it seemed like some kind of affirmation.

He was afraid to hope.

"I like the way you treat your enemies as the friends they could become," Luke said. "It reminds me of a verse in Proverbs. I'm not quoting exactly, but says something like, 'A man's wisdom yields patience. It's to his glory to overlook an offense.'"

And with those words, Luke headed out the door. He paused to say something to Gracie and Hallie, who still stood in the doorway; then he disappeared from view, and Zeke assumed he returned to the *haus* and the visitation in progress.

Zeke blinked at the burn in his eyes and looked up to find that both Gracie and Hallie had left. Hopefully to find the people she needed to talk to. Timothy. Cliff. Someone—anyone—who would listen and help to stop the wedding.

Gracie might never be Zeke's, but she deserved better than Timothy. Unless Timothy cleaned up his act and actually fell in love with his bride. Which wouldn't happen before Thursday.

* * *

Grace and *Mammi* followed Debbie Fisher out to her buggy. Debbie was as old as Grace's *mammi*, and her husband was the silent type who never seemed to leave home. Since she was going home to fix dinner for her husband, she offered to give them a ride. Grace was thankful for it but dreaded the time spent with the community's chief gossip.

As Grace settled into the back seat, she mulled over the look on Zeke's face at Vernon's threats. Hopefully, there wouldn't be trouble for him tonight. And she needed to talk to *Daadi* Cliff, if he had returned, and to actually speak with him about Timothy like Zeke had told her to. Her thoughts were a confusing jumble.

While *Mammi* got in, Debbie untied the horse, then climbed in next to *Mammi*. She glanced over her shoulder at Grace. "I was ever so glad to hear you and Timothy settled your differences and decided to get married after all. I just can't wait to see you two get hitched."

It seemed bad news traveled fast. Grace squirmed, not sure how to answer. Settling differences was hard to do when she'd only seen Timothy twice. Once, he said his name was James, and the other time she dumped soda on his head. Not exactly a settling of differences. Echoes of Zeke's words to talk drummed in her head. Except, he'd said to talk to *Daadi*, Timothy, and the bishop…not to the gossip queen.

"Did he make you eat crow for cheating on him with that Zeke person from Indiana?" Debbie's eyes were all wide innocence, as if she weren't waiting for the next tidbit of gossip.

"Really, Debbie." *Mammi* frowned. "She didn't even meet Zeke until after Timothy didn't show up for the wedding. Zeke is a rescue worker, you know, and he was helping Gracie look for her dear groom."

And that was one way to shut the gossip up. Grace looked out the buggy window.

"And they found him. So romantic." Debbie sighed.

Well, it wasn't exactly that easy, or romantic, but Grace didn't plan to share her thoughts on the matter. Not until she could talk to *Daadi* Cliff or *Daed* to see if she had any options. Surely, Timothy wouldn't have jumped the gun like this without talking to her. Was he even calling himself Timothy? Or James? No, the whole thing seemed contrived. If he was hanging around the hospital last night, when had he gone home to reconcile with his parents anyhow? Last she'd seen, he'd pretended not to know them. It must be a desperate measure by Timothy's parents to bring their boy back under their thumbs. And Grace, too. By proxy. Kind of like he had treated her. Was that where he'd learned the bossy measures?

"I just can't begin to tell you how boundless my joy is." Debbie reached over the buggy seat and patted Grace's leg, drawing her attention. "You must be overjoyed."

And again, not exactly.

"And it was so nice of him to forgive you." She set the horse into motion.

"For what? Looking for him?" Grace burst out without thinking.

"Cheating on him with Zeke, dear," Debbie said patiently. Slowly, as if Grace was hard of understanding. "He says quite firmly that your baby isn't his."

"What!" Grace would've jumped from the buggy if she could without climbing over the two older ladies in the front seat. "When did you see him to ask him that?"

"At the hospital yesterday. We went up to visit with Peter's parents. And he was quite horrified to hear you weren't the angel everyone calls you."

So much for *Mamm* squelching that rumor. And when yesterday had Debbie seen Timothy? Was it before or after the cafeteria meeting, because Grace didn't run into him until evening after the barn was built and she was having a late supper. And since when was he admitting his identity and not "amnesia"?

Mammi's face had turned an alarming shade of red.

Grace was pretty sure that her expression matched.

"Debbie, our Gracie did not cheat, and she is not expecting." *Mammi*'s voice was firm. "Not only that, but that boy is from Indiana, and according to my husband, he's not allowed to date here. Which is really too bad since Cliff is quite fond of him. In fact, he told him to skip the dating and cut straight to marrying."

"Oh, really?!" Debbie's eyebrows darted up as she stared at Grace through the rearview mirror.

Grace liked that idea, but she hated to see where Debbie Fisher would go with that tidbit. She stared out the window so Debbie couldn't see her expression.

"So she's not going to marry Timothy, after all, but her lover?"

Grace's stomach threatened revolt. Not at the idea of marrying Zeke but where the woman was going to take this conversation. Really, was Debbie even right in the head?

"Again, Zeke is not her lover. Besides, I'm happy to say that the bishop approved Timothy and Gracie marrying next Thursday." *Mammi* sighed. "Let us out at the next mailbox."

Amen. We'll walk from here.

CHAPTER 26

Zeke glanced up as movement in the doorway caught his attention. Was it Daniel Zook, the head missionary, finally arriving to read him the riot act?

An elderly Amish man hobbled into the room.

"Ready to go, boys?" the man shouted. He shoved his glasses farther up the bridge of his nose.

"He's the semiretired buggy repairman we're staying with," Kiah said, without lowering his voice. "Deaf, unless you shout at him."

"It was good seeing both of you," Zeke said. "Guess I'll see you again when you return to Shipshewana." A heavy weight settled on him. Never in his wildest dreams had he anticipated being sent home in disgrace.

Kiah punched him lightly in the arm, but his face screwed up. "I'll miss you."

Henry nodded, face sober. "Keep the faith." He followed the old man out the door.

Kiah hesitated, then pulled Zeke into a man hug, pounding his back, before he followed the other two.

Zeke blinked at the burn in his eyes and looked around at the bases for six chairs. It wasn't enough, but considering it was the first time any of them had made furniture, at least they'd made some progress after Vernon left. Very little, but some. And Luke had already nodded at this start, so the chair bases wouldn't need to be remade.

Cliff strode into the shop promptly at five, just as Zeke finished putting the last tool away. "Where's Vernon?" Cliff glanced around.

Zeke turned to close the lid on the toolbox and bent to knock the worst of the wood shavings off his legs before he looked around for a broom. "I have no idea. I haven't seen him since before lunch." And if Daniel Zook had come to pick Vernon up, he would've taken the time to talk to Zeke, because they promised the punishment would be swift and severe. He picked up the two empty lunch pails. "One of the other guys ate Vernon's lunch." After much joking about the pink lunch pail.

"I'm sure that's fine." Cliff came farther into the shop and inspected the chairs. "Looks like they're off to a good start."

Zeke stood a little taller. "*Jah*, Luke said something about somehow curving a piece of wood for a rounded back, but I don't know how to do that." And he wasn't likely to learn, either, even though he was curious and would like to have the chance. Zeke swallowed, walked over to the doorway, and flicked the gaslights off, shrouding the room in near darkness from the dusty windows and almost completely set sun. "Any word on Jon? Or the lame horse?"

"I called the vet. Horse will be fine. He said he left some sort of ointment for a long gash on the horse's leg and recommended rest. As for Jon, it's too soon to tell. He's still alive, which is a miracle in and of itself. Aubrey, his fiancée, claims that his fingers are flexing when she holds his hand, but Seth says he hasn't noticed it yet. Doctors aren't saying one way or another, but he survived the first night, which they said was critical." Cliff rubbed his shoulder as if it ached, and sighed.

"Are you okay?" Zeke eyed him. This wasn't a heart attack coming on, was it?

"I'm fine. Just aggravated an old injury." Cliff leaned to inspect a chair more closely in the dim light. "So, Vernon. Where is he if he isn't here?"

Zeke shrugged. He was tired and sore himself from leaning over the workstation, but the extra chores tonight would do him good. He swung the lunch pails as he moved away from the doorway to rejoin Cliff. "Again, I don't know." He didn't want to tattle about Vernon's temper tantrum or threats. "He walked out after I accidentally shut a cat into a pine box. The cat didn't like it so much."

Cliff grunted. "And neither did Vernon, I'm guessing."

"I fired him." Luke came through the door and turned the lights back on. "He had a bit of an attitude about my putting Zeke in charge. Vernon apparently messed up and blamed Zeke. So, he walked out after making a few threats, made a couple phone calls, and someone picked him up by the mailbox."

Zeke raised his eyebrows. Who had picked him up? When? And why hadn't they come inside to talk to him? Very odd.

Cliff scratched his head. He said nothing for a long minute; then he made a "hmm" sound. He glanced at Zeke. "Sounds like you and I need to have a talk, boy."

Was he blaming Zeke?

That figured.

Zeke swallowed and nodded.

"Don't come the next two days, Zeke, since Sunday is the Lord's day and Monday is my son's funeral. I'll see you Tuesday." Luke looked exhausted. He ran a hand over the wood as if to check Zeke's sanding skills. "Good job."

"I'm not sure I'll still be here on Tuesday." No, he'd be sent home in disgrace, with an overflowing bucket of fiery, hot coals ready for *Daed* to heap on his head.

"You'll be here." It was a statement. Cliff punctuated it with a decisive nod. "We want to keep you around."

"How can you be sure?" Zeke wasn't being a smart-mouth but was curious. These two men liked him. And it was so nice to be appreciated. Valued. Looked upon as an equal. Hallie's *daed* liked him, too. Allies in a strange land. It was a rather amazing feeling.

Cliff glanced around. "Sweep the floor while I have a word with Luke." The two men left the room and shut the door behind them.

Zeke eyed the shut door. He wanted to hear what was being said, but peace filled him. No matter what would happen, *Gott* knew. He knew and He cared. And for now, Zeke was here in this community to help. And he'd keep on helping until they dragged him away.

He set the empty lunch pails on a worktable, looked around again for the broom, and found it leaning in a corner. No dustpan. The sawdust was probably swept right out the door. He gathered it all into a large pile, ready to push out.

With time left to spare, he grabbed a bottle of window-washing fluid and an old copy of *The Budget* and washed the shop windows.

The door opened, and Cliff peeked in. "Let's go, boy."

"I need to sweep this out the door first."

"Let me get out of your way before you do that. I don't want to disappear in a cloud of dust." Cliff pushed the door wide open, then stepped behind the outside wall.

Cleanup complete, Zeke returned the broom to the corner, grabbed the pails, and turned the lights off again.

He followed Cliff to a closed buggy and they both climbed in. "Where'd this come from?"

Cliff waited until they were on the way before answering. "It's mine. I asked one of my grandsons, Dan, to return Seth's buggy. I'll give him a ride home when I drop you off. I have a few more errands to run before supper."

Zeke nodded.

"Tell my wife and Gracie to expect a few more guests for supper."

"Okay?" It was a question, but if Cliff recognized it as one, he decided to ignore it. None of Zeke's business anyway.

"I have a couple pounds of ground lamb in the buggy, if they want to use that." He gestured over his shoulder at a bundle on the back seat. "I thought to grab catfish fillets, but one of the men coming for dinner has an aversion to fish."

This was getting stranger and stranger. "Okay."

"And tell my granddaughter to bake a few cherry pies. Just to sweeten things up."

"Are you celebrating something?" Or would this be his last meal in Illinois? Zeke frowned. He loved cherry pie, and Gracie was already sweet. He couldn't wait to see her.

Cliff ignored that, too. He stopped the buggy by Seth's back porch. A brother, Dan, came out of the barn and approached. "There's also a potted mum in the back, if you want to get it. I meant to take it up to the hospital for Jon, but my wife suggested it'd be better to have it here. If Jon and Aubrey are still able to marry as planned, it'd be nice to welcome them back home with a potted mum. After their wedding tour, of course."

"Of course." But with Gracie's news about her pending marriage to Timothy, it might welcome them home first. *Please,* Gott, *don't let that happen.*

Zeke climbed out of the buggy. Dan climbed in.

"Don't forget the lamb and the flowers, now. Oh, and tell them to expect the guests around six thirty."

Zeke retrieved the items from the back seat and carried them up the porch stairs.

"And don't forget cherry pies. You can sweeten that up with a kiss."

Zeke stumbled. He caught himself on the handrail and turned to stare at Cliff. "What?"

Dan's eyes widened. "*Daadi* Cliff—"

"On the cheek. From me." Cliff laughed and drove off.

It took Zeke a moment or two to recover as memories of Gracie's kisses teased his senses.

A kiss.

Oh *jah.*

* * *

Grace folded the clean clothes, still warm from the dryer, and carried the basket up from the basement. She entered the kitchen as Zeke came inside, carrying a white-wrapped package and a potted garden mum in a pretty shade of purple.

Her heart hitched as he looked at her. There was something glimmering in the depths of his eyes that made her senses sit up and take notice.

His lips curved into a smile, fleeting, to be sure, but a smile all the same. His eyes softened.

"What's that?" She nodded toward his load.

He looked down. "Um, the flowers are for Jon—"

She caught her breath. "Nooo!" Tears pricked her eyes. The laundry basket thudded to the floor at her feet. The top layer of clean clothes flopped out on the floor.

He set the package and the mum on the table and reached for her.

She launched herself into his hug. He smelled of saw-dust. Sawdust and pine and something citrusy.

"No, Gracie, Jon's still alive. Your *daadi* just thought the flowers would be better here than cluttering the hos-pital room."

She sighed. "Oh, *danki*, *Gott*." But she didn't leave his arms. The strength of him seemed so capable of carrying her burdens just for a moment longer. And even though she'd spent the afternoon praying about Jon and the ru-mors and her supposed wedding and wishing *Daadi* Cliff would come home so she could talk to him, there was no place she'd rather spend her future than in Zeke's arms.

"Gracie." His hands trembled against her back for a

moment before he set her away. He glanced around as if to check for witnesses.

"*Mammi* is taking a short nap."

Still, he shook his head and backed up as if distancing himself. "The white package is ground lamb. Your *daadi* said to do something with it for supper. He's bringing a few guests. He said to expect them around six thirty."

Grace frowned. "Oh? Who?"

"I don't know. He also said to make a few cherry pies."

She stared at him. "The bishop is coming?" Maybe she'd get a chance to talk to him about Timothy.

"I don't know." Zeke shrugged.

"Bishop Nathan absolutely loves cherry pie."

"Then, maybe he is." Zeke glanced around again. "Where's . . ." He exhaled. Inhaled. "Vernon?"

"I haven't seen him since he stormed out of the shop." Gracie whirled and ran out of the kitchen into the living room and upstairs to the room Zeke and Vernon were staying in. "His bags are gone." The words emerged on a breath. When had he come in to take them?

"They are?"

She caught her breath. Somehow she'd missed that Zeke had followed her.

"They are," he said again. "Gone. His things are gone." There was a note of panic mixed with relief in his voice. But before she could ask him about it, his arms wrapped around her from behind. She shivered as his head lowered and his warm breath tickled her neck. "Your *daadi* said to give you a kiss, from him, on your cheek."

His lips brushed her cheek; then he pulled back.

She grasped his hands as he started to release her and held on tight. His strong arms held her so gently, unlike Timothy's strength that often hurt her. The sawdust peppering his arms meant he wasn't afraid of hard work and would be a good provider.

"Do you always do as you're told?" Her voice came out breathy. She swiveled her head to look at him. He was so noble to try to do the right thing. If he ever promised to love her, she'd be the luckiest woman alive.

He chuckled. "Hardly ever, but I've been trying to do better. Oh, Gracie." His gaze dipped to her lips. Lingered. "I want to kiss you again, but—"

He did? Then what was the holdup? She didn't intend to stop him. "Then kiss me." Her voice was husky. If things didn't go well talking to the bishop after supper, if he indeed was coming, then this moment with him was all she'd ever have, and she couldn't bear the thought of never kissing him again.

He sucked in air, his hands trembling against her. "Gracie, I want to, but your *daed* trusts you. And me." He hesitated a moment. "Maybe not me. But you've got pies to bake and supper to cook for guests, and I urgently need a shower."

"If you want to, you can." She twisted in his arms. Wrapping her arms around him in a hug, she pressed herself against him. "Supper can wait a minute longer."

Please, whatever it takes and no matter how foolish I seem, just kiss me one more time...

He groaned. "Gracie—"

"Unless it's a pity kiss." She frowned and edged away.

His arms tightened, holding her in place. "It's not a pity kiss. It never was. But your *daed*..."

"*Daed* knows better than to trust me. If you want to, you can kiss me." She tipped up her face. *Please. One last kiss. Let me have this memory to warm me during the coldness of my loveless upcoming marriage.*

Zeke caught his breath. "Gra—"

"Unless the chocolate cream pie truly was better than my kiss." She pretended to pout and shifted to teasing. That was better than manipulating, though she had valid reasons. Maybe.

A chuckle, low and rumbly. "You'll never know. But I'm content in the knowledge my kiss was better than peanut butter pie." He winked. Released her.

"I changed my mind. Peanut butter pie is way better than your kiss." *Fine. Have it your way.* She tossed him an impish grin and flounced toward the door.

She didn't get far.

He caught her by the waist. Turned her to face him. "That's not fair. Now I'm obligated to defend my honor."

Her breath hitched. She shivered. The next moment she was caught up against him. Right where she wanted to be. Her heart rate surged. He was close to the target but not close enough...yet.

"Take it back." He brushed a tiny kiss across her lips.

She might have whimpered. "Never."

He kissed the corners of her lips. "I'll have to torture it out of you."

Her back arched. "You'll never change my mind."

He kissed her eyes shut, then blazed a trail of fire to her ear. He nibbled it. "Last chance," he whispered.

"Not happening."

His lips burned a path to her neck. He nibbled her pounding pulse.

She moaned. She couldn't help it.

"Do you surrender? Admit it."

Oh jah. But that would only free her. Not what she wanted. "No. Never."

His fingers tickled her ribs. She squirmed closer. And then joy of joys, his lips were on hers, and he was kissing her the way she wanted him to.

She tried to pretend to not to be affected, but oh…she whimpered. Pressed closer. Her hands rose to tangle in his hair.

He growled, deep in his throat. "Do you admit it?" Another kiss that stole the breath right out of her.

"No." She might've gasped.

His lips worked magic that left her clinging, unable to do anything but lose herself in the moment.

"Gracie." The faint call was as annoying as a needy fly. She ignored it in favor of the dangerous fire Zeke was lighting inside her. *Mammi* could wait a few more minutes.

He pressed her even closer to him and stopped kissing her long enough to whisper another "admit it."

"Peanut butter pie wins," she teased.

He growled, and the assault on her senses began anew.

"Gracie?" The unwelcome call came again. Louder.

She whimpered. Again.

"Grace Lynn Lantz!" a man said.

Zeke released her so quickly she stumbled. Her knees buckled. She struggled to stay upright.

He bent to pick up his bag. Shoved something into it. *What?* "No. Zeke, no."

He straightened, his gaze going from her to the door. "Hi, Timothy."

*   *   *

Apparently, no one would be getting a happy ending. The only possible outcome here would be for Zeke to be returning home in shame. Especially with Gracie's still-fiancé standing in the doorway, eyes wide, mouth agape as he caught Zeke in the process of seducing a woman who wasn't his.

A woman who'd gasped, turning to stare at the man in the doorway. "Timothy..."

Zeke had known better, of course, but with Grace teasing him so relentlessly about the peanut butter pie being better than his kisses when she so obviously hated it...and then flouncing away, hips swaying...

He knew better, but his honor was at stake there.

Okay. He crossed the line.

Big-time.

Admit it. He groaned. Caught enticing another man's woman into his arms with a foolish challenge. One he'd been able to avoid—though not exactly easily—when Gracie offered to let him kiss her when he stupidly admitted wanting to. But the second she sashayed away, his overactive male hormones kicked in, and...

And Timothy had actually caught his fiancée in another man's arms. Kissing another man.

Never mind that Timothy had cheated first. It was still wrong.

And after Zeke had promised it wouldn't happen again.

The consequences would be stiff and severe. And if Vernon had witnessed it, Zeke would be caught in more than quicksand. Still, there was no way he'd still be around on Tuesday. Might as well pack after all . . .

He deserved it.

He bent to shove another pair of socks into his bag.

"Zeke, stop." Gracie tossed the words over her shoulder. "Timothy, I have a few pies to make. Let's take this to the kitchen." She moved toward the door as if she'd been unaffected by Zeke's kisses. As if peanut butter pie had actually been better.

"Your *mammi* sent me up." Timothy still stared at Zeke, betrayal darkening his eyes.

"Well, I'm sending you back down. Go on, now."

Timothy didn't move.

Zeke found his voice. "I'm sorry. We were just goofing off." Not exactly. Because the twin bed had been too close and too present in his mind, and they would've crossed another line. One of no return.

Really, the interruption was a blessing.

His words earned him a glare from Gracie.

"I meant we were settling a debate," he amended.

Timothy's expression didn't change. Well, maybe it did. It darkened and mixed with hurt. Acute betrayal.

Zeke found his pajama pants. Stuffed them in the bag. There. All packed. Except for his toothbrush.

A clatter came from the kitchen. Followed by a crash.

Gracie pushed past Timothy and ran.

Timothy stared another moment before he turned away to follow Gracie.

Zeke collapsed on the edge of the bed, closed his eyes, and waited for the ax to fall.

The line was drawn in quicksand.

And he'd crossed it.

Willingly.

And for just a moment, he'd had a taste of heaven. Of his dream future.

One that was lost to him forever.

CHAPTER 27

Grace dashed into the kitchen to find the iron skillet on the floor in front of the stove, halfway between *Mammi* and a Mennonite man she didn't know standing in the open doorway. Another man who appeared to be Amish stood in the shadows behind him. And behind the second man, Vernon. *Mammi* stared, unmoving, holding a rolling pin as a weapon. Had she dropped the iron skillet when the men appeared, or had she flung the iron skillet at the man? Or men? More importantly, had *Mammi* lost her mind?

Grace bent and picked up the skillet, setting it on the stove. She turned to the men. Someone had to be hospitable. She winced at the memory of Vernon's last words and threats and the realization these men might be here to send Zeke home, especially if Vernon's self-satisfied smirk was any indication. She added a quick prayer for sanity since this situation couldn't get any weirder with Zeke's kisses still burning her lips, Timothy upstairs, and *Mammi* threatening violence. Although, she'd like to toss the skillet at Vernon and knock the smirk off his face, too. But instead of being impulsive, she took the high road and pretended everything was fine. "May I help you?"

The first man didn't look away from *Mammi*. Apparently she was the larger threat. "Daniel Zook, miss. We're here to speak with Ezekiel Bontrager."

Oh. Judging by the first man's grim expression and Vernon's folded arms, it wasn't for a good reason, either.

Could she lie and say he wasn't here? She picked up the clean clothes, returned them to the laundry basket, and moved it to a chair.

But no. Lying would be a sin, and not only that, Vernon was here and he'd know…not to mention *Mammi* would scold her for telling falsehoods.

"Um, take a seat on the porch," Grace said. It was chilly outside, but since *Mammi* was armed with a rolling pin and possibly throwing dangerous frying pans, it somehow seemed the best place for them. "I'll get him."

"I'll get him," Timothy said rather sharply.

Grace whirled to see him standing in the doorway of the kitchen. She fought a giggle at how absurd this whole situation was turning out to be. If only *now* she could be dreaming. But no. Instead, storm clouds gathered, dark and scary looking, on her personal horizon.

The look Timothy gave her was downright possessive. As if now that he'd caught her in an embrace with another man he suddenly found her desirable. But now that she'd had that embrace, she could never say the same about Timothy.

Lord, get us through this storm. And if I can marry the man I love, I'll never doubt Your ability to calm storms again. A weird sense of peace in the middle of it filled her.

She puffed out a breath. "*Danki*, because I have pies to make." Despite the faint sense of peace, she desperately grasped for some anchor of normal in the middle of this swirling storm.

Timothy nodded and turned away, retreating upstairs. The three men returned outside. And instantly, she had more breathing room.

"Oh, and *Mammi*? *Daadi* Cliff sent ground lamb for supper. I think Bishop Nathan is coming because *daadi* requested cherry pies."

And oh, please, Lord, let me have a chance to talk to him before Timothy does.

She set the package of meat beside *Mammi* on the counter.

Mammi made some sort of weird noise and didn't move. She kept staring at the porch window. The men were still visible, making themselves comfortable on the porch furniture.

"*Mammi*?" Grace waved a hand in front of her face to end the statue pose.

Mammi shook her head. Hard, as if to clear it. "Bishop Nathan. Right. He's especially fond of shepherd's pie."

"*Daadi* Cliff requested a few cherry pies, too. I'll get started on that," Grace repeated, in case *Mammi* hadn't heard her the first time. She carried the canister of flour over to the table.

Timothy appeared in the doorway. His gaze pinned

Grace's. "I told Zeke some guys are here for him, but he's taking a shower first. Hopefully, it's a cold one."

Grace's face burned.

Mammi ignored him. "How many did Cliff invite for dinner exactly?"

"I don't know," Grace said.

"Me." Timothy pointed to his chest. "He said Gracie and I need to talk about our wedding plans." He raised a brow.

Grace sagged and braced her hands on the table. A storm raged to life inside her, a roaring noise in her ears just like that tornado, twisting, twirling, and wreaking havoc. A flash flood threatened to flow from her eyes. *Dear Jesus, no. Please calm the storm.* She hadn't actually thought of Patience's prayer until it emerged.

She closed her eyes for a moment as the prayer emerged, then opened them to look the source of the storm in the eye.

"And I can see we have plenty to talk about," Timothy added glumly, maybe a bit of hurt in his voice, still staring at Grace. There was also a glint of jealousy in his eyes and a silent promise of punishment or a lecture later that she rebelled against.

"*Jah*, we do." Grace opened her mouth to let loose with a torrent of words, starting with the obvious *Where have you been, and why did you pretend—*

> Be still, and know that I am God: I will be exalted among the heathen, I will be exalted in the earth.

A verse from Psalms dammed the words on her tongue.

Be still? When Zeke had told her to talk to Timothy and she had so much she wanted to say. Not the least being, *Please, let me go. Release me.*

Timothy sat at the table and stared at her. He said not a word.

But then, neither did she. At least not verbally. She dumped ingredients in the bowl and mixed the dough. She still didn't have any answers. She picked up *Mammi*'s rolling pin weapon and applied it to the dough. *Be still. Impulsive is so much easier.* She bit her lip and pressed down; then a noise caught her attention.

Zeke emerged, hair damp, in clean clothes, and carrying his packed bag.

Her heart lurched, and the storm swirled again. *Oh, dear Lord . . .*

"They're on the back porch," Timothy said.

Zeke stopped, shook Timothy's hand. "I wish you every happiness."

He glanced at *Mammi*, who'd finally started to brown the ground lamb, then looked at Grace. "*Danki* for your hospitality."

Timothy snorted.

Shadows filled Zeke's eyes as he gazed at Grace. He swallowed, his Adam's apple bobbed, and his jaw firmed. "I'll think of you on Thursday. I'll, um, never forget you." His voice was raw.

She whimpered. Only their audience kept her from launching herself at him. And that was by a badly fraying thread.

Is this it, Lord? Did you want me to come to a com-

plete and total end of myself? Well, I have. Now what? Will you finally calm the storm, or will it be like the other two times when the tornado destroyed our barn and Jon almost died? How am I supposed to be still? How are You exalted in any of this? She'd prayed the first part of the prayer twice before, but He hadn't answered. There was no reason to expect He would now. Well, the tornado had postponed the wedding and brought Zeke here, but what good did that do her now?

Tears blurred her eyes as Zeke moved toward the door.

A car pulled into the driveway and parked behind the missionary's van.

Zeke stepped outside.

Grace gulped and ran after him, ignoring the floury mess on her hands. If there were some way of stopping this…

Daed emerged from the van. He paid the driver, then stooped to pick up Timothy's rusty green bicycle from where it lay in the yard. He pushed it far enough to lean it against the *haus*.

Slush howled and ran from the barn, launching himself at Zeke as the driver left.

And Zeke stumbled to a stop as he glanced at the trio waiting on the porch. "*Daed*?"

CHAPTER 28

This was worse than Zeke had thought. His behavior had brought *Daed* to Illinois to berate him among strangers. He cringed, glancing from *Daed*'s irritated grimace to Vernon's perpetual smirk to stern Daniel Zook. Hopefully, they would try to make his scolding less public. At least away from Gracie. He didn't want her witnessing the harsh words. He wanted her final memories of him to be positive, with them laughing, teasing, kissing...

He sighed as he dropped his bag, ran a hand over the dog's head, then turned to Seth, postponing the inevitable. "*Danki* for your hospitality, Seth. I hope Jon is doing okay?" He wished he'd be around to know Jon had fully recovered. Maybe Cliff or Gracie would write and let him know. He hated leaving behind the man who could have been like a brother or friend, although not as much as he hated leaving Gracie.

Seth climbed up on the porch. "He's showing some

involuntary hand movements. And he opened his eyes briefly."

"Oh, praise *Gott*," Gracie murmured behind Zeke. He stepped to the side so she could see more than his back.

"His *mamm* insisted on staying again tonight, but I needed to pick up a few things here and then I'll head back in the morning. Plus, my *daed* said there was something I needed to be here for." Seth's gaze landed on Zeke's packed bag. "Are you boys leaving us?"

That would seem obvious. Zeke gulped and glanced at Vernon leaning against the porch railing.

Daed stood, extending his hand. "Ezekiel's father, Elias."

Seth shook it. "Seth Lantz. What can I do for you gentlemen?" He eyed Daniel Zook, where he sat on a bench, with a confused frown.

Daniel Zook opened his mouth but shut it again as a buggy rolled in, and Cliff and Bishop Nathan emerged.

Oh no—more people to witness Zeke's disgraceful expulsion. At least his allies were now equal in number to his judges, until they hear of the most recent kiss. And with Timothy sitting inside and the door wide open, they surely would.

Cliff glanced at Timothy's bike as he bustled up on the porch. "Oh good, we're all here. Send Timothy out and let the party begin! Gracie, are those pies done?"

Party? This was no party. Zeke frowned.

"No." She sounded stressed. "I sort of got sidetracked, but—"

"Well, get in there and make them. This doesn't involve you." Cliff pointed toward the door.

"It does involve me," Grace objected.

Zeke glanced at her. *Please, obey your* daadi. The dog nuzzled him, and he looked down at a smiling Slush. As if there were something to smile about. "I don't want Gracie to hear this." His shame would only be compounded if she witnessed it. And why did Timothy need to be here? So he could gloat over emerging the victor? It was hard enough for Zeke to have wished him happiness. But also, what about the audience of Vernon smugly watching? That was bad enough.

Gracie touched his arm, sending fire to his heart. Oh, the ache. "But—"

"Go inside, Gracie," Cliff reiterated.

She made a frustrated and hurt sound but went inside. The door didn't click, though, so she must've left it open a crack.

Zeke glanced at *Daed*.

And...and was that a smile?

He blinked and looked again.

It was.

When was the last time *Daed* smiled at him? Certainly, he'd never smiled when Zeke had messed up, which was more often than not.

That smile. Oh, how he'd missed it and the relationship they used to have. If only he could feel his father's love again.

Slush nudged him, knocking Zeke off-balance. He took a step, and then something propelled him forward— an almost physical pressure against his back.

Daed met him halfway.

Zeke almost cried as *Daed* folded him against his chest.

When was the last time they'd embraced?

Zeke might've clung.

"I love you, son. I'm proud of you."

Proud? Of what? And who told him something good, because it definitely couldn't be smug Vernon. Zeke rubbed his eyes. Perhaps he was dreaming.

The door creaked open, then slammed shut behind them. "You requested my presence?" Timothy sounded a bit cocky.

It wasn't a dream. Zeke released *Daed* and half turned. Maybe what he'd thought was a nightmare humiliation might not be so bad after all. No matter what happened next, at least he'd heard those amazing words from *Daed*'s lips, and he had one reason to celebrate today, even if nothing else turned out well.

Slush growled.

"Shut up, dog." There was a bit of that wild *I need a fix* light in Timothy's eyes.

"Slush." Zeke crouched. The dog leaned into him.

The bishop coughed and pulled a hot-pink, zippered cell phone case out of his pocket. The one Zeke had found in the underwear-strewn field. Bishop Nathan glanced from Cliff to Seth as he handed the colorful plastic-protected phone to Timothy, who winced. Paled. His hands shook as he took the phone.

Zeke's stomach dropped. Even without the text message open, Timothy obviously recognized the phone, and that alone convicted him of wrongful behavior toward his intended bride...Oh, and based on their cafeteria conversation, this other woman Timothy loved wouldn't let him into her new apartment. Zeke's heart hurt for Timothy. He had some explaining to do—explaining that might postpone or cancel the wedding.

Bishop Nathan frowned. "We need to talk about this and a few other things, Timothy. Come with me to the barn. Seth, please join us."

Cliff nodded at Seth. "I've got the rest of this conversation, son. Go with the bishop and keep your mind on *Gott*."

Timothy's hands shook harder. He dropped the phone.

Seth picked up the phone, handed it to the bishop, but frowned at Cliff. "*Daed*, what is going on?"

Jah, exactly. Was this a dream or reality? Zeke ran his hand over Slush's head. What was going on? Something that might result in Gracie being set free. *Please, Lord.*

"We're clearing the storm-muddied waters, son," Cliff said. "Now, go do your part."

Those storm-muddied waters were crashing over Zeke in waves that gave him moments of hope mixed with equal parts of terror.

"Come, Timothy." Bishop Nathan gave him a stern look, turned, and headed to the barn.

After a moment, Timothy followed. Except, he stopped and grasped his bicycle handles. Straightened it. Started to swing his leg over.

Seth grabbed Timothy's shoulder. "To. The. Barn. Now."

Timothy stumbled, dropped the bike, and obeyed.

Except, he pulled what might be a homemade cigarette out of his pocket. Lit it.

After a moment, the breeze brought the unmistakable odor of marijuana to the men on the porch. Hopefully, *Gott* would show Timothy a way up from rock bottom and help him get the help he so desperately needed.

Seth grabbed the joint, threw it on the ground, and

crushed it with his shoe. He said something Zeke couldn't hear to Timothy, then picked the crushed cigarette up and carried it into the barn. Probably to show to the bishop. As if there weren't enough evidence against Timothy already. Just like there was plenty of evidence that Zeke had crossed the line and broken trust.

Zeke patted the dog one last time, then stood. "I suppose we should go. It was nice getting to know you, Cliff." He swallowed a sob, grabbed his bag, and moved toward Cliff and the stairs.

Cliff grabbed him by both arms. "Stop right there, boy. We aren't done with you."

"Have a seat, Zeke." Daniel Zook pointed to an empty chair across from Vernon—which would put Zeke in the hot seat.

He grimaced. "Do we have to do this here?"

"Sit." Cliff gave a gentle shove.

Zeke sat. And tried to keep his eyes on Jesus and find that same peace he'd felt yesterday over there in the partially built barn when he prayed with the missionaries. He shifted his gaze back to the man in front of him. He'd take his punishment like a man.

Daniel Zook leaned forward. "So, I heard from Vernon—"

"Yes, sir. And I'm sorry—"

"There is no rule against a girl developing a crush on you. Especially since you didn't date her. Although I did hear the story of her kissing you." Daniel Zook glanced at Cliff and smiled slightly.

Zeke's face heated.

Daed chuckled.

"From what I understand from reports coming in to

the rescue/relief center, everyone loved you, while"—
he glanced at the silent Vernon still leaning against the
railing—"Vernon kept complaining about being stuck
with jobs like finding lost cows."

Zeke had wished he'd had that job over washing a dog
or fixing a mailbox with a pink hammer. To think they'd
been jealous of each other's jobs.

Daniel Zook nodded at Vernon. "I already had a heart-
to-heart talk with Vernon about reasons for the assignments, motives, and jealousy."

Vernon squirmed.

In what universe did perfect Vernon get the lecture?
And how that must have stung!

Wait. Everyone loved him? Zeke didn't know quite
what to say to that. Maybe he wasn't as much of a loser
as he'd thought. But would they still love him if they
knew how he'd kissed Grace upstairs? How he'd hoped
Timothy wouldn't be found so Grace was free?

Daed reclaimed his seat next to Daniel Zook and
clasped his hands over his knees. "Back home, I was getting phone messages from Daniel Zook reporting how
you saved a man from falling off his roof. How you comforted a grieving man. How you rescued a family stuck in
a storm shelter. Positive comments from everyone here.
Seth called. Cliff called. Then Vernon called, and I knew
I had to come."

Zeke cringed. So, all the positives were lined up on
one side, and it only took one voice from home to erase
it all.

"I know I let you believe I was the bad guy," Vernon
said with sincerity and a glimpse of admiration in his
eyes, "and I know I poisoned your relationship with your

daed over the factory job, and I'm sorry about that. But you were wasted there. I fired you because I knew you needed to sacrifice the good to get the better, and now you need to sacrifice the better to get the best."

Zeke blinked. Was that supposed to make sense?

"Everyone needs someone who believes in them more than they believe in themselves," Vernon continued, glancing down at his feet. "I didn't explain myself back then. I should've, but I didn't know how until I talked to Daniel Zook today. And *jah*, I was jealous then, and the last few days brought those feelings back even more. He helped me see that, too. Everyone loves you. Even cows, dogs, and special-needs people. I'm good for nothing but bossing people around. And they resent that." He gave a short laugh. "The world is chaos. I must be in control."

Zeke's mind struggled to process it all. A dull ache began in his temples.

"I'm sorry for acting out toward you. I called your *daed* to tell the truth about everything I lied about. So many things." Vernon hung his head. "I'm truly sorry."

"I'm truly proud of you, son." *Daed* rubbed a fist over his eyes. "So when Vernon called after talking to Daniel Zook, I dropped everything and left on that four-hour drive. Vernon is going home tonight, but I'm staying until Monday."

"So I'm not leaving now?" Zeke pressed against the ache.

Cliff chuckled from his guard post by the stairs. "If things go as I hope in the barn, you aren't leaving ever. Luke wants to hire you as an apprentice in his furniture-making business." Cliff glanced toward the open barn doors.

"Really? But I don't know what I'm doing." But he'd love the challenge.

"Or, your current boss is talking about expanding into this area," *Daed* said.

That was news to Zeke, but he would enjoy that.

"But no dating while you're here as a mission worker," Daniel Zook said with a bit of a teasing smirk.

Cliff laughed. "We'll do that skip-the-dating-and-cut-straight-to-marrying thing."

Zeke was afraid to hope. But *jah, please, Lord*.

The three men emerged from the barn wearing matching grim expressions.

And the hope died.

CHAPTER 29

The cherry pies were prepared and ready to slide into the oven when the shepherd's pie came out. While *Mammi* took care of the folded laundry, Grace wiped off the table, washed the baking dishes, then prowled by the porch window, attempting to hear the men's words.

But other than *Daed*'s very good news about Jon before *Daadi* Cliff sent her back inside, she hadn't heard anything since Timothy joined the men and slammed the door.

If only she had the courage to open the door a crack and eavesdrop. But the hinges creaked and would give her actions away if she did.

Worry growing, she dipped her head and prayed. *Jesus, calm the storm. All the storms. The Timothy storm, the Zeke storm...Help me to be still and know you are* Gott. *Help me to trust.*

There was a moment of peace, then she glanced out

the window at the Mennonite man's stern expression and Vernon's smirk, and she yanked her worries right out of *Gott*'s hands and started stressing over them again. So she had to give them back. Over and over.

The oven timer buzzed, and since *Mammi* hadn't returned downstairs, Gracie removed the shepherd's pie, covered it with a towel to keep it warm, and adjusted the temperature for the pies.

Voices rose outside, and she peeked out the window. *Daed* and Bishop Nathan herded a sullen-looking Timothy toward the *haus*.

She *had* to know. Were they being forced to marry, after all?

She flung open the door.

Daadi Cliff straightened from his position guarding the stairs and pointed her back inside.

Her stomach churned, but she didn't dare disobey with *Daed* and the bishop there. Still, she left the door open a crack.

Low murmurs came from outside. Not loud enough. She moved to stare out the window and attempted to read the bishop's lips. But no. That was impossible with his beard and the slight angle of his body.

Except, *Daadi* Cliff grinned and gave Zeke a thumbs-up before turning away to say something.

A thumbs-up. That meant something good, ain't so? *Oh, please,* Gott.

Zeke stood, a slight smile on his face.

Timothy stared down at the ground.

Daed met Grace's gaze through the window, but she couldn't understand his expression. Sadness, definitely, but… She squinted. The glare from the lanterns and shadows on his face made it hard to see. And her internal worry meter rose a bit again.

The oven chimed that it was heated to the temperature the pies needed.

She swung away from the window, slid the pies in, and reset the timer for twenty minutes. She'd cover the edges with tinfoil at that point.

The door opened with a squeak of the hinges.

"Gracie. You can come out now," *Daed* said. There *was* sorrow in his voice.

She turned and studied his expression for a moment.

Her heart lurched. Had Timothy told them about catching her and Zeke kissing the way they had?

She stumbled toward the door and out.

Zeke reached for her hand. She grasped it as if it were a lifeline.

Please, Gott…

Timothy looked up, his expression broken. "Gracie…" He gulped. "I…I…You don't love me the way you love him." He nodded toward Zeke. "I can't marry you. I don't love you the way I should, either."

"I wish you the best and *danki*," she murmured because it was polite. She and Timothy used to be friends, and now all she felt for him was pity.

Free! Oh, glory. She was free! Free, and no longer bound to the promise she'd made to *Mamm.* She wasn't promised to anyone now and was free to choose the man beside her…

But why the frowns? Her stomach clenched.

Timothy jerked, tears appearing in his eyes. He glanced at the bishop, made a sound as if he were in pain, then bolted for his bike. The next instant he was pedaling away.

"He's being excommunicated tomorrow during church," the bishop said with a slow head shake and a twist of his lips.

Oh. *Oh.* Pain shot through Grace, and her eyes burned. Timothy was shunned until he came to repentance. He'd been mean at times to her and to Patience, but a shunning? Ouch. Compassion for his family filled her. Their son was alive...and yet "dead" to them for a season.

"He'll be a special project of mine while I'm here." The Mennonite missionary gazed after him.

"Supper is ready," *Mammi* said behind them.

"I need to hit the road," Vernon said as he glanced at the missionary. "It was nice meeting everyone. It's been a real...eye-opener." He slapped Zeke's shoulder in a friendly way.

Zeke released her hand and returned the gesture.

What had she missed?

"They are my ride, so I guess I'll go, too," his *daed* said. "I'll be seeing you, Zeke, before I leave." His *daed* hugged him.

"Since you'll be in the area, stay for dinner," *Daadi* Cliff said. "And if you haven't found a place for the night, you can stay here."

Mammi counted the number of people staying for supper and then went back inside.

Daed nodded. "You'll be welcome."

"*Danki*. Let me grab my bag." He went out to the van and removed a black bag.

The missionary shook everyone's hands, except *Mammi*'s, since she was inside, and he and Vernon left.

Daadi Cliff headed for the door. He showed the

bishop inside, then stopped and pointed at Zeke. "Now, you gct to proposing, boy, so we can celebrate."

Grace's face heated. But inside she was a flurry of emotion. She was free from Timothy, and was it truly possible she might get her first true proposal instead of an "I'm telling you"?

Zeke's hand closed around hers, and he chuckled nervously.

Daed winked at Grace as he followed *Daadi* Cliff and the bishop inside.

Zeke's *daed* stepped forward. "I'm looking forward to getting to know you, Gracie." The door shut behind him.

Leaving Grace and Zeke alone.

Except for the four male faces pressed against the window.

Zeke glanced at them, then tugged Grace down the steps and around the corner of the *haus* where there weren't any windows.

She dipped her head to avoid looking at him. "*Daadi* Cliff is a tease. You can ignore him." But oh, she hoped he wouldn't.

His fingers gently raised her chin. "Gracie...*Ich liebe dich*. I know I've only known you for a few days, but I love your kindness, your humor, even your temper. I want to spend the rest of my life getting to know everything about you." He shifted nervously. His gaze dipped to her lips and then back to stare heatedly into her eyes in a way that made her hot from head to toe and all the parts tingling in between. "Grace Lynn Lantz, how do you feel about marrying me this Thursday?"

That would be a dream come true beyond her wildest imagination. Like the glorious rainbow after a storm. Tears beaded, clustered, overflowed. "Are you serious?"

He looked a little worried. "I kind of like the whole skip-the-dating-and-cut-straight-to-marrying idea. If... if you do, too. Will you marry me?"

"*Jah*! *Ich liebe dich*, Ezekiel Bontrager."

He grinned and pulled her into his embrace. Her face was tucked under his chin with his warm arms around her back. She held on tight and swayed, listening to the steady beat of his heart.

This wedding she wouldn't dread.

Gott had let the tornado stop her wedding to Timothy and brought Zeke here as a rescue worker. *Gott* had saved Jon's life in a miraculous way. *Gott* had used the storm to catch Timothy's attention and bring him low, to reveal his sins so he could confess. *Gott* had saved her from a disastrous, loveless marriage and gave her Zeke instead—a man who could be a valuable member of the community.

The inner storms were calmed, and *Gott*'s hand was clearly seen and exalted. "*Danki*, Lord."

"Amen."

She glanced up at Zeke.

"Gracie, I promise to always love and honor and take care of you."

Jah, she promised the same. She opened her mouth to say it, but Zeke lowered his head and kissed her.

And kissed her.

And kissed her.

Until *Daadi* Cliff clapped his hands from an upstairs window. "Enough of that. Now, let's celebrate!"

Zeke chuckled as he pulled away. "Your family," he murmured.

"Soon to be yours as well," Grace said.

"I can't wait. I hope your bishop agrees to a wedding right away. It just feels right." He grasped her hand.

It did. Grace didn't suffer a bit from cold feet. Instead, she couldn't wait.

Together they strolled around to the back door as Slush came running from the barn. With a big grin, he jumped up on Zeke and wrapped his front legs around Zeke in a big dog hug, as only Siberian huskies can do.

Grace giggled. "He's welcoming you to the family."

Zeke released Grace's hand and returned the dog's hug.

The door opened, and Patience came out. "Reuben walk me home from next door to get clean dress. *Mammi* say stay supper, we celebrate. What we celebrate?"

Zeke stepped forward and grasped Patience's hands in his. "I'm going to marry Gracie as soon as the bishop allows me to."

Patience frowned. "I knowed that. I told you marry Gracie day you came."

"I want you to be a sidesitter," Grace said.

Patience's lips turned up. "I be bridesmaid?" She threw her arms around Zeke and hugged him. "You be brother."

"Yes. Brother-in-law." Zeke returned her hug. "Now, let's go celebrate."

Celebrate they did, with cherry pie and homemade root beer.

And Grace felt absolutely surrounded by love... and eager to be loved by Zeke for the rest of her life.

ACKNOWLEDGMENTS

Even though Hidden Springs is a fictional community, thanks to Marilyn Ridgway for information about the Amish in Arthur, Illinois, where the story is set, buggy snapshots taken with her cell phone, and answering questions. I've been there a zillion times, but you are an excellent resource and so patient answering my questions. Also thanks for the prayer support.

Thanks to Jenna, Candee, Lynne, Linda, Heidi, Marie, Christy, Kathy, Julie, and Marilyn for your parts in critiques, advice, and/or brainstorming. Also to my street team for promoting and brainstorming. Candee, this story would not be what it is without you.

Thanks to author Loree Lough for the picture of a cow stuck in a shed.

Thanks to Jenna for taking on the bulk of the cooking while I'm on deadline.

Thanks to Hachette Book Group (Forever) for taking a chance on me, and to Tamela Hancock Murray for representing me.

Are you loving the Hidden Springs series?
Don't miss Kiah and Hallie's story in
The Amish Secret Wish.

Available in summer 2020.

Please keep reading for a preview.

Chapter 1

*Gott, I don't know what to do. I wake every morn-
ing hoping the darkness will be less oppressive, but
each day is as bleak as the one before.*

Hallie Brunstetter bent over the lined white paper in
front of her on the table, penning her innermost thoughts
by the dim flickering light of the candle. She should
write the article due for *The Budget*, and she would,
but first, she needed to talk to *Gott* in a physical way.
Maybe then He would answer. Besides, she used to love
keeping a prayer journal and seeing how and when *Gott*
answered.

The darkness permeated the kitchen, and she
squinted. She didn't dare light the lantern or the gaslight.
The brighter beam might wake someone. And she
wanted to be alone. Needed to be alone. *Mamm* and
Daed slept right through the open doorway on the full-

size bed pushed up against the wall in the living room. A visiting preacher and his wife from someplace in Indiana were staying in their bedroom for the weekend. They were supposed to have arrived late last *nacht*, long after Hallie had gone to bed. She'd heard the low murmur of voices but rolled over and went back to sleep.

She glanced at the clock, faintly backlit by a battery. Since she'd need to head into work in about an hour, she probably wouldn't meet them until this afternoon.

She should have time to finish her prayer, though. She turned her attention back to her letter to *Gott* and reread the words she'd written. Would it be selfish of her to pray for a special male friend so her loneliness and depression would ease? Maybe one like her secret pen pal . . . but no. Love equaled hurt and eventual loss. She didn't want to live through that pain again.

> *Gott, please comfort us. Me. Toby's family. Send the light.*

Light flickered across the page.

She caught her breath and lifted her head. A thin beam from the rising sun filtered through the sheer lace curtain hanging over the window.

Outside, the darkness of night receded, and soon the world would brighten.

Perhaps the same would be true of her life.

Or not.

But for right now, she would cling to hope.

Because if she didn't, she might not make it through another day.

Creaks came from the bed in the living room, and

Hallie quickly slid the paper she'd written on under a few other pages filled with notes for her article, gathered them up, and stashed them in the drawer in the hutch where she kept her writing supplies.

A few minutes later, *Mamm* shuffled into the kitchen wearing fuzzy bunny slippers. The long, fluffy, pink ears wiggled with movement. Those slippers used to make Hallie giggle. Now...when was the last time she'd smiled at something, other than in a polite, forced way?

It had to have been sometime in November, when life was good. Before the off-season tornado destroyed everything, slaying her dreams along with her beau, Toby. Six long, painful months ago.

Hallie blinked back the sting in her eyes as *Mamm* lit the lantern. *Daed* smiled at her as he went past on the way to the barn, but concern filled his eyes. It always seemed to be there these days. In fact, it was there every time he'd looked at her since that horrible day when he'd been the only one home with her when she got the news.

"Were you writing the post for *The Budget*?" *Mamm* asked as *Daed* shut the door behind him. She extinguished the candle and pushed in the chair Hallie had abandoned.

Hallie grabbed her purple pen and put it away in the mug with the other writing utensils. "Gathering my notes and my thoughts for it." It was a truth-stained lie. Her notes now waited in the stack of papers she'd put away, and she always prayed before she wrote her weekly article. She tried to think of a way to change the subject. The guests would distract *Mamm* from discussing what she thought Hallie should write. "Did the visiting preacher arrive?"

"Very late, around midnight. He brought his son along as well," *Mamm* said as the door off the newly built, attached *dawdihaus* opened and Hallie's grandparents came in. They'd lost their home during the tornado and opted to move in with Hallie's family rather than rebuild.

"Aw, how sweet. I guess I'll meet him when I get off work." Hallie glanced from her grandparents to the clock again. "I'll feed the chickens and gather the eggs, then get ready to go. Unless you think the little boy would like to go out with one of our neighbor's younger children to see the chickens."

"I'll hitch up the horse and buggy for you," *Daadi* muttered as he headed out to the barn.

"He's not so lit—"

"Good morning." A strange voice entered the conversation. Male. Must be the preacher. Hallie forced a polite smile and turned to stare at a handsome, beardless man with green eyes and dark-blond hair. He held a straw hat in one hand. He most definitely wasn't a preacher. He'd have her undivided attention if he stood behind a pulpit. Something odd and unexpected pinged her heart. And for a moment—a very brief moment—interest flared.

She steeled herself. Despite her crazy unwritten wishes and her prayer, she needed to guard her heart.

He looked familiar, as if she'd seen him before. She narrowed her eyes, trying to figure out where. When.

A spark of recognition flashed in his baby, uh, greens. So they *had* met. He smiled. "I remember you. Holly, right? But you said you're not a Christmas baby."

"Hallie. Not Holly," she corrected automatically. But oh. That explained where and when. Her forced smile died. Six months ago, he was in town as a volunteer after the tornado...during the most terrible time of her life. Toby's funeral.

His smile widened. He winked. "Holly and Hallie sound the same to me. But I would love to help you collect eggs."

And he was a flirt. Lovely. Just lovely. She ignored *Mamm*'s not-so-subtle head tilt toward the door that urged her to take the boy out to the barn and to be polite. She didn't have the patience today. Unfortunately, she'd have to put up with flirts all morning at her waitressing job. Most of them were retired, traveling with their significant other, and harmless. There were always a few she had to watch out for, though. The ones who reached out to pat, touch, or pinch waitresses in inappropriate places. She shuddered.

The green-eyed man's smile faded.

"I forgot your name." She glanced at *Mamm*, who frowned at her with narrowed eyes while beating batter for pancakes; then she made an effort to be polite. "I mean, nice to meet you. Um, make that welcome to the area."

"*Danki.*" His lips quirked. "Hezekiah Esh, at your service. My friends call me Kiah."

They weren't friends. Not even close. But his name...Her heart lurched as she thought of the stack of letters hidden in her locked hope chest upstairs, forwarded to her by *The Budget*, all written by Kiah Esh. Letters she'd responded to, using her initials. Maybe they were friends. Secretly. So secret he didn't even know. At least he didn't know her in person.

Mammi adjusted her trifocals and tapped nearer with her wheelless walker. She peered up into Kiah's face, reached her hands up to touch his cheeks, and studied him. Then she pinched his cheeks before she released him and patted his arm. "So you're the one who's going to marry our Hallie."

Kiah's eyes bugged, and he spluttered, then coughed.

Hallie's face burned. She stared at the floor. At least *Mammi* had good taste in men. But oh what Kiah must think. "I need to go to work." No point in trying to correct *Mammi*. She wouldn't understand.

"What about the eggs?" Kiah's voice sounded somewhat strangled.

"You can collect them with my sister." Hallie pushed past them.

Her arm brushed against Kiah's as she passed. Weird sparks shot through her. An electrical charge? She shook her head and went upstairs.

Kiah's last letter, one she hadn't responded to, had said he would be coming to Hidden Springs, Illinois, and he wanted to meet her—GHB. He hadn't said when. Or where he'd be staying. And if only she'd known so she could have been better prepared. But too late now. She'd have to make the best of it and make sure he'd never find his mystery girl.

Because the safest place to hide was in plain sight.

* * *

Kiah turned away from the disconcerting *mammi* and watched Hallie hightail it for the stairs—the ones he'd just come down. Intriguing girl—and he'd felt sparks when they'd accidentally touched—but he wasn't interested. He'd fallen in love, sight unseen, with the scribe for *The Budget*. He just had to find out her real name and then convince her she was the one he'd been waiting for. Or he was the one she was waiting for.

Her real name—would it be Gabby? Gizelle? Gina? Gail? Whatever the *G* in GHB stood for, he'd find her. And woo her.

Of course, that would be assuming she was young and not married to someone else.

His *mamm* said it was pure craziness, because the scribe was probably eighty if a day. But the handwriting in her return letters didn't look old. *Daed* shook his head in wonder or dismay and called it a "wild goose chase," because if she were available and interested, she would've told him her name. And maybe they were right. But he wanted to find out for himself.

He turned back to the kitchen to face the unsettling *mammi* and the now pancake-frying *mamm*. He cleared his throat. "I'm not on the market, but Hallie seems like a really nice girl. I'm actually already involved with someone else from this area. Perhaps you know her? She writes for *The Budget*, and her name starts with a *G*. GHB."

Both women stared at him. The *mamm*'s mouth gaped, her eyes wide, startled. A measure of doubt clouded Kiah's vision. Maybe G *was* married.

The troubling and bothersome *mammi* cackled. "Talk to Hallie," the older woman said, with a gleam in her eyes.

Right. Because she believed he was going to marry Hallie. But then again, maybe Hallie would know where to find G.

A floorboard creaked, and Kiah turned to see *Mamm*

and *Daed* emerging from the hallway. And Hallie coming downstairs, carrying her purse.

"Hi." Hallie greeted his parents with an overly polite smile. "I don't mean to be rude, but I'm running late for work. I'm looking forward to getting to know you this afternoon."

Kiah didn't think she meant it. She'd sounded too sugary sweet. And she didn't quite make eye contact. He caught her *mamm*'s frown.

Hallie's smile faded as she skittered past Kiah with her head dipped, gaze down, and careful not to brush against him. So she must've felt the sparks, too. Interesting. The scent of lavender trailed her.

"My husband's in the barn," the pancake-frying *mamm* said.

Daed nodded. "Come, Kiah. We can make ourselves useful."

Kiah put his straw hat on and followed *Daed* and Hallie out of the *haus*. A small barn stood on the other side of the circular driveway. The air smelled fresh, as if they'd had a heavy dew overnight. There were no noticeable signs of the terrible twisters that'd touched down with destructive damage six months ago. A horse and buggy were already waiting, ready to go, in front of the porch. Hallie put her purse on the seat and climbed in.

Kiah stopped beside the buggy, adjusting his hat to better see Hallie. If he wasn't already so heart connected to the scribe, he might have been tempted by the beautiful woman. Or at least have accepted the challenge to break through her odd reserve around him. But he'd been different since the tornado, which led him to write to the scribe in the first place.

He gazed up at her. "Can we talk later?"

She paled. Shifted. Odd response. "I might be working a double shift."

"Whenever you get home is fine. Your *mammi* suggested I talk to you about some information I need."

Her glance darted toward the door and then back. She opened her mouth, hesitated, then shut it. She shook her head and muttered something he didn't catch. Probably something about her crazy *mammi*. His heart sunk to realize the woman might have steered him in the wrong direction, and yet he couldn't leave a possible avenue unexplored. Hallie clicked her tongue.

The horse slowly took a step forward.

Kiah took a step back to avoid getting run over. "Your *mammi* thinks you might know someone in this district with the initials GHB."

Hallie frowned and gazed over his head as if she was thinking. When she glanced at him again, her expression could only be called a smirk. "George Harold Beiler." She wiggled the reins and drove off.

A man?

Kiah mentally reviewed the handwriting. It was neat. Beautiful. But then some men had pretty writing. Kiah's best friend, Zeke, who'd recently married, had great handwriting. He said it was because he had to read his measurements.

But the writing had looked feminine.

And at least one of the return letters had used lavender ink. Not a usual male color choice.

Hallie's *daed* stood in the wide-open doorway of the barn watching his daughter drive away. He shook his head as his gaze shifted to Kiah. His head tilted as if he was sizing him up. He gave a tiny nod as if Kiah had passed some pop quiz. "She works as a waitress in town. I'll give you directions later if you want to go, order a slice of pie and conversation."

Did he think Hallie knew who GHB was, too?

Or...Kiah cringed. What was wrong with the woman that she needed so many obvious matchmakers?

*   *   *

Sometimes it seemed as if the breakfast crowd never left before the lunch crowd arrived. The Friday-morning coffee club had filled every seat in the entire overflow dining section. Hallie refilled coffee mugs innumerable times, dodged the expected and inevitable wandering fingers, and delivered breakfasts, doughnuts, pastries, and pies. Now she was left with messy tables, sticky chairs, and a floor that needed sweeping and scrubbing.

At least the coffee club left good tips.

She filled a gray tub to overflowing with dirty dishes, hoisted it up in her arms, and turned to deliver them to the dish room.

And there, in plain sight, was Kiah, legs kicked out under a small table, an infuriating grin on his oh-so-handsome face.

Her heart lurched. Why did he have to be so appealing? So handsome?

His green eyes met hers. "Service, please." Somehow he managed to infuse the words with enough humor that it wasn't an order but more teasing. Teasing like Toby used to do. But Kiah didn't resemble Toby at all. He was light where Toby was dark. Really, Kiah was much more handsome. Did they have the same sense of humor? The same careless ease appeared to be there, and Kiah's presence rubbed salt on the wounds of her loss. However, the man in the letters had an unexpected depth revealed there. Was it possible this teasing flirt had actually written those letters?

Her lips quirked before she caught the involuntary movement and stiffened them. She liked his teasing. Liked his boldness. It made a part of her heart come to life, as if his humor had slipped through a crack in her sheltered and barricaded heart just like that sliver of sun through the curtain. She couldn't allow it to gain any more ground. "This section is closed until the other dining room overflows." She tilted her head toward the exit.

"When I asked where you were, your boss told me to come back here. She said it was so nice to meet your new boyfriend."

Boyfriend? She used to have a boyfriend. Not anymore. Had he introduced himself that way, or had her boss merely assumed that any young man asking for her must be a boyfriend?

"What's with all these people matching us up?"

"I don't know, and I don't like it." Hallie shifted the heavy tub and sighed. If her boss sent Kiah back here, Hallie had no choice but to let him stay. She needed to think up more GHB names to "help" him. If he only knew... "I'll be right back to take your order."

"Coffee and a slice of pie for both of us. I don't care what kind. Your boss said to tell you to take a break. I ordered fifteen minutes of conversation, too."

He ordered conversation? That could be done? Hallie frowned at him, but she could see how he charmed her boss into giving her an unscheduled break. That smile? That dimple? Those good looks?

However, she wasn't in the mood for either coffee or pie. She *was* in the mood to be contrary. She carried the tub to the dish room and returned with a cup of coffee, a slice of caramel apple pie, a glass of cola with ice, and a bowl filled with grapes, apple and orange slices, and strawberries. She set the coffee and pie in front of him, then set her cola and fruit on the opposite side of the table before sitting across from him.

"Oh, it does feel good to sit down." If only she could kick off her shoes and socks. "I may not get up again." She only half joked, because she hadn't been able to find her shoes this morning and had borrowed her younger sister's sneakers. They pinched, and she'd definitely have blisters.

Kiah studied her name tag. "Your name really isn't Holly." As if he hadn't believed her. "H-a-l-l-i-e. That's an odd spelling. What's your given name?"

"You don't go by *your* given name. How do you spell Kiah?" No way would she share her real name.

"Touché." But his gaze remained fixed on her name tag. "Hal is short for Henry. Is your name Henrietta?"

"Good guess." But wrong, wrong, wrong. Her name was Hallelujah. She took a sip of her cola and tried not to smirk.

"Henrietta, in the attempt of full disclosure, I am here to find the woman I love."

She tried not to react. But… "Hallie, please. Not Henrietta." She'd forget to answer. "And is your girl-friend lost?"

He picked up his fork and toyed with the pie. "I only know her initials. GHB. And that she's a scribe for *The Budget*. Good thing I like puzzles." He chuckled. "Unfortunately, I'm not very good at them. Can you help me find her?"

ABOUT THE AUTHOR

Laura V. Hilton is an award-winning author of more than twenty Amish, contemporary, and historical romances. When she's not writing, she reviews books for her blogs and writes devotionals for the *Seriously Write* blog.

Laura and her pastor-husband have five children and a hyper dog named Skye. They currently live in Arkansas. Laura enjoys reading and visiting lighthouses and waterfalls. Her favorite season is winter, and her favorite holiday is Christmas.

You can learn more at:
Twitter: @Laura_V_Hilton
Facebook.com/AuthorLauraVHilton

Fall in love with these charming contemporary romances!

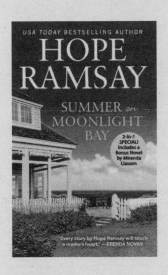

SUMMER ON MOONLIGHT BAY
by Hope Ramsay

Veterinarian Noah Cuthbert had no intention of ever moving back to the small town of Magnolia Harbor. But when his sister calls with the opportunity to run the local animal clinic as well as give her a break from caring for their ailing mom, he packs his bags and heads home. But once he meets the clinic's beautiful new manager, he questions whether his summer plans might become more permanent. Includes a bonus novel by Miranda Liasson!

WISH YOU WERE MINE
by Tara Sivec

When Everett Southerland left town five years ago, Cameron James thought it was the worst day of her life. She was wrong: It was the day he came back and told her the truth about his feelings that devastated her. Now she's having a hard time believing him, until he proves to her how much he cares. But with so many secrets between them, will they ever find the future that was always destined to be theirs?

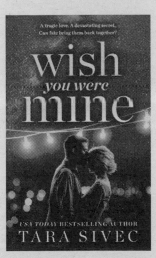

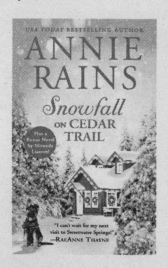

THE AMISH WEDDING PROMISE
by Laura V. Hilton

After a storm crashes through town, Grace Lantz is forced to postpone her wedding. All hands are needed for cleanup, but Grace doesn't know where to start—should she console her special needs sister or find her missing groom? Sparks fly when the handsome Zeke Bontrager comes to aid the community and offers to help the overwhelmed Grace in any way he can. But when her groom is found, Grace must decide if the wedding will go on...or if she'll take a chance on Zeke.

MERMAID INN
by Jenny Holiday

When Eve Abbott inherits her aunt's inn, she remembers the heartbreaking last summer she spent there, and she has no interest in returning. Unfortunately, Eve must run the inn for two years before she can sell. Town sheriff Sawyer Collins can't deny all the old feelings that come rushing back when he sees Eve. Getting her out of Matchmaker Bay when they were younger was something he did for her own good. But losing her again? He doesn't think he can survive that twice. Includes a bonus novella by Alison Bliss!